LEST BRIDGES BURN
DETECTIVE LIZ MOORLAND 2

PHILLIPA NEFRI CLARK

Lest Bridges Burn

Copyright © 2023 Phillipa Nefri Clark

All rights reserved.

No part of this publication may be reproduced, distributed, or transmitted in any form or by any means, including photocopying, recording, or other electronic or mechanical methods, without the prior written permission of the publisher, except as permitted by Australian copyright law. For permission requests, contact hello@phillipaclark.com.

The story, all names, characters, and incidents portrayed in this production are fictitious.

Cover design by Steam Power Studios

LEST BRIDGES BURN

AN IMPORTANT NOTE...

This series is set in Australia and written in Aussie/British English for an authentic experience.

Like to discover more about Liz, other titles, and Phillipa's world? Visit Phillipa's website where you can join her newsletter. www.phillipaclark.com.

PROLOGUE

The same routine every day was fine by Maureen. If it kept her kid happy, then she was happy. She could enjoy sitting in the sun without being nagged for attention every two minutes. Not as much, anyhow.

Eliza loved the park with its swings and sandpit and oversized timber climbing fort. There was a bridge above another play area and lots of interesting nooks. Left to her own devices she'd spend an hour at play. Longer if any of the other kids she'd made friends with were around.

Maureen settled on the bench near the fountain and pulled a magazine from her large handbag. A bag of lollies fell out and she scooped it up, ripping the corner and helping herself to a handful of sugary sweetness. Eliza's oversized backpack with her stuffed unicorn, jumper, juice, water, and a snack bar leaned against the back of the bench. She'd come and help herself when she wanted a breather.

'Marr-mee?'

So much for a few minutes peace.

'What's up, bub?' Maureen's voice rose in response.

Eliza waved from the bridge. 'Come and tie my shoelace.'

'No, you have a go trying first. If you get stuck then come

here.' Maureen flicked through the pages, stopping on a story about the latest game show host scandal. How on earth did those people get away with such bad behaviour? Not at all like the real world where good people—like Eliza's dad—made one mistake and ended up in prison. 'Place would be overflowing if the real criminals were caught.'

She finished reading the article as Eliza skipped across the grass.

'Did you do your own laces?'

Both were perfectly tied. But not how she did it and Eliza was only just learning.

'I need a drink, Mummy.'

'In your backpack. You said your lace was undone.'

'The man fixed it.'

On her feet in an instant, Maureen scanned the playground. In the distance, a couple of young teens tossed a ball to each other. Nobody else was around. It was the middle of the morning so no school kids were there, apart from the teens.

'Was it one of the boys over there?'

Eliza—who had forced a tiny straw into a fruit drink—followed Maureen's pointed finger. 'No. A nice man. And he has a little girl.' She frowned. 'He said he once *had* a little girl who died. That's so sad, isn't it Mummy?'

'Yes, bub. Very sad. Is the man still here?'

'He went home. I'm going to wear my backpack.' Eliza zipped it up and shrugged it on, sticking the straw back in her mouth and sucking loudly.

'Leave it here. That way it won't get in the way when you are in the tunnels and stuff.'

'I might get hungry and need to snack.'

Maureen kissed Eliza's forehead. 'Well, you go and play for another half hour.'

'And you stay right here, Mummy. I'll come and find you.'

With that, the little girl pushed the now-empty fruit box into Maureen's hands and skipped away. Maureen found a bin. She'd miss this all next year when Eliza went to kinder for real but at least she'd be freed up to look for more work.

She settled again, back in the magazine and humming along with the song Eliza loudly sang to herself in the distance. When the singing stopped she glanced up. Eliza was in a sandpit. Maureen turned the pages, stopping at some recipes and then a short piece of fiction. The sun was getting a bit too warm and soon they'd go and get an ice-cream each.

'Is this yours?'

Maureen's head shot up.

The two teens approached, one holding the soccer ball they'd been kicking around and the other carrying a backpack. Pink. Stickers of unicorns. Far too big because it was second hand and all Maureen could afford at the time.

'That's my little girl's. Where did you find it?'

The kid pointed. 'Behind the fort.'

Maureen grabbed it from him and glanced inside. Only the snack bar was there. Not the jumper or water or unicorn toy.

'Was Eliza there?'

He shook his head.

'Then where is she?' Maureen threw her magazine and the rest of the lollies into her bag. 'She was wearing this.'

The teens exchanged a look. 'We'll help find her.'

'She's probably under the bridge. She likes making up games with her toy there. Can you both go in opposite directions and look? Her name is Eliza.'

The boys split up, running to either end of the park.

'Eliza! Bub, where are you?'

This had to be a mistake. Eliza had taken her stuff out of her bag. Been cold in the shade and put on her jumper. Kids got confused with temperature sometimes. Didn't they? Put jumpers on even when it was warm?

Heart pounding, Maureen looked under the bridge. No Eliza.

Then the fort, climbing up to the top and using the extra height to look around the park.

'Eliza! Eliza, where are you?'

There was no cry of 'here, Mummy'. No sound at all.

Maureen part climbed, part fell to the bottom.

One of the teens puffed as he reached her. 'Not at the far end or the swings. Does she have a phone?'

'Phone? No. She's a little kid. Can you look in the bushes along the front?'

He took off.

Where was she?

It had only been a few minutes.

She checked the backpack again. Even the little wallet she'd zipped into an inside pocket with Eliza's address and Maureen's details, plus a few gold coins, was gone.

Had Eliza walked home? Why would she do that?

Tears fell unchecked, clouding her sight as she ran to the side of the park where they usually came in from the crossing. Their apartment was only a couple of blocks away.

Maureen came to a stop. Eliza was nervous about the traffic. She'd never cross without holding Mummy's hand. Never.

Throwing her head back, she screamed to the sky, 'Eliza!'

ONE
~DAY ONE~

It was too hot to be running in the middle of the day.

Liz sprinted along the concrete, avoiding prams and pedestrians who were texting as they walked.

Night shift was a devil she'd got really cosy with lately.

She'd never been good at sleeping anyway. Not for years. The downside with sleep was the risk of dreams. Or nightmares.

The pavement was unforgiving beneath her expensive runners. Sand was her preferred medium apart from when she trained for half marathons but today she only had an hour before a briefing at work. Something important, Terry had said.

Dodging cars, Liz crossed the road and barely slowed as she entered her building. Sweat poured down her spine as she took the stairs two at a time. Three floors up. The elevator was dodgy anyway but the added cardio never hurt.

Key in the lock she stopped as her neighbour called out.

'Best you get to work, Liz. Something terrible happened today. Something affecting one of our own.'

On the opposite side of the long, narrow hallway, and a couple of doors up, long-time neighbour Darryl Tompsett leaned against the wall outside his apartment. He had a beer in his hand. As usual. The singlet and jocks and knee-high socks weren't a good look.

'Meaning?'

Darryl shrugged. 'Little kid on the fifth floor vanished at the park. Ker-poof.'

Liz turned the key and pushed her way inside, slamming the door behind herself before sinking to the ground. Her arms covered her head. Ragged breaths in and out were loud to her ears. Blood pounded in her veins.

This isn't happening.

Another sound. A buzzing. Annoying, stupid buzzing.

With a gasp, Liz lowered her arms and dug her phone from her running belt. 'What?'

'Love you too.'

Detective Sergeant Pete McNamara. Sometimes work partner. Always a pain.

'Has something happened. Something at the park?'

'Crap, how the hell do you know already?'

Her stomach clenched. 'Neighbour. Tell me, Pete.'

Liz rolled onto all fours, putting the phone on the floor as she stretched her spine.

'I'm on the way to you. Twenty minutes and I'll tell you what we know.'

'Pete—'

But he'd gone.

His twenty minutes meant fifteen, tops. She forced herself to her feet and tossed her phone onto the kitchen counter as she passed it. Her top went over her head followed by a sports bra and the rest came off as she turned on the shower. All the clothing got thrown into a hamper and she stepped under the stream of water.

For one full minute she let the water cascade over her head, choking on tears which refused to come. This was meant to be over.

It will never be over. Not until I find you, Ellen.

Liz was outside when Pete drew up exactly fifteen minutes after he'd called.

'Tell me everything,' she said.

'You need to dig deep if you want to be on this one. They'll pull you off if you show any weakness or any—'

'For goodness sake, Pete. Tell me.'

He let the car idle in the no stopping zone. 'Five-year-old girl is missing. Last seen on the play equipment at the park—the same damned park, Liz. Happened less than two hours ago and we've already got some people on the ground. Uniforms searching. A canine team coming.'

'Then why aren't we moving?'

Pete gazed at her. They'd worked together for a few years, on and off. Most cops didn't want to buddy up with him but he was good at his job. Just not fun with people unless he was turning on the charm to get information or had a skinful of grog. Last winter he'd done something good. Saved the life of someone she cared about and he detested. It was a defining moment and her respect for him was solid. But now he was filtering facts.

'Stop messing with me, Pete.'

'She lives here, Liz. Two floors up from you. And you have to decide if you can do this before we leave. Terry will watch you like a hawk, let alone the higher-ups.'

'This child is not my niece. For all we know she's hiding somewhere as part of a game. Or wandered off and will be found before night falls. I've got it together so can we please get going?'

'Sure.' Yet he hesitated before pulling out with a quiet, 'I've got your back.'

Liz got up to speed on the way. It was only a few blocks to the park which was rectangular and surrounded on all four sides by busy streets, shops, and apartment buildings. An image popped up on her phone and she recoiled. Eliza Sharney Singleton. Cute as a button. Blue eyes and cheeky smile. Blonde hair. Light gold, same as Ellen. She flicked to another page. It might as well have been a history lesson. A distracted adult. A missing child.

This time will be different. You'll be found.

'What about our briefing at work? Is Terry still running it?'

Detective Senior Sergeant Terry Hall was their boss, a decent man who regularly spoke of retiring but didn't seem to have the heart to leave the job he loved.

'Delayed. He's here until Missing Persons make an appearance.' Pete parked in a no standing zone on the next block.

Other than a couple of patrol cars and uniform officers working their way along the parameter of the park there was no appearance of a crime. And why would there be? Kids disappeared all the time and nearly always showed up in a matter of hours.

"You coming?"

How had Pete got out of the car without her seeing?

Pull it together.

She followed him without a word. This was a coincidence. Nothing more or less. A tired mother. A kid wandering. They'd be reunited by dinner time, probably accompanied by a lot of tears and a smack or two. In whichever order.

The park wasn't fenced. Bushes—some kind of evergreen species about two metres in height—acted as a boundary, with intermittent entry points. The greenery created a sense of quiet and privacy, an oasis away from the suburban chaos only metres away. Paths led to a couple of rotundas with barbeques for the public to use. There were open spaces to play cricket or throw a frisbee. Benches. A fountain. And a sprawling play area for younger kids.

Just in front of that, Terry was in conversation with another detective and when he noticed Liz and Pete he cut it off. He was the best boss she'd ever worked with but at this moment, she wished he wasn't here. Those eyes of his were too observant.

"Pete, I need you to facilitate a square by square search of the park. And get bodies posted on every way in to stop curious eyes and possible contamination."

The minute Pete was on his way, Terry turned to Liz. "Would you like me to speak to the mother?" she asked.

"Are you right with this? And be straight with me, Liz."

"I almost threw up when Pete told me. But he was beaten by a few minutes by one of my neighbours."

"What the heck?"

"Has the mother been on her phone?"

"Of course she has. The call to us wasn't her first. Even her tenth. Her husband is in prison so she's no fan of the law," Terry said. "For all I know she's alerted the press and we're about to be descended upon. Which brings me back to my question."

"What do you want me to say? I'm gutted, Terry. But this has nothing to do with Ellen's disappearance. We'll find the kid, send someone to do a welfare check, and move on. So, can I do my job or are you going to waste more time interrogating me?"

"Check the attitude, Detective Sergeant. Go find the mother. And lean on her a bit."

Liz could have sworn Terry grinned as he pulled out his phone but she wasn't waiting around to be sure.

A pop-up trailer was being pushed into the park by several police officers in preparation to set up a mobile crime scene point. When Ellen disappeared, there'd been nothing apart from a few local beat cops that had come to help look. Here there would be a central unit with computers and dedicated staff to manage information as it came in.

If she'd had these resources then.

'Why haven't you found her?'

The screech was close enough to hurt Liz's ears and was directed at the officers pushing the trailer.

'Mrs Singleton? Maureen?' Liz hurried across.

Early thirties. One fifty five centimetres give or take a bit.

Pretty face. Blouse and skirt, both a bit tight for her build. Sandals. No rings. No makeup. Eyes puffy.

'I'm Detective Sergeant Liz Moorland.'

'What are you doing to find my baby?'

'As you can see, we have a number of officers actively searching and are setting up a mobile station to work from. My partner has the task of going over every inch of the park and he is very good at his job. There's a canine unit on the way. Can we sit and talk?'

'I've talked. And looked. If I can't find my daughter how can you? Police don't care enough about people like me.'

'We care a lot about a child who is missing.' Liz stared at the other woman. 'I know you've repeated yourself already but not to me. Run me through everything that's happened today.'

Maureen deflated. 'I was sitting on a bench reading. And some teens came over with Eliza's backpack and—'

'Let's go into the shade.'

Without waiting for Maureen, Liz moved to beneath a canopy of trees and sat on one of the benches scattered around the park. A moment later, the other woman dropped onto the seat at her side. Her face was red and her eyes darted everywhere.

'Do you have some water with you?'

'Water?'

'I understand how distressing this is but you need to stay hydrated. No point us finding Eliza only to have her mum unwell.'

It must have made sense. Maureen opened a big handbag and pulled out a water bottle, leaving the bag hanging open on the seat at her side. She sucked from the bottle, long and noisy slurps, then closed the lid and held on to it.

'Tell me about the whole day starting with when you got up. Was Eliza already awake?'

'No. She had a bad night. Yesterday was her birthday... she misses her dad something bad. More on special days. Wanted to stay up late and I let her, being her birthday and all. But she woke up crying for him and it took a while to settle her. So we both had a bad night.'

'So, you got up this morning – around when?'

'Eight, maybe.'

'And what happened?'

'Nothing out of the ordinary. I had breakfast and checked social media for a bit. Then Eliza got up and I made her breakfast and then tried to put on a load of washing. Where I live, we don't have a laundry in the apartment so I have to go down the hallway and load the machine. But I always lock Eliza in and I'm only gone for five minutes.'

'No laundry inside?'

'Can't afford a bigger apartment. Trying to get by on the little bit of money I can make around caring for Eliza. I'm doing my best.' Maureen lifted her chin, her face hard but her eyes swimming with panic.

'Keep going. I can see how much you love your daughter.'

The woman tried to smile and failed. 'There are two machines but one has been out of order for ages and the other was being used so I came back with the basket and we decided a walk to the park was a better idea.' Her voice caught. 'I should… should have stayed home.'

Liz forced down a rising tide of nausea. Her stomach was flip-flopping and the earlier desire to vomit returned with a vengeance. She dug her fingernails hard into her palms and drew a long, slow breath in through her nostrils. There'd be time for that later but losing control out here in the public eye would see her removed from the investigation on the spot.

'Do you remember what time you left home?'

'Ten-fifteen. We stopped at the convenience store on the corner to get a bag of lollies and I noticed their clock.'

'What then?'

Pete was barking instructions to some poor general duties officer not far away.

'We walked here and I sat at my usual spot and Eliza went to play. We come here a few times each week and she's a good girl. Always stays in sight and comes back to get a drink or snack or take a break.'

'Maureen, I understand you've already given one of the officers a good description of Eliza and the missing contents of her backpack. That's really helpful. And we are looking for the two teenagers who helped search for her, based on the info you remembered about them. I need you to think about what else was going on while you were both here. Particularly while Eliza was off playing. Did you see other people? Hear any conversations?'

The woman was shaking her head but then she gasped and her mouth dropped open.

'Shoelaces,' she whispered.

A ringing sound began in Liz's ears.

'What about shoelaces?'

As if unable to find words, Maureen gestured toward the fountain.

Liz took the bottle of water from the woman, opened the lid, and pushed it back into her hands. 'Take a sip.'

Instead, Maureen stood, dropping the bottle. Water leaked out onto the grass.

'Eliza said a nice man tied her shoelaces. She came over to tell me and that was when she took her backpack from the bench. From there.'

This time she pointed. Directly at the bench near the fountain.

And this time it was too much for Liz.

She ran behind a tree and emptied the contents of her stomach.

TWO

'Nobody saw a thing. The minute you dived into the undergrowth I distracted them.'

Pete stood guard between the bushes and open area of the park while Liz rinsed her mouth from a bottle of water he'd given her.

'How?'

'How did I distract them? Actually, I had found a soccer ball, maybe belonging to the boys who were here, and was waiting for you to finish with the mother before saying anything. But it seemed like as good a time as any to speak up and got most of the cops looking my way. Instead of yours. Are you good now?'

Liz nodded and finished the water. Emptiness replaced the nausea.

'Then come and see.'

'Where's Maureen?' Liz walked beside Pete, her voice low. 'She needs to be properly interviewed away from here. There's stuff she's remembering.'

'An officer is walking her home. She wants to be sure the kid didn't go there.'

'Oh for heaven's sake. Eliza isn't there. She's been taken.'

'Hang on, we don't know that,' Pete said. 'We're treating this as suspicious but there's stuff-all to go on.'

'Because none of you are looking in the right place.'

'Liz.'

He put his hand on her arm and she shrugged it off.

Unfazed, he put it back. 'Liz, stop for a sec. Before we are too close to the others.'

I don't need you running interference.

Yet she stopped and faced him. 'The reason I lost control? Maureen was sitting near the fountain. That's where I was sitting when Ellen disappeared. And you know what else? A man re-tied Eliza's shoe laces.'

Pete's brow furrowed.

'Don't you remember?'

'Lizzie, I didn't know you then and was undercover. It was Vince Carter who was involved in the case.'

Vince. I need to talk to him. He'll remember.

'Okay. Then read the file. Get up to speed, Pete. Eliza is almost a twin to Ellen in looks and age. Both disappeared after a man re-tied their shoelaces. Both disappeared after the adult they were with sat on the same bench. And both were connected to the same apartment building.'

'And the disappearances are how far apart? Fifteen years? Twenty?'

Liz knew how long. To the month, the day, the minute. It was etched into her mind. The day she'd lost her niece. A person doesn't forget that kind of awful.

Except you tried.

God, how she'd tried.

Her life had returned, eventually, to a semblance of normal. The job helped and when the paid hours were done she volunteered in the community to keep busy caring for other people. Some who were grateful and could move forward with a bit of direction. Others who didn't know they were desperate for help. And when the volunteering ended, the running began.

'Listen to me. If you are clear about this, that there might be a connection, then focus, Liz. Do not fall into a well of self-pity or grief or blame. It doesn't fix it.' Pete squeezed her arm until it hurt, his face inches from hers. 'It doesn't fix things, Lizzie.'

She nodded and he glanced around. They were out of earshot of anyone. 'I need you to take a look at that bench and fountain with me.'

'Just let go of my arm, Pete. People will talk.'

'As if. Like who'd even think you and me would be like that?' With a shake of his shoulder-length hair he started walking.

Liz kept up, ignoring the urge to rub her arm.

His phone buzzed and he answered without breaking stride. His conversation was short and he changed direction as he hung up. 'Boss wants us at the caravan.'

Terry caught Liz's eye as she and Pete arrived. There were already a dozen officers standing around, mostly detectives and a few uniforms. A canopy extended from the caravan and tables and a portable whiteboard almost filled the space below.

She nodded, keeping her face neutral. If anyone other than Pete would see through her expression to the distress bubbling underneath, it was Terry.

'Right. We've got people taping off the park. Bloody big job.'

Liz's heart sank further. This was a crime scene in Terry's eyes. He'd not waste resources if he thought it even fifty-fifty to be a wandering kid. He was taking this seriously.

Unlike the person in charge of Ellen's case.

'The mother is on her way to an interview. There was no sign of Eliza at their apartment. Just a lot of interested residents. I have more uniforms coming in and they'll be split up to door knock in a two block radius, shops included. Missing Persons aren't far away and they've been briefed every step of the way.

Canine unit will arrive any minute.' Terry gestured to the magnetic whiteboard. Already, a colour photograph of the child took centre stage, with her mother's image to one side. 'Everyone can read what we know so far once I'm done but to summarise, Eliza Singleton disappeared without a sound from the park somewhere between ten forty-five and eleven am this morning. There are two teenage lads who helped the mother look for her and we need to find them for interviews. Both scarpered when she called us, probably wagging school. Each of you will get the same information we have, updated as we get it. We want to find Eliza today. Unharmed. Get her back to her mum.'

Murmurs of agreement surrounded Liz. Devices began to ding as the data came through and officers moved away.

'Got to go.' Pete jogged away.

Terry indicated for Liz to follow him as he strode in the direction of the bridge.

In the distance a chopper approached.

They climbed onto the bridge and stood in the middle. It was a decently constructed arc with fort-style towers at either end above a sandpit and a sensory area. Liz gazed down. Any kid would love this with its interesting patterns and blocks of timber in different sizes as well as stepping stones and a dry river bed. It had been ahead of its time when it was built and not much had changed.

'Talk to me, Liz. Tell me what you think.'

'About what I've found out from speaking to the mother?'

'You have insights nobody else does so I expect you to be part of this team unless you can't handle it. If you want out, at any point, just say so. I won't judge you, Liz.'

'Is that why we're here away from prying eyes?'

Terry sighed. 'There's a connection, right? Minute I saw the kid's photo I knew it. Add on the apartment block and similar MO and I reckon I know what you're thinking.'

'Aren't you thinking the same? Boss, we've barely scratched

the surface but the resemblance to Ellen's disappearance is too close to ignore. Same age, same apartment block, same park.' Liz forced her voice to stop shaking, lowering it and speaking more slowly. 'Maureen sat on the same damned bench.'

Both stared across the park to the bench near the fountain.

'From over there, this bridge is only just visible,' Liz said. 'Under these big trees the perpetual shade makes the timber kind of blend into the background. Yet we can easily see the bench.' She tapped her phone. 'I'm asking Pete to sit on the bench.'

Terry grabbed his own phone and dialled. 'We'll need forensic attention at the bridge including the ramps and surrounding area. Soon as possible.' After he hung up he pulled a pair of shoes covers from a pocket and slid them onto his feet.

Liz followed suit. 'What about the apartment block? That was barely considered with Ellen.'

'We'll canvas the residents.'

Pete and a uniform officer were in the middle of an animated conversation as they came into view. He plonked onto the bench and looked their way, then took off his sunglasses and peered, hand shading his eyes.

'Clear as day from this side,' Terry said.

Liz's phone rang and she answered on speaker. 'We can see you.'

'Can you wave?'

Terry raised his arm.

'I can see the motion but it's pretty hard to identify more than that. Anything else?'

'Any news on finding those lads?' Terry asked.

'Nup. I'll check where we're at and get back to you.'

After pocketing the phone, Liz again looked at the area below them. 'So many places someone could approach a child. An adult might stand here and watch for other people. Wait for the right moment. Or be underneath where there is the dry river, sit on a boulder or the like. It wasn't as secluded back then. With Ellen.'

'We need to go back down. Andy Montebello's here and I want you involved in the conversation,' Terry said.

Her heart thudded as she followed him off the bridge, both careful to avoid touching anything and watching their step. She had to control her reactions. Finding Eliza was all that mattered today.

THREE

Detective Senior Sergeant Andy Montebello wasn't ready for this.

On paper he was qualified. Anyone who'd ever worked with him would consider him a perfect fit for the job. And even though his heart was set on Homicide, he'd been in Missing Persons for his entire time as a detective and rejoiced during some incredible results. At a bit past thirty he'd made a name for himself and been happy to use his degree in criminology and personable nature to his advantage. When the chance came along to step into one of the senior roles in MP, he wasn't about to say no.

But this one is different.

The heat of the day was only rising and he'd rather be sitting on a beach than working in a suit. Nobody wanted to be here and it had nothing to do with the job or the weather and everything to do with a little kid who was probably scared out of her mind—if she was still alive.

Andy stood on the footpath. Police tape was everywhere and a uniform eyed him off as he straightened his tie and buttoned his jacket. He had one job to do today and his mind had to stay sharp.

Before heading into the park, Andy slowly rotated to get a feel for where he was. Inner suburb of low to moderate income. Mix of cultures but Anglo dominance. Busy street with shops opposite this side of the park, most built into apartment blocks. The tramline followed the intersecting road, alongside the narrower end of the park. People gathered in small groups, curious about the heavy police presence. A chopper wasn't far away.

'Are we going to admire the dubious scenery or get started, boss?'

He hadn't noticed Meg come up behind him. With bright purple hair braided to one side and tiny, round, black tinted sunglasses, the forensic analyst looked too young for her experience despite having a decade on Andy. It fooled some people into overlooking her during an investigation or subsequent court case. Perps. Journos. Defence lawyers. The latter she could eat for breakfast. She didn't belong in Missing Persons but arrived a year ago as part of a trial which was recently extended after the team's results showed such promise.

Meg carried laptop bags over both shoulders. 'I hope those shops are being canvassed. And we need to access footage from the trams which would have passed here. And buses, taxi, Ubers, and crap.'

'Singing my tune. Apart from the crap. Need a hand?'

'Lift the tape, dude. I mean, boss.'

She grinned and ducked under the tape as he lifted it.

'Stop with the boss thing. Now I get why Ben always told me off for using it.' Andy followed.

'Ben *was* the boss. Pity he moved down the coast.'

'Sorry.'

'Well, wouldn't you rather be surfing or something like he gets to go? I'm jealous thinking about it.' Meg stopped a few feet along a path. 'I would. Or did you believe I meant he was a better boss than you?' She managed to take some photos on her phone of the scene ahead, despite the bulk she carried. 'Don't be hard on yourself. You'll improve with a few years' experience.'

Andy almost spluttered. 'Excuse me?'

'Got work to do, sunshine. Coming?' The sideways glance she shot him was rich with humour but she didn't wait around. Meg was intent on getting to the police caravan and he left her to go and start telling everyone there what to do.

He'd join her soon enough but wanted a few minutes to observe. Something Ben Rossi—whose role he'd stepped into—taught him, was to use his senses. Following a disappearance it might be the smallest thing which would lead to a recovery. Watch, listen. Smell the air. What struck him was how quiet the park was even with so many police and crime scene officers present.

And with the traffic so close.

The dense bushes between him and the road dulled the sounds.

This was where people would come to take a breather. Most locals would be apartment dwellers and not in the huge fancy type with rooftop pools and gardens. Lots of small boxes on top of small boxes, crammed into a box of a building. And the woman heading toward him lived in one of those boxes.

'Detective, nice to see you again.' Liz extended her hand.

She was a few steps ahead of Terry, who did the same. 'I know the Senior Sergeant in charge will want to talk to you but there's a lot of ground to cover. We could use you first.'

Although Liz wore oversized dark sunglasses, the strain on her face was clear. He knew her casually and their respective positions crossed over at times but they weren't friends as such. What he did know what that her niece had disappeared eighteen years ago. This situation was hitting home for her.

'Shall we go to the caravan?' Terry suggested. 'Did you arrange Air Wing?'

'I did.'

They crossed fifty metres or so of grass, past a fountain and bench which were under the scrutiny of a member of the forensics crime scene unit, and into the shade of the canopy extending from the caravan. Meg had already opened both laptop bags and was setting up a work station at the back. There were half a dozen officers at work, three of them seated at computers and two at a large whiteboard. They stepped back to let Andy look.

Liz helped herself to a bottle of water from a few dozen on the end of a table and opened it. She stayed back a bit, drinking, while his eyes darted over the notes on the whiteboard. Terry was on the phone and then excused himself and the other two officers were commandeered by Meg. The helicopter roared overhead and moved on.

'I'm glad of that,' Liz said.

'The chopper?'

She nodded and removed her sunglasses. 'They might not have got far. Might have waited until the first rush of panic eased off before he moved her on.'

The chance was slight. The helicopter was there in case there was a witness of who took the kid and what direction they went. But he nodded.

'The father is in Barwon Prison,' Liz said.

'You think there's a connection?'

'No. I think this was planned a long time ago. I think this was a crime of opportunity, borne of patience. And I believe that when we find him, we'll find the monster who took Ellen.'

Her voice hadn't faltered. Her body language was calm and gave nothing away, not even a tremor of the hand holding the bottle. But Liz's eyes tore into Andy's soul. She was hurting bad. How well she was holding it together was testament to her strength. He'd read Ellen's file more than once over the years and it was close to being filed with Cold Cases—already would be except for the connection with a cop. Liz's experience made her an asset with such specific knowledge if this was deemed related.

'You've spoken to the mother… Maureen?'

'I did and she's on her way to a formal interview after insisting on checking her apartment. Before that she was starting to recall small details—'

'And you let her go before she told you?'

A flash of irritation crossed her face. 'Yes, I let her go.'

'Alright. What *did* she tell you?' He crossed his arms. 'I mean anything not on the whiteboard.'

She glanced past him and scanned the information. 'Not much that isn't up there. The child spoke to a 'nice' man who tied her shoelaces and before you tell me you already know that, it was just before Eliza collected the backpack. She showed her mother how neatly they were tied. You should get an artist to work with her and see if we can work out handedness and any peculiarities. Anyway, guess where Maureen was sitting? It's not on the whiteboard yet. She was at the bench near the fountain.'

His mind raced back to the file on Ellen. There'd been a hand-drawn map with the play area, fountain and benches. The one beside the fountain had been circled.

Crap.

'Same bench as where you were that day,' he said.

'At least you know the case. Andy, listen. It is the same person who took my niece. We need to find Eliza and then we need to find what happened to Ellen.'

A serial kidnapper? His chest tightened even as an annoying surge of interest sparked in his brain. He'd never be able to suppress the response with any curious case. He stared at Liz. She couldn't possibly stay impassive and impartial under such pressure.

'Would you be better off stepping aside?'

'Not a chance in hell, Detective. You need me. *Eliza* needs me.'

Somebody was yelling. Pete McNamara. 'Did you hear me, Liz? Possible sighting, come on.'

Liz leaned so close to Andy that he could feel the heat off her skin. Her voice was low and intense. 'Don't even try to stop me. I have to be here, Andy. I have to.'

And then she was running after her partner.

Andy ran a hand through his hair and exhaled.

FOUR

'Ben would have said the same, Liz. Missing Persons has jurisdiction now.'

Their sirens parted traffic and Pete slowed the car through a red light.

'Yeah, but he'd say it to sound official then taken it back. Andy is different.'

And too smart for his own good.

'Different how?'

'He wants in—to Homicide. You know that. And he will do anything to get noticed to make it happen.'

Pete chuckled and she glared at him.

'What? Look, Liz, he's a kid and keen. But he's bright and educated and the future of the force. By the time you and I retire, all cops will have multiple degrees.'

Perhaps. But that didn't change having to deal with an ambitious detective who didn't know her enough to trust her. She pushed it away and read an update. 'Okay, another sighting two blocks ahead. Male, late twenties, T-shirt and shorts. Got off a tram. Carrying a small girl who is screaming. Damn, it isn't them.'

'And you know this how?'

'The male is too young and too casually attired. It'll be a father with an angry toddler.'

There was no answer. Pete had his hands full getting around a tram and he'd find out soon enough. Liz watched the road, hands tapping against her legs. How had they even found this person? Something didn't add up.

'There. Over to the left just past the second house.' Liz pointed.

A young man wearing a backpack and carrying a kid on his shoulders stopped in surprise as Pete pulled into a driveway in front of him.

'Told you,' Liz said. She climbed out.

'Everything okay, officers?'

The kid was no more than three, blonde and giggling at the flashing lights through the open front door of the car. Her father was maybe twenty-five and wore a 'peace' T-shirt over scruffy shorts.

Liz sat on the brick fence of the closest house as disappointment welled up.

'Sorry to stop you, mate. We got a report of a little girl screaming getting onto a tram,' Pete said.

'She hates them. But it's too hot to walk all the way home. But otherwise she's a happy kid... did I do something wrong?'

Pete shook his head. 'Nothing. False alarm.'

'Can we take your details?' Liz asked. 'Just to exclude you from an investigation.'

'Do I have to? I'd like to get her home.'

On her feet so fast that Pete didn't get a chance to let the man pass, Liz took out a notepad and stood inches from the young father. 'Not to concern you, but we've just come from the scene of a suspected kidnapping. A little girl, not much older than yours. Taken while her mother was only a few metres away. So rather than the general public sending us after you again when news gets out...'

His face paled and he lifted the kid off his shoulders to nestle against his chest. 'Yeah, of course. Where?'

'Watch the news later.' Liz wrote down his details and sent him on his way.

Back in the car she checked for updates as Pete backed out.

'Geez, Liz.'

'Shut up.'

'Coming from someone who goes too far all the time, that was a bit close to the line.'

'You are rubbing off on me,' Liz said. 'I said nothing he won't know in an hour, once the vultures sweep in with their cameras.'

'You scared the life out of him. Probably never take the kid anywhere again.'

Or at least never let her out of his sight.

Liz put her phone away. 'Who called it in? The tip-off which just wasted our time.'

Pete took a few seconds then shot her a look. 'Because there's nothing official out there yet? Maybe the mother. For all we know she might have posted on social media. Things like a lost kid can go viral and all of a sudden everyone is a sleuth.'

'Or the real perp sent us in the wrong direction.'

They turned onto the road to the park. Several media vans lined the sides of the street and camera crews and reporters were congregating as close to the park as the police would allow. Pete drove past and around the corner before going up on the pavement between the tram line and hedge.

'You complain about me.' Liz laughed shortly. Pete was the last person who should give advice on keeping to the rules and not just on police matters. He didn't mind drifting into dark corners in his private life. Probably what made him so good at his job.

'Between ten-forty-five and eleven this morning, Eliza Singleton left the park, either on her own or with another person—'

'Forcefully, Terry? Is this a kidnapping?'

Terry ignored the interruption. He'd arranged to speak to one reporter, a young woman who'd previously shown herself to act ethically with information, but the minute her crew set up, a dozen vultures followed. Pete had offered to send them packing but Terry wasn't fazed. He'd done this before too often and it reminded Liz why he was still running Homicide. She kept her eyes on the crowd just outside the corner of the park where Terry was making the announcement.

Sometimes perps couldn't help themselves and came back to the scene.

Or those who help them.

She'd always believed whoever took Ellen had to have had help. The little girl wasn't one to go quietly with a stranger.

'Eliza's description and a recent photograph will be made available momentarily and I'm appealing for members of the public to be watchful. If you see a child fitting this description or you have reason to believe a child is Eliza, then I urge you contact Crime Stoppers or your local police station.'

Terry cut the interview off shortly afterwards, speaking briefly to the reporter before turning his back on the rest of the rabble. Liz and Pete joined him to head to the caravan.

'Detective Hall! A moment please.'

Liz knew the voice and clearly, so did Pete and Terry. Nobody turned around.

'Teresa Scarcella from *At Six Tonight*. I can help you find her.'

Now they stopped. The woman puffed a bit as she caught up yet somehow her makeup and hair was pristine. 'I don't even have a camera, okay?'

'You have one minute,' Terry said, crossing his arms. 'Exactly how.'

'My reach is more than just television. I have live streaming across multiple social media channels and a large audience willing to listen and look for Eliza. I can call people to action, have them check up on any strange occurrences they witness, even create a hotline for sightings.'

Teresa drew breath and nodded at Terry as if they'd made a deal. Liz didn't have a high opinion of the press and this woman circled around the bottom of the pack. But she didn't lie. *At Six Tonight* was huge.

'What you're suggesting sounds like impeding our investigation, not to mention potentially putting innocent people at risk.'

'At risk from who, precisely? Do you have a suspect?'

From his body language and tone of voice, Terry regretted stopping. 'We don't even know how Eliza left the park, Ms Scarcella. There is no evidence it was with another person or persons but we are looking at all possibilities. If you are serious about helping then spread the word about her description, her photo, the area she was last seen. And get your audience, to phone Crime Stoppers or their local police station if they have any information.'

Unfazed, the woman leaned closer to Terry and crooned. 'I want to find this poor child. You want to find her. Why shouldn't we combine our efforts? We could compare notes over a drink.'

Behind Teresa, Pete looked ready to burst into laughter.

'Your minute is up. Please follow the instructions which will be sent to your editor, or whatever they are called these days.'

'Sure, honey.'

With a smile which didn't reach her eyes, Teresa spun around and stalked off.

'New friend, boss?' Pete grinned.

Terry muttered something uncomplimentary and took off in the opposite direction, leaving Pete and Liz to follow.

'She's trouble,' Liz said. 'This isn't the first time she's tried to use somebody's tragedy to make a name for herself.'

'Yeah, I remember her almost sabotaging the Bannerman case. But this is worse, Liz. Nobody should profit off a missing kid. Nobody.'

Liz snuck a glance at Pete. His face was grim and his hands

were clenched. She'd known Pete a long time and seen him at his worst. But also his best. He was as tough as they got but she knew once something or someone touched him, he would move heaven and earth to protect them. She tapped his arm and he gave her one of those 'what?' looks she was used to.

'We're going to find Eliza. And then we're going to find Ellen. Okay?'

'That bloody reporter—'

'Isn't what we need to focus on. Pete, I have to talk to Vince. And you and I need a plan.'

He snorted. 'Vince is a waste of space.'

'Well, as you said earlier, you weren't around when Ellen vanished. He was. Anything else to say?'

'Just don't expect me to go with you.'

'Afraid he'll thank you for saving his life?'

Pete rolled his eyes.

FIVE

Two police dogs were working. The officer who'd gone to Maureen's apartment had returned with some clothing from the unwashed basket and the dogs had had no trouble picking up her scent.

Liz stayed close without getting underfoot. She'd tossed her jacket into the car and wore a lightweight Police vest. One dog was insistent on going under the bridge several times, his interest on one of the stumps. A crime scene officer turned their attention to it and the dog was directed to keep working the scent, then pulled its handler away from the bridge. They all jogged across a short open grassy area to an opening between the hedges.

The dog and handler scooted through, turning left and following the footpath. This was the least busy of the four surrounding roads, with apartment buildings opposite and angled car parking on both sides. No shops or businesses and less traffic.

A hundred or so metres along the dog paused, sniffing the ground and the air before doubling back. But he stopped again and whined.

His handler tried to engage the dog but it was obvious the

trail was cold.

'We'll get the other dog out here. But I'd say the kid was put in a vehicle.' The handler turned away and spoke on his radio.

Liz dialled Terry. 'Trail went cold on the street. We need to get bodies over here canvassing and finding some video footage.'

'Wait until Pete gets there then come and see me.'

He hung up before she could ask why. His tone of voice was odd.

If Andy is causing issues about me…

What? What would she do? Detective Sergeants didn't get to make the rules. If the higher-ups told her she was out then she had no recourse. Liz loved her job. Really loved it at the core of her being except for times like this. Autonomy wasn't exactly what she wanted—structure mattered—but being shunted off this investigation? Heat rose in her body and she yanked the vest off and ducked under a tree for shade. It didn't make much difference.

The second police dog led its handler to the same spot but then veered onto the road. Liz ran out, holding her hand up to stop an oncoming car as the dog weaved around some parked vehicles and back toward the pavement.

'Good boy, good lad. Detective!' The handler moved the dog to beneath a tree and pointed at what nobody else had seen.

On the bitumen between two cars was a shoe. A child-sized shoe.

———

'Maureen has identified it as matching the pair Eliza wore.'

Andy had been on his phone since Liz had called Pete. They'd both arrived at the same time, followed closely by a crime scene officer and several uniforms. Terry wasn't far behind, and between them and the dog handlers, they'd kept the media at bay and put up some barriers around the space where the dogs had indicated.

'She's sure?' Liz was. The size looked right for an average five-year-old girl and had unicorns on the side.

'Without seeing more than some photos, yes.' Andy gestured for Liz to follow until stopping close to the kerb. 'This will help.'

'The laces are still tied.'

A photographer took images from every angle before the shoe was carefully collected in an evidence bag.

'How long, Andy? When can we get a result on trace?'

'Fast tracking it. But, Liz, you know as well what the backlog is like.' He ran a hand through his perfectly cut hair, then smoothed it. 'Frustrating as hell.'

'Two girls' lives might depend upon a fingerprint. Or a skin sample.' How she kept her voice controlled was beyond her. He might be frustrated about forensics but all Liz could feel in her bones was the ticking of the clock. 'Time matters.'

'I'm aware.' His answer was short. Tense.

About to snap back at him, Liz reined the response in and excused herself. Terry had his eyes on her from the entry to the park. If she got booted from the investigation it wasn't going to be because she'd contributed to it.

'Boss, you wanted to see me earlier?'

'Walk back to the caravan with me.'

It was surreal being here. In the past couple of years she'd only ventured into the park a handful of times. For the first few months after Ellen vanished and the so-called investigation ended she'd spent far too much time sitting on the bench for hours at a time, in blistering heat and downpours. Just in case her niece returned.

'Lizzie? You hanging in?'

They stopped at the fountain. Water bubbled up in the centre, flowing down a couple of levels to a shallow base. Lots of kids and even adults would splash around in it.

'Ellen loved this,' Liz said. Even to her own ears she sounded listless. 'Had to chase her out of it almost every visit.'

'She used to stay with you when her parents were away?'

'Yeah. Let them have couples time, keep the spark going kind of thing. Lots of short breaks.'

It made her feel like a mum. Something she'd never be except by borrowing her sister's kid. Board games and pyjama parties for two. Ice cream cones in summer and pizza sitting on the floor watching cartoons in winter. Five-year-olds were chatty and fun. Tram rides. Ellen lived in one of the outer suburbs and unlike the little kid earlier who hated the trams, used to squeal in delight at their iconic bells and clacking wheels. And the park. Always the park.

'Boss, we need to talk to everyone in my apartment building.'

He raised both eyebrows.

'How do two kids disappear under such similar circumstances let alone two kids of the same age and from the same building?'

'When Ellen disappeared, was there a door knock in the building?'

Liz snorted. 'Apart from my floor, it was left to me.'

'You're joking.'

'I spoke to every resident and made myself even more unpopular with a lot of them. I try to keep my head down as it is.'

'Why the hell are you even living there? It's a shithole and you make more than enough to have your own townhouse or whatever.'

Terry had asked her this in the past. Lots of people had. The answer was simple but she wasn't in a sharing mood.

'So, can we get some uniforms in there today?'

'I'll ask the Senior Sergeant but Liz, we're stretched.'

'Then can I do it?'

'You just said you keep your head down there.'

'Then give me a job to do.'

'Does your building have CCV?'

'Some. Outside and in the common areas. I can ask the manager to give me access.'

'Do you need Pete?'

'Does anyone?' She grinned, already walking backwards.

'Don't you need a warrant?'

Brian 'Bing' Bisley wasn't friendly at the best of times, not unless there was something in it for him. His short sleeved shirt had a stain from a recent meat pie or the like and his desk was cluttered with takeaway coffee cups. The room stank and the overflowing ashtray was the obvious offender.

'Isn't this a smoke-free building?' Liz asked.

'My office, my rules.'

'Fair enough.' She pulled her phone out. 'I'll call my boss to arrange that warrant. Have you got one of those complaint forms you like so much?'

He scowled. 'Why?'

'So I can complain about this office. Isn't this where residents have to come to communicate issues? Pretty awful if you were asthmatic. Or pregnant. Or a kid. And I believe one of the washing machines on floor five has been broken for a while. Want me to fill in a form for that as well?'

Bisley pushed himself upright and rummaged around in a drawer. He pulled out a set of keys. 'You can look at the footage. But I need a warrant if you want to take the tapes.'

Tapes? In this day and age?

'Perfect.'

Liz was happy to be out of the disgusting office and followed Bisley down the hallway past the rooms for the cleaners and switchboards. She was about to make it her business to gain access to every one of these locked up rooms and anywhere else she hadn't been inside.

He unlocked and pushed open a door. 'Need me to run you through it?'

'I'll call if I do.'

She waited and he huffed, pulled the key from the door, and

lumbered off.

After closing the door behind herself Liz gazed at the mess of monitors and stupid-old surveillance equipment. None of it was hard to work out but lacked functionality. Pulling up a chair she took a few photographs first, then ensuring she wasn't messing with a current recording session, spun a tape back to eight this morning.

Putting it onto treble speed, she texted Pete while keeping an eye on the monitors.

Watching surveillance video at the apartment building. Tell me the minute you get any kind of news. Any.

Her heart had been racing so much today. The adrenaline high was bound to kick her butt when it came down but she'd push through. She didn't remember Eliza. Liz never took the elevator, which didn't work half the time anyway – another issue to raise – and kept to herself. There was only one reason for living in what Terry kindly called a shit-hole. It was the only place Ellen would remember.

Stupid. Stupid, ridiculous reasoning.

But there it was. She forced her shoulders to relax but that hurt more than keeping them tense so she stood and stretched, eyes darting to one screen then another until her phone beeped.

Tapes? Did you fall through a time warp?

The monitors covered several areas—the front of the building, inside the entry area before the lift and stairs, the roof, behind the building in a laneway, and along one hallway— notable by its darkness, and one she didn't recognise. Was there a basement floor?

The first hour of footage was busy with movement and she rewound several times to cover all the monitors. People leaving for work. A few of the elderly residents gathered in the entry and left together. Deliveries came in. The lack of coverage on the main floors was frustrating. Liz had no way of knowing where the delivery people were going but she made notes about arrival and departure as the footage rolled.

At almost nine, a fire door opened onto the laneway at the back and a woman carried a full laundry basket out. Her back was to the camera and she struggled a bit with the weight of it as she walked to a parked car. The boot popped and she lowered the basket in and shut it. Someone stuck their hand out of a window with an envelope which the woman took. As the car drove away she returned to the fire door.

Liz paused the tape. 'Found a way to get a machine working, huh Maureen?'

She rewound a bit and then took video with her phone. This she sent to Terry with a comment.

Eight fifty five this morning.

The woman was probably making a bit of cash on the side doing laundry for others. Not a crime and the only people who'd care were whoever she got her welfare from and possibly the tax department. But it raised more questions.

Sending one of the young GD's across to take over. Show him what you need done and then go and talk to Maureen Singleton please.

'Best suggestion all day,' she muttered and messaged back.

There's a stack of utility rooms and an underground floor I've never seen before. Any chance of getting these searched?

Liz jumped the video forward to the time Maureen said they'd left. No sign of them after ten this morning. She went all the way through to almost eleven and then back to ten and began to run the tape backwards.

'Ma'am?'

The same officer who'd escorted Maureen back to the apartment stepped inside.

Pausing the footage, Liz got to her feet. 'Ever seen something like this? Constable…'

'Lou Barker.' The young officer shook his head, his eyes wide, and she grinned.

'Okay, Lou, two minutes to teach you then I'm off. But I'll make a list of what I need. First though, I have some questions for you.'

SIX

The shoe was a good find. It was a tangible connection to the child and unless the person who'd tied her shoelaces wore gloves and was lucky, there'd be trace on it. When the CSS van had rolled in he'd asked them to treat the tiny shoe as the priority.

In a perfect world trace would reveal the identity of whoever tied those shoelaces.

In a perfect world nobody would take a child.

The patrol Senior Sergeant had to leave thanks to another major crime and Meg had jumped into the role of communicating directly with the office of Public Transport Victoria which monitored the trams in the area. She had several feeds going at once on the monitors and had a uniform watching like a hawk while she calculated how far Eliza might have travelled under different scenarios.

'She could be in one of the neighbouring apartments or halfway out of the state,' Meg said, eyes on her screen. 'I trust the dogs and they both said the trail ended on the road.'

'What can we access on that side? Or can we see from other cameras?' Andy looked over her shoulder. He didn't understand half of her calculations but he didn't need to. Trusting the right people to do their jobs was core to policing and he trusted Meg.

She turned to gaze up at him. 'It was a clever spot the adult with Eliza chose. Only two obvious security cameras point in the general direction of the shoe and seriously, why? I mean, in this day and age everyone should use technology! Anyway, my recommendation is that we focus door knocking on the apartment buildings opposite and apply whatever pressure we can.'

'Pressure?'

'Come on, Andy. This isn't a cop-friendly zone so nobody is running over here offering information.' She smiled sweetly. 'If they won't offer, we have to... ask.'

'Happy to volunteer to apply pressure.' The officer next to her commented.

'I'd rather you focus on that tram footage. If you don't mind.'

Again, the sweetness in her tone belied the heart of steel Andy knew drove Meg. The officer grumbled but went back to his job.

'Where are we up to with that, boss?'

'Door knocking? Almost done along the tram side and—'

'Really? But there is a ton of surveillance there. Can you move breathing bodies to where I suggested? *Please.*'

With that, Meg was back tapping on her keyboard and Andy felt dismissed.

Breathing bodies.

She had a way with words but it was her brilliant mind he admired most. And she was right. They needed to expand the search now.

'A minute, Andy?'

Pete was tapping on an iPad as he approached. 'Liz is on her way to ask the mother a few more questions but the officer looking at footage of the apartment building just sent this to me.'

'Why is she doing that?'

'Terry told her to go do it.'

'Hang on, why—'

'Look, you and Terry sort out who is in charge of telling everyone where to go but while you do, the rest of us will get on with finding this kid.' Pete stared at Andy and then turned the iPad to show the screen. 'This is at nine-forty-five today.'

The video was from outside the apartment building. Maureen and Eliza walked in the opposite direction of the park.

'Time on the video is correct?' Andy asked.

'It is.'

'So Maureen made a mistake and was half an hour off.'

'She said she was at the corner shop at ten-fifteen. The officer is going there now to ask to see any footage but we might need a warrant pretty fast if they won't assist. The corner shop is the other way so where did she and Eliza go for half an hour and why didn't Maureen mention it during several conversations?' Pete turned the screen back. 'Liz spotted footage of her putting a basket of washing in a car behind the building earlier this morning and being paid for it. Or it looked like it.'

'Ah. Liz wants to know how long Eliza was alone for.'

Pete waggled a finger. 'Now you're catching up. I'll let you know if we need that warrant.'

I don't have time for your bull, McNamara.

But at least one of them could be professional. 'Anything else, Pete?'

'Word of advice. When there's a kid involved we're all after the same thing. Every cop here is giving their best. Now, whether you get the glory or someone else… it doesn't matter. So you see, your permission or not, Liz is just doing her job.'

'As am I, Detective. But chain of command matters.'

'Like I said, Liz is just doing her job.'

'And she can. As long as she is looking for Eliza, not Ellen.'

Turning on his heel, Pete stalked off. His middle finger might have shot into the air but it was too fleeting to call him back. And the little shit was partly right, at least about everyone having the same goal. But the lack of respect and way the man represented himself was pathetic. Andy had heard the stories about Pete McNamara. His devil-may-care attitude and scruffy appearance was a throwback to the force of the eighties and earlier. He'd worked in task forces and been undercover but surely now, as a Homicide detective, McNamara should put some effort into how others viewed him.

Andy ignored the voice taunting him about his own failure to get into Homicide.

It would happen in time. He just needed to prove himself.

And finding Eliza Singleton will help get me there.

SEVEN

'Everything she's said matches what you briefed me on. And the original report which came through before Mrs Singleton arrived.' Senior Constable Annette Benski shook her head as she outlined her thoughts in the police station's hallway. 'She's just worked with an artist to get the shoelaces right but I understand you found one. A shoe?'

'The dogs did. It was still tied and CSS have it as top priority.'

'Poor kid. Must be terrified,' Annette said.

'Unless she knows the person who took her.'

'You've got something new?'

'A hunch. You know me.'

Liz and Annette went way back. They'd crossed paths often and liked each other without having stepped into a proper friendship.

Maybe a friend would be nice.

'I'll go and have a chat. Does she need a coffee?'

Annette shrugged. 'I keep offering coffee, tea, water, everything but she's gutted.'

'Ta. I'll find you once I'm done.'

The woman needed sustenance or at least hydration. Liz slotted coins into a couple of vending machines.

Maureen slumped in her chair, eyes puffy with dark rings of exhaustion. She looked up as Liz entered, her face expectant as she straightened. 'Did you find her?'

'I'm sorry, no, not yet. But we will, Maureen.'

A tear slipped down Maureen's cheek as the hope fled her face.

'You must be so tired. And thirsty. I've got a selection because I needed a coffee.' Liz laid out her small haul. 'There's two coffees, one white and one black and I'll drink either so you take what you prefer. And two chocolate bars and some crisps and there's a couple of rolls. No idea what's in them. Salad I suppose.'

'I can't.'

Liz pulled up a chair and sat. 'You must, Maureen. I know this is mainly junk food but you are depleted.' She pushed a roll across the table. 'When we get a lead on Eliza we will need you close by. Having her mum there will make all the difference but if you refuse to drink and eat…'

Maureen's head dropped. 'How do I do this?'

Like I did. Except your child will come home.

'I'm starving. Eat with me and we'll talk. And then I'll get you out of here once we're done, okay?'

'So I'm not arrested?'

'Good god, no. Why would you think that?' Liz unravelled a ridiculous amount of plastic wrapping. 'Your insight matters and being here, with someone like Senior Constable Benski, gives us the best chance of putting together information which all of our officers—and there are so many—who are looking for Eliza right this minute are able to access. Eat. Please.'

Both salad rolls disappeared first and once Maureen started to eat she couldn't seem to stop, ripping open the crisps and then the wrapper of the chocolate bar. In between she gulped the coffee. Her energy was higher, probably from a nasty sugar boost. Liz ate her own roll without any appetite but the coffee staved off the headache from caffeine withdrawal. She never drank coffee before running and was getting edgy. She read a couple of messages from Pete and watched the video he'd sent again.

All they did was confuse the situation.

'Hope that helped a bit, Maureen,' Liz said. She placed her phone onto the table and rolled the wrappers up for disposal.

'So we can leave?'

'Couple of questions first. You told me you'd tried to put on a load of washing this morning, sometime after Eliza had breakfast. Do you remember what time?'

Maureen pursed her lips and leaned back in her chair. Her eyes darted around the room. Anywhere but on Liz, who pressed harder. 'You said you got up at about eight. And you did some social media stuff for a bit and then made breakfast once Eliza was up. A rough idea is fine.'

'Maybe nine. Maybe a bit later. Yes, later. Because when I couldn't put the washing on we decided to go to the park. Probably half-past-nine.'

'Talk me through it.'

'Through what? I'm really tired of questions.'

'Not many more. How far is the laundry from your apartment?' Liz watched Maureen closely. At what point would the woman tell the truth?

'We are one end of the main hallway. The laundry is right down the far end then around the corner.'

'Okay. You got to the laundry. How long did you stay there?'

Maureen mumbled under her breath.

'Sorry, can you repeat it?'

'I said, a minute.'

'You stayed a minute. Took a minute or two to walk back to the apartment. And can you remind me what time you left to go to the park?'

With a huff, Maureen looked at Liz. 'I told you we went to

the corner shop first and bought bottled water and it was ten-fifteen according to the clock behind the counter. But why does any of this matter? Why aren't you searching for Eliza?'

'I have been. Part of searching was going through surveillance footage from the apartment building looking for anyone or anything unusual. A person following you, for example. Or loitering around the front. Or back.'

Maureen's face and neck flushed bright red.

Liz picked up her phone and located the second video, turning the screen to show the other woman. 'Please watch this. It was from earlier today. There's you and Eliza. You turn in the opposite direction of the corner shop and the park.'

Tears welled in Maureen's eyes and her shoulders dropped. 'There was an errand I had to run. I forgot.'

Taking out her notepad, Liz nodded. 'Tell me where you went and who you saw.'

'Um, er, I don't remember.'

'There are police knocking on every door in a two block radius of the park, Maureen. Shops, apartments, businesses. And other police are going through footage from trams and buses so I imagine you and Eliza will appear on at least some. If you went past a petrol station or crossed a road… get my drift? Does that help you remember?'

Tears flowed down Maureen's face as her mouth opened and closed.

'We want to find Eliza. If there's something missing from the timeframe you gave us then fill me in.' Liz wasn't falling for the emotion, fake or real.

'What do you want from me? I've lost my child. My husband is in prison. Everyone wants a piece of me. Everyone.'

'Who?'

The woman's voice dropped to a whisper. 'Please don't make me tell you. I need the extra money.'

'I can help you. I can arrange emergency assistance. But

finding your daughter is my sole focus and I should be working on that rather than having to baby you.'

Maureen gasped.

Liz didn't care. 'Be offended if you must. I know many women whose husbands are incarcerated and some are like you, waiting for them to get out and barely surviving. Others make their own futures. At the end of the day it is up to you how to live your life but when there is an innocent child involved—'

'Bing.'

What?

'I do stuff for Bing. Brian Bisley. He lets me pay less for rent if I run errands and I don't ask what's in the packages. I just do it.' Maureen's voice turned croaky as the tears continued. 'I can't stand him but I was behind in my rent and he said he'd kick us out unless I helped once. And then it was all the time and you know what, miss smart-mouthed detective? I will do whatever I must to keep Eliza safe. I would do anything.'

With a cry, she dropped her head onto crossed arms on the table and sobbed.

―――――

The whiteboard in Missing Persons already had photos, diagrams, and notes when Liz arrived an hour later. Pete met her at the doorway as Andy and Terry shared a quiet conversation and a dozen detectives found seats.

'There's no point us being at the park now. The caravan has moved closer to the main entry and we're encouraging the public to visit it. The bosses are about to announce something,' Pete said.

'They need to hear my new information.'

'Terry knows.'

'Not all of it.'

'Can we get everyone's attention?' Terry asked. 'Liz, thanks for getting back in time.'

She perched on the edge of a desk at the back. Pete pulled out a chair and she could have sworn he groaned as he sat. Just about every time she'd seen him today he'd been jogging or striding somewhere. It was on her lips to ask if he was getting old but one glance at his exhausted face and she decided teasing was best done another time.

'Today is shit. Shit for the mother, for us all. Shit for Eliza. But dealing with shit is what we do and in this room alone I see some of the best people able to bring this little girl home.' Terry's eyes roamed the room, landing on Liz. 'We're all tired but we've got some decent leads and I reckon we'll find Eliza alive.'

He nodded to Andy and took a seat.

'Thanks, Terry. I agree with everything you've said.' His eyes scanned the room, barely pausing on Liz, and then to the whiteboard. 'This department is fortunate to have a forensic analyst in-house. What began as a trial has thankfully continued and Meg is an asset. She's in her office with some assistance from a keen youngster who was there from the beginning. At this point, they are working their way through curated footage—there's too much for the two of them so all of it is being vetted first.'

'Vetted?' One of the detectives asked.

'Narrowed down. Discarding anything without a child, for example.'

'Not going to find us a bad guy,' Pete said. 'The kid is one thing, but excluding any suspicious activity—'

'Did I say that?'

'You did.' Pete folded his arms and trained what Liz had once nicknamed his 'death stare' on the other man.

Andy started to respond and must have changed his mind, glancing at the whiteboard as though giving himself time.

What has gone on with you two?

The hostility in the room crackled and Terry shook his head ever so slightly.

'We are fast tracking all the forensic evidence from the playground. The shoe is our best lead and is top of the list both for trace and for the way the laces were tied in a manner which is apparently not typical. Thanks to where the shoe was located, our door-knocking teams are now focused on the same side of the park and we are getting a few hits with security cameras and the like.' Andy paused and now his eyes rested on Liz. 'Media are spreading the information we want out there and there's a hotline already receiving what appear to be credible calls. Every police officer in the state knows what's going on, as do all forms of public transport and the airports.'

'Docks?'

Andy didn't bother to look at Pete to answer his question, but kept his eyes on Liz.

'Docks as well. This level of saturation is both helpful and problematic so Terry and I have handpicked you all for a taskforce.'

At last his attention moved, this time to the whiteboard.

'What we know is that Eliza left the park between ten forty-five and eleven this morning. Hopefully we'll narrow that once we access footage from the road where her shoe was located. We also know that her mother hasn't been forthcoming with all of her information and Liz has the latest about that. Would you come up here and address the team?'

Andy moved to the other side of the whiteboard and Liz took his spot. The detectives in front of her were people she knew. The team was solid.

'I've come from an interview with Maureen. She's had a long day. Spoken to several of us. And kept to the same story. But while I was checking footage in her apartment building for signs that she and Eliza were followed, I caught her in a lie. Several lies.'

She had everyone's attention.

'One. She is doing laundry on the side for cash and put a load into someone's car at eight fifty-five this morning when she'd told us she was in her apartment. We have the rego of the vehicle and it is being followed up. Two. Maureen was adamant she and

Eliza were at the corner shop at ten-fifteen and it looks as if that is true, however she claimed they went there as soon as they left the apartment building. Instead, she ran an errand first.'

Andy was tapping a pen on his fingers. 'What, shopping?'

'No.'

Just wait for this.

'Maureen has an arrangement with the manager of the apartment building. She gets cheaper rent and god knows what else, and in return, she couriers packages around the area for him.'

Now she really had everyone's attention and she snuck a look at Andy. He wasn't tapping his pen but he was frowning.

'She claims not to know what is in the packages. But this manager has been there for longer than I have. He is a creep. And just maybe, he is more than that. Maybe he deals in kids.'

EIGHT

'Boss? We found something.' Meg's head appeared around the doorway. 'Can I borrow Liz?'

Pete was on his feet in seconds.

'Sure, you can come too,' Meg grinned.

'Actually, McNamara—'

'Back soon, Andy.' Pete wasn't waiting for anyone and as soon as Liz caught up with him in the hallway, he rolled his eyes. 'About done with him.'

'I leave the two of you alone for a couple of hours and all hell breaks loose.'

'He started it.'

'Faark.' That was under her breath. There was no time for grown adults to be embroiled in arguments.

Meg worked in a long and narrow office filled with monitors and whiteboards and counters, the latter which were often covered in maps, books, or whatever was being investigated. She sat behind two keyboards and three monitors and nodded for them to join her.

'I sent the young dude to get food for us both. He's good. I might keep him.' Meg didn't look up, instead pointing to one of the screens. 'Keep an eye on the footpath.'

The video was footage taken a distance from the park, pointing toward the side the shoe was found. It was looking down, probably from a second or third floor of a building. It wasn't the clearest Liz had seen but she identified the make of several angle-parked cars and assumed Meg would be able to get licence plates from stills.

A figure dressed in shorts and a hoodie hurried along the footpath away from the main road, glancing around and over their shoulder. They moved out of sight.

'What are we looking at?' Pete asked.

'Keep watching.'

Within a few seconds the same figure returned, almost running in the direction they'd come from.

Meg moved the cursor and changed to a different angle, this time from the main road and almost aligned with the footpath. The figure emerged from the park, close to the corner but definitely through a gap in the hedge. Their back was to the camera as they walked with that nervous looking around.

The hair on Liz's arms rose as he ducked between two cars, leaned down, and then ran toward the camera, pushing the hood back as he shoved his hands into the pouch at the front of his top.

'Crap. Crap, crap, crap.'

'I know him,' Pete peered closer as Meg paused the video. 'Why do I know him?'

Liz stalked a few feet away, running a hand through her hair to stop herself exploding.

'Who is it, Lizzie?'

It wasn't possible. How could she have missed it?

She returned to the monitors. 'I didn't even question how he knew Eliza was missing but he did. We need to find out who Maureen told in the apartment building before I arrived home.'

Meg and Pete both stared at her.

'That's Darryl. He lives on the same floor as me.'

Terry had called a meeting in his office, behind closed doors. Him, Andy, Pete, and Liz.

After the revelations from Meg, Liz had visited the bathroom to have a moment to control the urge to find Darryl and get him into a dark alley somewhere. Fury bubbled up in her body, ready to spill over into action. But this wasn't her. She played by the rules and relied on them to guide her through difficult times.

Had she stepped outside those rules when Ellen disappeared then perhaps the little girl would have been home within a day instead of still missing, presumed dead. And as she'd gazed at herself in the mirror, the hardness in her eyes almost shocked her. But this time was different. Nothing was off the table.

'Darryl Allan Tompsett. Born 1973 in Melbourne. Trained as a paramedic and was injured by a patient in 1998. Awarded a reasonable sum in a claim. Never worked a day since.' Terry looked up from the file he held. 'Served time three years later for breaking and entering. Turns out it was the house of the patient who'd attacked him and while Tompsett managed to keep his compensation money, he spent a year behind bars for assault. What do you know about him, Liz?'

That I want to string him up by his balls.

'He's lived in the same apartment for around as long as I've lived in mine, which is a bit over eighteen years. As a neighbour he's quiet, unless he's on a bender which happens once or twice a year. Gets noisy. Walks the hallway banging on doors looking for his wife.'

'Wife?' Terry frowned, eyes on the file. 'No mention here.'

'Tina something. De facto when he had his accident. She left him after the attack on him and he never forgave her.'

'Pete, find me Tina,' Terry scribbled a note.

'But isn't Andy the better choice for missing people?' Pete whined.

'And while you're at it, interview the person who assaulted him.'

Pete shut up. Terry knew exactly how to handle him and for once, Liz wasn't up to chiming in. She needed Pete to be close by and the best thing he could do was follow orders and not make it worse.

'What else, Liz. Ever see him with kids? Or acting odd?'

'If I had, it might have clicked that there was more to him than the down-on-his-luck persona he portrays. He's complained about his life since I moved in but as far as I know hasn't done a thing to change it. Boss, I need to access all the reports from when Ellen went missing.'

Andy shuffled in his seat so he could look her in the face. 'Her disappearance was investigated. Residents in your apartment block were questioned and nobody came up as suspicious.'

'Who questioned Darryl?'

'You don't know?'

'I don't recall but it wasn't me. May I have access please? As well as diary notes and anything filed. Eighteen years ago something went wrong with the whole damned system and my niece was given up on far too soon. If there's even a small chance of a connection it has to be worth me looking at it.' Pausing to draw breath, Liz was well aware how angry she sounded and tried to filter her next words. 'You were still in the academy. Ben Rossi wasn't in Missing Persons. I'm not blaming either of you. But I was treated as if I'd neglected my own niece.'

Andy nodded. He wasn't taking it as an attack and that was one thing Liz did admire about the young man. Ambition didn't get in the way of logic.

Terry cleared his throat and all eyes went to him.

'Mate, any chance of Liz taking a look? Might be worth it given where she lives and the similarities. And Liz… go and talk to Vince Carter.'

Pete snorted but wisely kept his thoughts to himself.

Not waiting for anyone to speak, Terry continued. 'Tompsett

is going to come in for a chat but Liz, stay clear. Act like the concerned neighbour who doesn't understand why he'd be questioned because it might pay off in the long run. While he's here, we'll have a look at his place and see where he's put the second shoe. Anything else for now?'

Andy stood and the others followed. 'I'm heading to a meeting to get more people power. And Liz, I'll make a call for you.' He nodded to Terry and left, closing the door in his wake.

'Thanks, boss.'

'Wish I could give you someone to help.'

'I might borrow that young officer. The one helping Meg.'

Pete grinned. 'Better you than me trying to prise someone away from Meg. Remember, she knows how to hide a body.'

———

'Maureen wants to see her husband and I can't say I blame her.' Pete had just got off the phone and sprinted to catch up with Liz at the car. 'I'll drop you home and collect her at the same time.'

'*You'll* drive her to Barwon?'

'I'm sitting in on the conversation between them. Only way it's happening given the circumstances.' He unlocked the car. 'She's been told I'm picking her up.'

Once they exited the carpark, straight into late afternoon city traffic, Liz leaned her head back and closed her eyes. Nobody had stopped for more than a loo break in the last few hours. If she rested for too long she'd lose focus. She forced her eyes open and straightened.

'That was hardly a power nap.'

'I'm fine.'

'Just phone Vince. Don't drive all the way out there when you're already stuffed, Liz. Stay closer.'

He had a point.

Until she'd gone through the file on Ellen—which she likely wouldn't get until tomorrow or later—she was relying on her memory of events. Vince might remember more. It wasn't so much the drive which was an issue but being too far from the apartment building and the park should there be news.

'Maybe.'

'Good.'

'Do you have any friends worth asking?'

Pete grinned, knowing exactly what she meant. Covert ops might be in his past but he'd managed to keep connections and wasn't above using them.

'Keep your friends close and all that? Yeah, I've reached out to someone. Couple of someones.'

There was a peculiar comfort hearing that. His seedy, underground contacts weren't people who would speak to her or most cops but he had a way with them. More than his way with his peers.

'What's the issue with you and Andy?'

'Could ask you the same, Liz.'

'He thinks I can't be objective and Terry probably thinks the same. Just says it a different way. But the two of you don't have that problem.'

Pete didn't answer.

'It just isn't helpful to have the two of you sniping at each other, mate.'

'Then he needs to stop... look, it doesn't matter. We'll both get on with the job, okay. You need to watch what you say to him and how you say it and before you tell me off, I'm just looking out for you. If that kid has a hope of being found alive then you need to keep your barriers up when it comes to people like Montebello.'

'What I need to do is work on this case,' she sighed. 'I'm bloody exhausted from stopping myself getting Darryl into a dark alley.'

The look Pete cast her was comical. He'd rarely heard her say a word about stepping outside the rules. That was his thing, which he curtailed these days but his reputation and past run-ins with superiors had once got to the point where he'd risked losing his job. He'd smartened up but all it would take was some encouragement from her to be in that metaphorical alley with Darryl at the wrong end of his fist.

And Brian Bisley.

If she had any say in it, the entire apartment building would be searched from top to bottom.

Somebody knew where those kids were.

NINE

Liz didn't want to be in the apartment. Shadows of Ellen accompanied by her sweet laughter appeared and then faded before Liz could hold onto them. It was just like the days and weeks after the disappearance and would drive her mad if she didn't stay busy.

The intention was to be here long enough for a phone call and change of clothes. She pulled the curtain open in her bedroom and stared down to the street. Terry hadn't given her an idea of when a warrant would come through to facilitate a search of Darryl's apartment but she assumed he wouldn't be picked up until that happened.

There was a general duties officer across the road keeping an eye on the front of the building. From here she could almost see the park. If there was one less building in the way it might be a clear view and she had no doubt that some of the higher floors would be able to see at least some of it.

She stripped off all her clothes and threw herself into the shower again, wanting the dried sweat gone and a moment to feel something other than the relentless, dragging grief in her heart. Water ran over her head and she visualised it taking the pain with it as it streaked her body and circled the drain.

After flicking on the kettle, she dressed while it boiled. Before making coffee she checked the hallway. It was quiet. She left the door open a crack and moved a chair from her small dining table to where she'd see any movement. After one sip of her coffee, she dialled Vince.

Vince Carter was her first partner when she got started all those years ago but he'd been as much mentor and friend as work colleague. He'd been in the middle of his career and was a popular and respected cop… until the day they'd been assigned to an Anzac Day march. He'd saved her life that morning, along with potentially dozens of other people but at home, his wife was losing her battle with an asthma attack. He'd never been the same as misplaced guilt and remorse overwhelmed him. Left with his small daughter to raise, Vince had changed, burning bridges in his wake until he'd abruptly retired a few years later. Last year he'd lost his daughter and history was repeating as he raised his grandchild. But recently, things had changed and Vince was a happier man.

'Lizzie. Has she been found?'

Typical Vince. Not even a hello even though they'd not spoken in weeks.

'No. But we have some leads this time.'

'You think it's the same perp.'

'I do.'

'How do I help?' Vince's gruff voice was steady, reassuring. And he believed her.

'I've requested access to everything on Ellen but it might be a day or two and my gut feeling is that we need to move faster than that.'

'My diary will be there. In the file. And yours, and don't overlook them, Liz. Eighteen years is a long time to clearly remember details no matter how much you think you do. Read your own notes first. Hang on a sec.' Vince must have moved the phone a bit away. 'Be back before dark, okay?'

'It doesn't take *that* long to lead Apple back from Lyndall's paddock.' The voice was young—Melanie, who was nine.

'Get Lyndall to help if you're not sure.'

'Apple loves me. See ya!'

'See you too.' His voice was closer again and with a new warmth. 'Who'd have thought she'd want to be in charge of the pony.'

Someone went past Liz's door and she went to look but it was just a neighbour heading for the stairs.

'I hadn't realised you'd moved into the new house.'

'Last week. Building finished earlier than expected and Mel was keen to be home. Been too long.'

Liz chuckled. 'I got the feeling Melanie was comfortable living up the hill at your neighbour's house. Both of you.'

'No idea why you'd think that, Elizabeth.'

Ah… you do have a thing for Lyndall.

He returned to the original subject. 'I've been watching what passes for journalism since the first broadcast. The little girl… Eliza? She looks like Ellen.'

'More than that, Vince. Almost the same age. Both from the same apartment building. Her mother and I both were sitting at the same bench in the same park while the girls played on the same equipment. Sure it might be a copycat but there's all the stuff not made public. Do you remember anything about Ellen's disappearance, particularly concerning her attire?'

She didn't want to lead him to a conclusion.

'She was dressed in a green t-shirt and white shorts. Green socks with dragons on them. Sunhat. White shoes. Ponytail.'

Damn he was good.

'Anything else?'

Vince was silent for a moment.

People were in the hallway. Heavy footsteps. More than one.

'Ellen told you a man had tied her shoelaces. You went searching and found nobody but the laces were different from how you'd done them that morning. You figured it was someone in passing who'd left the park.'

'And that happened again, Vince, except this time a shoe was found. Eliza's shoe tied in a specific way.'

'Geez.'

'I have to go. My neighbour is about to be taken in for questioning and his apartment searched.'

'Go. But Liz, call me later. No matter how late.'

There was a commotion in the hallway and Liz hung up and flung the door wide. Three uniform officers and two detectives were at Darryl's door, which was open a crack.

'We have a warrant, Mr Tompsett, and rather than us break the security chain, how about you just unlock it.'

'Go away. I'm a victim, not a criminal.'

Darryl's voice was whiny and pathetic.

Liz caught the eye of the lead detective. 'May I?'

Everyone stepped back enough to let Liz be visible to the man inside.

'Darryl? It's Liz. Listen mate, I have no idea what's going on but if the police have a warrant then you're best to let them in. Okay? You can come and sit in my apartment if you want.'

Liar.

The detective frowned. Did he seriously believe she'd allow that cretin inside her home?

'Liz? Are you arresting me?'

'Why would I do that, Darryl? Come on, this is probably just a routine check or something and I'll find out for you. But let them in for now.'

One of his eyes peered at her through the small gap and then he closed the door and undid the lock. It opened again and he stepped back. The lead detective motioned for the others to enter. 'Darryl Tompsett, I have a warrant to search these premises. I'm also asking you to attend an interview with me.'

'Now?'

'Now.'

'But why?' His face had drained its colour and his hands shook. 'What did I do?'

'Routine questions around the disappearance of Eliza Singleton.'

'But I don't know anything.'

'Darryl, just go and answer some questions and then once you get back this will all be over,' Liz said. 'Lots of residents are going to be interviewed. Not just you.'

'You sure?'

'I am.'

'Will you come with me?'

Not even in your wildest dreams.

'I would. I really would Darryl but I have to be somewhere else. Just came home to change before following up some leads on the little girl. But these detectives will take good care of you.'

'It was me who told you she was missing, Liz. That has to count for something cos I was helping. Doesn't it?'

'Do you remember who told you about her?'

His face was blank.

Liz moved out of the way as Darryl left the apartment. 'The detectives will look after you. We all want to find Eliza, don't we.'

He nodded but his eyes darted inside. 'They gonna mess my place up? Better not. Do I need my lawyer?'

The detective took over, gesturing with his head for Liz to go. 'You can have your lawyer at any time, Darryl but all we're doing is going to the station to have a conversation. Do you need to get your wallet and phone?'

Once she closed her door the voices were too muffled to hear. She unclenched her hands. Wanting to pound the man until he told the truth wasn't helping but if he believed she was on his side then she'd have his trust later on. Let him believe she cared about him as a long-time neighbour and just maybe he'd let something slip.

She ran a comb through still-damp hair and refilled her water bottle. After locking the door behind her, Liz let herself into Darryl's apartment. The officers doing the search had closed the door to avoid prying eyes and they glanced up when she entered the living room, but didn't tell her to leave. The place was a shithole. Rubbish piled up in a corner was likely the reason for a disgusting aroma of something rotting. The carpet was filthy. An open beer bottle, partly drunk, barely stayed upright on a coffee table overflowing with fast food containers.

The kitchen was even worse, if that was possible.

'Careful. Floor is sticky.'

'Ew.' It was. 'Anything yet?'

The officer shook her head. 'We'll be a while.'

Liz wasn't hanging around. With Pete doing the run to Barwon Prison, she was going to chase up Darryl's ex. She'd have preferred to be in on the interviews with Darryl and Bisley but at least she could do something.

———

Tina Pollock lived across the city in a townhouse and arrived home the same time Liz pulled up out the front. She was a nurse and in her scrubs as she unlocked the door, immediately offering Liz coffee when she showed her badge.

'Let me get out of these. Grab a seat.'

Liz perched on a stool at the kitchen counter as the coffee machine heated. This was the opposite of Darryl's apartment in cleanliness and homeliness and from her brief introduction to the occupier, it was hard to imagine the two of them living together in the past.

'Sorry about that,' Tina said, hurrying back. 'I long to be back in trackies by the time I end a shift. Black coffee okay? I don't have any milk.'

'It's perfect, thanks.'

'What's Darryl done?' The woman wasted no time once she brought the coffees over. 'Was he arrested?'

'Being questioned. He's my neighbour and there's been an incident affecting one of the families in the apartment building we live in. He's one of a number of people being interviewed.'

Liz sipped the coffee to give herself a moment.

'You don't mean the little girl who disappeared today?'

'Unfortunately, yes.'

'But he'd never harm a child. An adult? Well, he's proven he's capable of that, but not a kid. You don't suspect him of taking her?'

'Nothing points toward him taking her, no.'

Only helping the person behind it.

Tina stared at Liz. She had a kind face. Gentle eyes which looked worried.

'How long since you've seen or spoken to Darryl?' Liz asked.

'A while. Every so often he phones and we have a nice talk. Just like the old times. He'll promise he's put the past where it belongs and is making a new start and has plans to get a job and I tell him I'm pleased for him. But he doesn't change. You said you're his neighbour?'

'For a long time. Eighteen years,' Liz said.

'And he's still forgetting to dress most of the time and spending his money on grog and fast food?'

'You haven't been to see him?'

Tina shook her head. 'Only went there once, when he first moved in but he'd got the idea I would move in with him and was angry when I made it clear it would never happen. These days I keep it to phone calls. He was a good man. Still is, I imagine, beneath the hurt and failure he feels.' She sighed deeply. 'After he was attacked, he was never the same. Kept saying I'd leave him for someone else just because he had some scars. He refused help with his anger about it all and there was only so much reassuring I could do.'

'Was he violent? Toward you?'

'After a day of boozing it up and swallowing pain meds he slapped me. And then fell onto the sofa in a stupor. By the time he woke up I'd packed his stuff and his brother was waiting to take him to his place. He pleaded and promised to get help but I don't give second chances when it comes to my life. I probably sound cold-hearted.'

'You sound sensible.'

Over the rest of her coffee, Liz asked routine questions to help build up a picture of Darryl but there was little she didn't already know. 'One more thing, and it will sound weird.' She took her phone out and located the image of the front of Eliza's shoe, just the laces. 'People tend to have their own way of tying shoelaces and I wondered if this is familiar.'

Tina took a long look than sat back. 'Sorry, not at all. Looks tight, doesn't it? And the way the loops are perfect... but if you're thinking it might have been tied by Darryl then I'd so no. He was taught by his father to do those rabbit ear loops and then doubled them. Funny how we learn odd things from our parents.'

After leaving Tina, Liz sat in her car gazing at the image of Eliza's shoe. There was a perfection about the laces and a memory tugged at her, too deep to reach. Perhaps Meg had still images of it she could view. There was more to this lost shoe than a clue to where Eliza got into a car.

TEN

'I already told you, and the other detective. All I did was go for a walk.'

Arms crossed, leaning back in his chair, Darryl was unfazed by his situation. If anything, he was becoming more confident with every passing minute.

'Before I showed you the footage, you claimed you'd not left your apartment all day.' Andy had taken over from the detective who'd brought Darryl in as soon as he'd finished a call with Terry. Thanks to the Senior Sergeant's efforts there were a dozen more officers coming to help with the door-knocking which was only half they'd requested but better than none.

'Got confused. I thought I was asked if I'd gone anywhere.'

'You were asked if you left the apartment building today and answered no.'

'Nah. What I heard was about me going away from the area. Shopping. Visiting the city. That kind of thing. Not a walk around the park which I do every day.'

It was sad seeing a formerly productive member of society fall through the cracks to such a degree. Paramedics bore the brunt of violence more than some other services and too many good people walked away from the job they loved thanks to the dangers. Darryl had worked in a particularly high crime region. Despite a decent payout and offers of support to help mentally and with a new job, he'd harboured such anger that he'd ended up in prison himself.

'Tell me about a typical day in your life.'

After rolling his eyes, Darryl uncrossed his arms and leaned on the table. 'Not a lot changes, mate. I live in a crap apartment building overlooking an alley. My back still gives me hell after the attack and I spend much of my life in pain. Couple of times a week I go to the local pub for the evening. Shop once a week for groceries. Rest of the time I'm watching tellie. And I walk around the outside of the park every day, rain or shine.'

'What happened today when you went for your regular walk?'

'Nothing. I walked. Came home.'

Keep digging yourself in deeper.

'Where exactly did you walk? From the minute you left your apartment, please.'

For the first time, Darryl's eyes darted side to side and he sucked air through his lips. Andy kept still. He was good at reading people and Darryl was nervous. As he should be.

'Alright. I threw on a hoodie. From the window it looked pretty cool outdoors and I feel the cold. Got my keys and that's all. Don't take my wallet or phone in case I get mugged. Stairs take a while down and up because it hurts and that lazy bastard who manages the building does nothing to keep the lift working. I stood outside the building for a couple of minutes to recover then went to the corner and crossed. Walked to the park. Walked around the park. Took the hoodie off on the way back as it was too hot. Whole thing took half an hour max.'

Darryl was impressed with himself, going by the smirk on his face.

'Care to look at the footage again? There's cameras everywhere these days including over the road from the quiet end of the park and straight along that footpath you took. Here. Have another look.'

Andy pushed his iPad over and pressed play. Everything was lined up to show Darryl's progress from both angles but the man didn't even glance at the screen.

'No? You just told me you walked around the park. Here it shows you walking partway along one end, stopping long enough to stoop down between two parked cars, and then you turn around and go back the way you came. Pretty quickly. And before any more lies leave your mouth, Darryl, our forensics analyst has viewed footage from all angles around that time and we know you didn't go all the way around the park. So what were you doing?'

Face set, Darryl didn't respond.

'This is what I think,' Andy continued. 'You picked something up.'

'I bent down to stretch. Look at it again. I was in agony, okay, and didn't want to say that and sound weak. I know what your kind think of men who've been to prison. People down on our luck. We're fair game and that's what's happening now, isn't it? You need to find someone to blame for that little girl disappearing and I tick all of your boxes.' As if to prove how much pain he was suffering, Darryl got to his feet and leaned against a wall.

This was going around in circles. Andy took his iPad back.

'Tell me about your relationship with Maureen Singleton. And Eliza.'

'No relationship. Since my missus threw me out I've sworn off women.'

'But you know her.'

'Sure. Just to say hello though if our paths crossed.'

'And where would that happen? Your paths crossing?' Andy asked.

'Laundry. She'd come and use the one on the end of my floor.

Probably most of the floors because hers only has one machine working properly.'

The state of Darryl's clothing made it unlikely the man spent much time near a washing machine.

'This is part of her laundry business? Who else uses it?'

Darryl clammed up and gazed at the ceiling.

'Where is Eliza while Maureen goes from floor to floor using multiple laundries? Doubt she'd traipse along behind her.'

'Ask her. I only saw her now and then and have no idea. Can I leave?'

'Take a seat, Darryl. New footage from security cameras in the area between the building and the park is coming in constantly so it is only a matter of time until we catch sight of what you were carrying. Why did you stop there?'

The other man dropped back onto his seat with a grunt. 'Told you. Stretching.'

Andy leaned forward in a sudden movement which startled Darryl. 'A child is missing. A little girl who was playing in a public park and expected to go home with her mother to get lunch. No doubt she's terrified and I don't like that. No kid deserves to be taken from a playground and into a stranger's car, away from her mum and everything she knows. But we know that the shoe found on the road was Eliza's and then we see you hurrying along, looking over your shoulder, to the exact spot and you know what else, mate? You weren't stretching. You were picking something up. I want to know where the shoe is that you took.'

Darryl began shaking his head.

'Stop that. You can make this better for yourself, Darryl. Tell me what happened and give me something to help me find little Eliza.'

'Nah, I didn't do nothing wrong. Public footpath, public road. I want to see a lawyer.'

Damn it.

Andy concluded the interview. At the door he turned. 'Think

long and hard, Darryl. And tell your lawyer what you've done so they can help you help us.' He closed the door behind himself. There was an officer with Darryl and nothing more would be discussed until a legal representative spoke with him.

'Sure you don't need to take air freshener in with you, boss?' Meg was far too happy about Andy's next interview. She was in the observation room with her laptop as well as watching the monitor in the interview room.

'He looks alright from here. Semi-business like.'

She snorted. 'Ignore my advice then. I'll just sit on this side of the glass where it smells nice and observe while you suffer.'

Andy shrugged into his suit jacket. He'd taken a short break after leaving Darryl, just time enough for water and a protein bar. 'How do you know how he smells?'

'Liz said he smokes non-stop in his office.'

'In the apartment building?'

'Yup.'

'Lovely. Anything new on Darryl?' Andy glanced over Meg's shoulder to the laptop. The screen was continuous rolling text updates, a bit like a message board. 'Heard from Liz yet?'

'No and no. Do you want her to join you when she gets back?'

'Not just yet. I'd rather let our visitors think Liz is being kept out of the investigation as much as possible. Wish me luck.'

'You don't need it,' Meg said. 'Air freshener though...'

Andy stepped inside the interview room and wrinkled his nose. She'd been right, not that he'd tell her. He nodded to the uniform officer with a quick, 'take a break'. The man looked thankful and vacated the room in seconds.

Brian Bisley grunted when he stood and offered his hand to shake. His skin was clammy and the stench of cigarettes permeated the small room. 'Brian. But call me Bing.'

'Detective Sergeant Andy Montebello. Please take a seat. I'm part of the Missing Persons unit and appreciate you coming in to speak to me today.'

Bisley's chair creaked alarmingly when he sat. He wore a freshly ironed white shirt, tie, and suit pants and his hair was combed to one side over a balding dome. Several fingers of each hand were adorned with thick rings and his phone, which was face down on the table, was housed in a glittering gold case.

Night club or apartment manager?

'Could kill a smoke right now, Andy.'

'Sorry, smoke free building. Can arrange a coffee though?'

'Shouldn't be here long, eh? Terrible thing to lose sight of a child in your care.'

Interesting choice of words.

'We're putting together as much information about the events of today as possible and you'll be aware we've begun speaking to residents in the apartment. There are a few people we've asked to come in, such as yourself. As the apartment manager you have a unique understanding of the complex and those who live there.'

Andy wasn't above using flattery and tapping into a suspect's nature and he'd seen the little flash of pride the minute he mentioned Bisley's position. The man almost preened himself but there was also a glint in his beady eyes. He was smart and probably suspicious.

'It would be helpful to have your opinion on the Singleton family. And a bit about their background since they moved in, if you don't mind giving us a hand? I know you'll appreciate that the quicker we have good intel, the faster we can act and all of us want nothing more than to see Eliza back with her mum.'

'You think you'll find her then?'

'Yes. We have some promising leads. What can you tell me about Maureen Singleton?'

'Don't really know her well. She's quiet. Never had any complaints about her or from her. Pays her rent on time. Says hello if you pass her in the hallway but that's about the extent of what I know.'

Not even close to how much you know.

'How long have Maureen and Eliza lived in their apartment?'

'Hm… I'd need to check my records but off the top of my head I'd say two years. We did an interview when she applied and she mentioned her husband had just gone into Barwon on some trumped-up charge… sorry.' He smirked. 'Showed her the apartment and then she and the child moved in a few days later.'

'And she works?'

Bing shrugged. 'No idea. Well, not quite true because I see her in the building with the child a lot so doubt she has a regular job. Maybe she does one of them online jobs from home. Actually, I heard she's a cleaner a couple of hours a week somewhere.'

'Not laundry?'

His neck reddened.

'By laundry, I mean does she do washing and ironing and the like for other residents? For people outside the building as well?'

'Against the rules to run a business from the building.'

'And you might be a kind person who knows she needs a bit of extra cash to keep her head above water. You might overlook something as harmless as a few loads of laundry a week.'

Bisley removed a crumbled handkerchief from a pocket and dabbed his forehead. 'Need to turn the heating down, Andy. I don't do so well in the warmer weather.' He licked his lips and shoved the handkerchief away. 'Could lose my job if the building owner thought I was letting anyone do the wrong thing.'

'I won't keep you much longer. Your office is on the ground floor, looking out at the street?'

A nod.

'Anything you remember about people coming in our out of the building today might help us. Deliveries, residents, anything at all.'

Even though he didn't need his notepad in here, Andy made

a show of opening it, and then waiting what he hoped was an expectant expression.

'I'm sure you can appreciate how busy my job keeps me. Paperwork up the kazoo and people dropping in for a chat.' Bisley screwed up his face as if trying to remember. 'Couple of deliveries for me first thing. Regular stuff like office supplies. Think I saw a supermarket home delivery guy go in. Couple of the older residents get those. Yeah, that's right. There's a few of the old ladies who meet up to go for breakfast on pension day and I did see them just outside the building.'

'Time?'

'Dunno. Eight. Bit later?'

'What time did Maureen and Eliza leave?'

Again, the reddening of the other man's neck, but this time it extended up to his cheeks.

'Never saw them.'

'No? How about Darryl Tompsett?'

Bing glanced at his watch. 'Didn't even know he was out of the building. I do have an appointment soon.'

'Last questions. Any routines you've observed? Residents going for a walk the same time of day or similar? Or anyone out of the ordinary hanging around?'

'As I said, I'm usually bum up and head down.'

The imagery wasn't pleasant.

Andy stood. 'Thanks for your time. I'll get someone to walk you out.' He held the door open and after Bisley lumbered through, let it close behind them. 'If you remember anything out of the ordinary, you have my card.'

With a nod, Bisley followed the uniformed officer away.

Meg appeared from the next door along. 'The search of Darryl's apartment hasn't turned up anything of interest, but I have some more footage.'

Back in the other room, Meg tapped the keyboard. 'Footage is from the dashcam of a parked car of all things. Driver came forward with it.'

This footage was much clearer than the grainy videos of the same area. Taken from the rear camera of a car parked diagonally across from the spot Eliza's shoe was found, it was immediately obvious there was nothing on the road. No shoe. Along the footpath, the man with the hoodie paused for a second, glancing this way and that, before stepping onto the road near the curb and leaning down. At the same time, he pulled something from the pocket of his hoodie and lay it on the bitumen. Then as quickly, he returned to the footpath and was out of sight in a few steps.

'He put the shoe there,' Meg said, pausing the video and looking up at Andy. 'We've got it all wrong. He wasn't taking one of two shoes but planting one.'

ELEVEN

Meg wasn't in her usual place. Homicide was quiet, with only support staff who couldn't tell her where everyone was. Pete wouldn't be back for a while and even Terry was absent from his office. Something must have happened and nobody had alerted her. She texted Terry.

Where is everyone?

She dropped onto her chair. If she was the only detective on the floor then either everyone had gone home—which was impossible—or there was a breakthrough. Her phone beeped.

Meet me in Andy's office.

Liz groaned as she stood. Her muscles and tendons and even her bones hurt. No warm-down after her run this morning then hours of stress and tension. And she was hungry. Forcing it all away, she took the elevator instead of the stairs. Just for once.

This floor was active. Detectives were in small groups working around whiteboards. Phones rang. Meg held court in front of a large television screen, talking to a handful of uniformed officers, including several of higher rank.

So everyone's working out of Missing Persons now?

Terry and Andy had their heads close, sitting on the same

side of Andy's desk, gazing at an iPad. Both looked up when she tapped on the open door.

'Come in. Close it, Liz,' Andy said.

'How did you go with Tina?' Terry rotated his chair and gestured for Liz to sit.

She took the remaining seat which was opposite the men. 'A bit to unpack. Darryl told me years ago—and reiterated it a few times a year—that Tina left him just after he was attacked while tending a patient. In reality she threw him out after he hit her. He was home from hospital and doing physio and the like and lost it with her while drunk. She sent him packing.'

'So his violence toward his attacker was not the one-off incident the courts heard,' Terry said. 'What else?'

'Basically she swears he'd never harm a kid. She hasn't seen him in years but does stay in touch with occasional phone calls. And she's a solid witness.'

Terry and Andy exchanged a glance.

'What's happened?' If only they'd tell her they'd found Eliza.

'Short version,' Andy said. 'I've interviewed Darryl and Bisley. Both are claiming no knowledge of anything dodgy, let alone when it comes to Eliza.'

'Did Darryl say it wasn't him in the footage?'

'Initially. Then he claimed he was stretching because his back hurt. And now he's lawyered up.'

Her heart sank.

'Why?'

'I pressed him. He panicked. But there's more, Liz.' Andy pushed his iPad across the desk. 'Meg found this half an hour ago.'

Liz tapped play.

'We had it the wrong way around. He wasn't picking up one of a pair for some nefarious reason. It didn't make sense that he'd have left one behind.'

Liz could barely believe her eyes as Darryl removed the shoe from a pocket and placed it on the road. This act was deliberate and gave rise to so many questions. She rewatched in silence then handed it back.

'I'm afraid to ask what you're thinking,' Terry said with a small smile.

'Lots which would have me arrested. Andy, you said he lawyered up so he's still here?'

'Yes. Legal representation hasn't arrived.'

'Let me talk to him. As his neighbour.'

Both men shook their heads.

'Not yet, Liz. I'd rather keep you off his radar in case we don't get any further.' Terry grimaced. 'I'm frustrated, too. Have you spoken to Vince yet?'

We need to force Darryl to talk.

Saying that aloud would have her booted off the case, even if Andy and Terry were also thinking it. Laws and processes could go to hell if she had her way. Put someone like Pete in there with the slimy little creep and see how well Darryl talked then.

'Liz?'

'Sorry, Andy. Vince has a sharp memory. Recalls fine details such as the colour and type of clothing and shoes Ellen wore. I wish we'd had the luxury back then of a shoe because there's something about the way those laces were re-tied on Eliza's and I don't remember what they looked like. Oh, Tina says the way those laces are done is not Darryl's work. He does the rabbit ear thing like a kid.'

Andy made a note on his iPad. 'You're sure you don't remember anything about Ellen's laces?' His eyes met Liz's. 'If the same perp is involved, it might help.'

'Vince told me to reread my own notes from her disappearance. To do it first.'

'There's boxes on their way. Should be at your desk within the hour.'

That was the first positive all day and she exhaled slowly.

Terry glanced past her as the door opened. 'Pete, join us.'

'I heard about the new footage.' With no chairs left, Pete

perched on the edge of a sideboard. 'Like me to have a quiet word with our friend?' He grinned. 'The cameras and audio could malfunction briefly. Wouldn't take long at all.'

There was a faint smile on Terry's face. He'd heard it all from Pete over the years. 'Update us on Maureen please.'

'Barely said a word on the drive over. Didn't want me listening in on her visit with hubster but he didn't care about me being there. Poor bloke is beside himself with worry. Had already been told the kid's missing and wasn't getting much help dealing with it. He talked to me more than his wife and I can't see either of them having a thing to do with this. Lot of love for Eliza.'

'Bit of a waste then,' Andy muttered.

'Haven't finished, have I? From Barwon to the apartment building I couldn't shut Maureen up. Not that I tried but it was like a dam burst. She's been running her laundry business for a year and brings in a few hundred dollars a week. But here's the thing. She hands half of her earnings over to the manager there, as well as acting as his sometimes delivery person for free. Otherwise he'd dob her in to Centrelink.'

'Why doesn't this surprise me?'

All eyes turned to Liz.

'Brian is a dreadful excuse for a building manager and makes it too hard for most of the residents to do more than have a whinge about any issues. The elevators are a perfect example. There are two, one at either end of the building. One works fine but the other, which is closest to the street entry, is either out of service or too slow most of the time. He does just enough to keep the building compliant but prefers sitting on his arse smoking to doing what he's paid to.'

'He went to great lengths to tell me how little he knows about the Singletons,' Andy said. 'I agree he is dodgy as all hell but did he have anything to do with Eliza's disappearance?'

'Doubt it.' Terry pushed his chair back and stood. 'Too high a risk of losing his disgusting little empire. And what motive would he have?'

Pete caught Liz's eye. He wanted a private word.

Terry wheeled his seat around the desk. 'We're upping the door-knocking around the park and Meg is in close contact with PTV and so on. There's a team focused on tracking Darryl's movements from the time he left the apartment and then after he dropped the shoe. Somewhere in there has to be imagery of where he's picked it up or been handed it. And that is our best bet so far on finding Eliza.'

―――

'I don't agree with Terry.'

Liz hit the elevator button harder than was called for.

Pete raised his eyebrows but was smart enough to keep his mouth shut.

She glanced around. Saying stuff to Pete was fine but Terry didn't need to hear her angry thoughts. Nobody was close enough to listen in, even if they were paying attention. Everyone on the floor was occupied. The elevator doors opened and she stormed in.

The minute the doors closed she pushed 'stop'.

'Good thing I'm not claustrophobic,' Pete said.

'Sorry. I just need a moment.'

'What don't you agree with?'

'Not letting me in with Darryl is the first one. And I see why he's so keen to find out where that shoe came from but I don't think just finding out is enough. We need to haul Brian's behind back in here and get a warrant for his office. For that matter we should search the entire building.' She drew in a rapid breath. 'Put a tail on Maureen. Actually, where is she? Shouldn't she be here?'

'Okay, stop.'

'No, we aren't doing enough, Pete. Two missing kids need

finding.' She turned away, whacking the wall of the elevator with her hand before dropping her forehead against the cold metal.

A firm hand gripped her shoulder and for a second Liz wanted to fall against Pete and sob. It was a stupid response and would horrify him as much as her and had nothing to do with Pete and everything to do with a moment of support when the rest of the world had gone crazy. She couldn't keep reacting so strongly because she'd mess up.

'If you want to visit the gym and beat the crap out of a punching bag I'll hold it for you. Even name the thing. Let me see... Bing? Darryl? *Andy*?'

The last name was said in a hopeful tone and it was enough to pull Liz out of her mood. She straightened and turned to face Pete, whose hand dropped away. 'We can take turns with the bag and you can name it Andy when you put your gloves on.'

'Deal.' Pete went serious. 'You okay, Lizzie? I can cover if you want to go eat. Or have a drink.'

She pushed the button and the elevator kicked into motion. 'Pleasant thought. A drink or three. Was there anything else from the Barwon visit?'

'That's what I wanted to talk to you about. Away from the others.'

The doors opened and they stepped onto a still-quiet floor— apart from an impatient officer at her desk. He'd dropped two boxes on the corner and met her halfway, holding out a clipboard.

'As requested.'

Taking the clipboard she headed for her desk and checked the details on each box against the paperwork while the officer glowered.

'Don't you like overtime, mate?' Pete asked.

'Is that what you get? Overtime?'

'Good point.'

'This is all of it?' Liz asked. 'There must be more boxes than this.'

'Checked them out myself. Everything is there. Can I grab your signature please?'

She signed and handed the clipboard back and waited until the officer left the area. 'How can this be it, Pete? Is this really all a little girl's kidnapping was worth?'

'Kidnapping?'

'Maybe. Maybe not as such. There was never a ransom request. Never any kind of contact from whoever took Ellen. But what else do I call it?' She didn't want an answer. Her heart was heavy with renewed grief and he needed to leave. 'Where are you going now?'

'I can help.'

She shook her head.

'Or I can see if Meg has anything new. And get food. Want food?'

'What were you going to tell me?'

'Maureen said she was surprised to get approved for the apartment. Everywhere she'd tried knocked her back and she was preparing to go to a shelter but she got a call from a friend of her husband saying to go and see Bisley. He rented it to her without any questions.'

'So he might have criminal contacts?'

'That. And probably a stupid idea but what if it wasn't just a helping hand but someone thinking ahead?' Pete shook his head. 'Nah, doubt it. But I'll dig around.'

Liz waited until Pete had gone, taking the stairs. She was the only person on the floor and that was a blessing. Her heart thudded as she removed the lids from both boxes and the musty smell of long-closed cardboard rose. Neither box was neat. Perhaps the officer had been so annoyed at having to bring them here so late in the day that he'd shaken them. More likely, whoever had last touched them left them in disarray.

On the side of each box was a sheet with names, dates, signatures of who had access.

She took photographs. That part would keep for now. Until the girls were found.

'Eliza. Until Eliza is found.' Saying the words helped. Ellen was as close to a lost cause as a person could be but Eliza was somewhere nearby. It was still the same day as her disappearance. Still hours rather than weeks. By car she might no longer be in Victoria. By plane it was possible she wasn't even in the country. But it was inconceivable that Eliza was long gone. There was a personal feel to all of this. Too many similarities. Not random.

Taking out a large lined notepad, Liz began to write.

What is in common?
What is not?
How were the girls chosen?
What kind of person does this?
Do he/she have help?

It was a he. How do two girls report a man tying their shoelaces and it not be the person who took them?

She pushed the notepad away and made space on the desk.

Then she began to remove everything from the boxes.

TWELVE

There were several folders of photocopies taken from the diaries of dozens of police, including Vince, who'd been involved in the investigation, sorted by date. Only Liz's diary was there in its entirety. She'd insisted it go with Ellen's case rather than be filed at the secure facility which housed millions of words recorded by officers over the decades. Going through all of this was daunting and she put the folders to one side to come back to.

There was evidence in clear bags, mostly items of Ellen's taken from Liz's apartment. As far she knew not one thing was found from the park after the disappearance. No shoe. Not the little bag Ellen took everywhere or anything which might otherwise have led to the child or the monster who stole her.

Liz opened a fresh bottle of water and sucked in liquid fast. This job ahead of her—revisiting a time so painful—was impossible. Except it had to be done. The chance of her niece being alive was close to zero but another little girl needed Liz at her best. She was a decent detective and it was time to approach this impartially as if someone seeing and reading the contents of the boxes for the first time.

Item by item she checked, making notes and then replacing each in the appropriate box. A sample of Ellen's childish handwriting. Pictures of her. Details about her parents and other family, including Liz. Photographs of the park and the apartment building. These she put aside to come back to. When all that was left was her diary, Liz opened it. And closed it.

She got up and went to the window. It was almost night and the city's skyscrapers hastened the darkness. Below was a riot of colour from head and tail lights as traffic filled the streets. Delivery bicycles zig-zagged between cars sitting across the intersection.

Her city. One day she'd buy a place along the river, close enough to walk to the restaurants which lined it or a little further to see a show. She had the money, thanks to a lifetime working with very few expenses. What kept her in the apartment was the stupid need to stay where Ellen could find her. After all these years, even if Ellen was somehow alive and made her way to Melbourne from wherever she'd been, how would she remember a place she'd only stayed a dozen times?

'Lizzie?'

Why was Andy here? For that matter, she'd never heard him use her name that way and it felt a bit odd.

'Is there news?'

She met him at her desk.

'No. No, sorry if you thought that.' He lifted his arm to show the plastic bag he carried. 'I had to walk away for a bit. Clear my head. And eat. I have more than enough for two if you'd like to share?'

Liz gazed at him. If he was trying to put things on a better footing then food was a good start.

'I'm starving. Thank you.'

She cleared space on her desk by moving the boxes onto the floor and the files and her diary to the edge. Andy unpacked half a dozen takeaway containers.

'Thai okay?'

'Love it.'

The aromas as they opened the containers made her stomach

growl and for a while, both ate in silence. Food would help her concentration and she'd get more achieved tonight with a full stomach. A couple of other detectives came and went, collecting things from their desks and calling goodnight.

'Everyone has worked so hard.'

Andy nodded as he slid fat noodles into his mouth.

'Unless Terry needs me elsewhere, I want to stay here until I've read everything.'

He eyed her as he finished his mouthful.

'There might be something, Andy. Something to help Eliza.' Her voice was quiet. She had no more fight in her and needed him to understand. 'I feel she's still close to the city somewhere.'

'A hunch?'

'Logic. How far could a stranger go with a little girl in a car? Assuming it is a car because now we have to revisit where she left the park. Even if she went willingly—if he'd coerced her with the promise of something nice—she'd work it out after a while and start making a fuss.'

'There are ways to keep a child quiet.'

How Andy said that, so matter-of-fact, was chilling. She pushed away the remaining food.

'This is distressing for us all, Liz but we may be dealing with a killer. But what you said before? What if he isn't a stranger to her?'

Liz leaned forward. 'I think he is because she told her mother a 'nice' man tied her shoelaces. No mention of him being familiar but what if he knew enough about her, or Maureen… or her father? Yes, what if he lured her away with the promise of taking her to visit her dad? It was Eliza's birthday yesterday.'

'Maybe. Are you thinking someone who knows her father?'

'Apparently a friend of Maureen's husband put her onto the apartment.'

'Let's get more intel,' Andy said. He made a note on his phone. 'I'll get someone on it.'

Sitting back again, Liz's fingers tapped on the desk. Andy

took another mouthful. Like Pete, he seemed able to eat anytime. She picked up her iPad and opened the notes she'd made when she'd originally spoken to Maureen.

'Okay, she said Eliza told her a nice man tied her shoelaces. There's got to be more.'

'With Ellen… did she say anything about a man to you?'

After putting down the iPad, Liz opened her diary, all too conscious of her elevated heartbeat.

The first part was a mix of her observations and speculation. She read snippets aloud.

'The park was quiet with no other visitors. Warm day. Ellen played for a while under the bridge in the shadiest spot. Returned for her water bottle and drank. Then back to climb along the bridge. At one point she ran back to the bench and said she wanted an ice cream. I said we'd get some on the way home but she didn't want to leave at that point.'

Liz gazed in the direction of the window. If only they'd left then.

'Not your fault, Liz.'

She drew in a sharp breath and forced herself back to the diary.

'Ellen pointed at her shoes and said a man had done up her laces. I asked who and where was he and she pointed to the bridge. We both walked back there and I spent a few minutes looking for him. Nobody was in sight and I returned to the bench. She said something else. Oh god, I'd forgotten.'

Andy's eyes were on her but he stayed silent.

'She said the man's little girl had died and he was sad.'

There was no way to stop the tears filling her eyes but Liz blinked them away. 'Where is Maureen?'

'At her apartment. She has an officer staying with her.'

'Have you read all of her statements so far?'

'Yes. And there's nothing like that.'

'She's been in shock today, Andy. We need to talk to her. See if there's anything new she remembers. Can I do that? Now?'

He glanced at his watch. 'We'll both go.'

'How's she doing?' Liz asked the officer who was staying with Maureen. They were just outside the apartment.

'I've let her know you are coming over but that there isn't news about Eliza. She jumps at every sound and keeps checking her phone is working. But she has some sleeping tablets and will take one in an hour and try to sleep.'

'Take a break. We'll be here for fifteen or so if you want to stretch your legs.'

Andy pushed the door open. The officer came back inside long enough to collect her jacket and then slipped out again. Liz followed Andy into the open plan apartment. Only two doors went off the combination living/dining/kitchen area which were presumably the bathroom and bedroom. It was a lot smaller than hers and faced onto the building behind. Same as Darryl's, with a view of the alley.

Huddled under a blanket, Maureen lay on her side on the sofa, channel surfing on the television, news program to news program. She barely glanced at Andy and Liz.

'Do you mind if we sit for a few minutes?' Liz asked.

Maureen nodded and turned the sound down. 'The officer said there's no news yet but it's everywhere on the telly. Why hasn't anyone seen her yet?'

Andy perched on an armchair. 'We've got a hotline set up and there's a team fielding phone calls. Lots of people are ringing it and even though—so far—there are no firm leads, it is just a matter of time. As well as the television, a media release went out to all the major networks, including radio and social media, and they in turn are pushing it through to their regional outlets.'

Pushing the blanket aside, Maureen straightened and put her feet on the floor. She was in the same clothes as this morning.

'Is it true about Darryl?'

'What have you heard?' Andy asked.

'That he's been arrested. His apartment has been turned upside down.'

'Not arrested but he is helping us with our enquiries.'

'Well what does that mean? You think he took my Eliza?' Maureen's voice rose as her attention turned to Liz. 'He lives near you. Why didn't you know? You must have seen him act suspicious but did nothing. Not even after your own niece was taken!'

'Hold on, Maureen—' Andy started.

'It's okay, she has good points.'

All of Liz's training and experience in pressure situations kicked in and shoved her personal feelings aside.

'Darryl is being interviewed because he was walking around the outside of the park after Eliza disappeared. We're working with him to see what he might remember. And yes, he is my neighbour but across the hallway and a couple of doors up so not close enough for me to be aware of comings and goings,' Liz said. She maintained steady eye contact with Maureen. 'I spoke to Darryl after Ellen was taken. So did other police. There was no reason to suspect him then either.'

'Oh. Sorry. I shouldn't have said that.'

'Maureen, of everyone, I understand. I imagine reporters have raked up stories about Ellen and I'm not going to watch any of that because I reckon they'll get it wrong and make up their own version of events. But whatever you've heard, the truth is that my niece went missing from the same park. She's never been found. I blame myself every day even though logically, I understand it would have happened no matter how vigilant I was because whoever took her, wanted to take her.'

Tears poured down Maureen's face and Liz moved to sit beside her, grabbing a box of tissues on the way. She put the box onto the other woman's lap.

'Eighteen years ago we didn't have the technology of today. We're going to find Eliza and bring her home. It's what I want, and Detective Sergeant Montebello wants, and the entire police department. Everyone is on your side. Eliza's side. Okay?'

Maureen nodded, dragging tissues down her cheeks.

'Every little thing makes a difference. Any observation which didn't matter at the time, might matter now. Do you recall anything else?'

'I've gone over and over this. With the first police who arrived at the park and then another one, and then you. I can't even remember what I've said. Not really.'

'Well, one more time? And let us do an audio recording because then we will know exactly what you've remembered. Would you mind? It might make a difference.'

After looking from Liz to Andy, Maureen nodded.

Andy set up his phone to record.

'Talk us through this morning from the time you and Eliza arrived at the park.'

For a few minutes, Maureen went over the same information Liz had heard. She was firm with the details. Probably etched into her brain the same way Ellen's disappearance was in Liz's. When she got to the part about Eliza coming back to get a drink, she frowned and paused while she thought. Her eyes shot up to look at Liz.

'Did I tell you what she said? I'm sure I told you. Her shoelaces were tied and she said that a nice man tied them. And then she got a bit quiet.'

'Why… why was that?' Liz could barely speak.

'She said the man's own daughter had died. She thought it was sad.'

There was the familiar ringing in Liz's ears and she was afraid to move in case she fell. Bile rose in her throat but then with a tide of relief she realised how much this changed things. Nobody could deny it was the same person. She was going to find Eliza and then she'd pursue the monster who'd stolen Ellen. Even if it took the rest of her life.

THIRTEEN

Although Pete had told Liz his idea was stupid, it wasn't. The more digging he did into Ellen's disappearance and Eliza's, the more he leaned toward the theory that a lot of planning had gone into both abductions.

Trouble was that nobody else was going to use up valuable resources on his theory. Not when they were stretched to the max with door-knocking and a hundred other tasks which all had priority. *His* time however—when he wasn't on the metaphorical clock—was another story.

Pete ran across Bourke Street between trams and traffic, waving back at a bus which honked. His special brand of waving. Donna was already on the balcony upstairs at the noisy pub she favoured for their occasional chats.

He grabbed a beer, and another wine for her.

Out here wasn't as loud, not yet. Once the after-dinner crowd arrived that would change but at the table on the very end of the balcony they could hear each other speak.

'Six months between drinks is pushing a friendship.' Donna Miles was forty, thin as a rake, and liked much younger women. She also worked for Teresa Scarcella on *At Six Tonight* and didn't mind exchanging a bit of information. 'Pity it took a missing kid to see you.'

'You do have my phone number.'

'*I* called last time.'

Pete grinned. 'Change preferences and I'll call more often.'

As if. Donna had a perpetually scary look in her eyes. A hunter, out for prey.

'Darling, you'd be far too old for me for a start.'

'Nice. Do you have anything on the person I mentioned?'

She screwed her face up. 'Work, huh? Very well. My contact at Barwon knows the kid's father and says he's straight up honest. Guilty as sin for breaking and entering but a nice guy compared to most of the inmates. He also knows the man who arranged the apartment and reckons it was a favour. Heard that Singleton's missus and kid were heading for a shelter and put the word on the manager of the building.'

'What favour?'

'If my contact knows he didn't say. What I can help with, assuming you can repay this and soon, is the name of the go-between. Not in prison any longer.'

'I'll repay it.'

'Can you get Teresa an interview with your boss?'

Pete almost spluttered out the mouthful of beer he'd just taken.

'I shall take that as a no. What about with Liz Moorland?'

'Forget it. She has enough going on. Tell you what. I'll try and line up Detective Sergeant Andy Montebello. He's personable and good looking. And young.'

Donna gave him a long stare. 'Fine. I'll text you the name the minute you tell me the time.'

Pete's hand snaked out and grabbed her arm. She glared at him but didn't try to pull away. They'd played this game before.

'A little girl is at risk of losing her life and you want to quibble over an interview. I promise I'll try but Donna, if you know something and don't share it right here and now, you can kiss any future intel goodbye.'

FOURTEEN

Whatever Andy had presumed about Liz went out the window after the last hour or so. She had a steel backbone and a relentless desire for justice and she wasn't going to let anyone down by being part of the task force. More than that, she had a way of looking at pieces of information and turning them into a cohesive whole. So if she needed a moment to herself now and then to manage what had to be an overload of emotions about this case, then so be it.

Since they'd returned to his car she'd been on her iPad and hadn't spared him a word or glance as she worked. They stopped at traffic lights and she suddenly looked up, as if remembering she was in the car. 'Sorry. I had an idea.'

'I'm listening.'

'This might need Meg's expertise because I'm not quite sure how to find a man whose daughter died in a city where there must be countless people meeting that criteria. I've created the bare bones of a profile and hope there might be something else of use to add from the files on my desk.'

'It is another part of the puzzle, Liz. Every bit is worth looking at.'

Her face relaxed and she nodded.

The lights changed and Andy turned onto the road to the police station carpark.

'How you handled Maureen... you have an excellent way with people. Even when she began to blame you for not seeing Darryl as a danger, you let it wash over you.'

'The poor woman is stressed to the max and exhausted. And those are just words.' Liz yawned, quickly covering her mouth. 'Everyone is tired.'

He struggled to contain his own yawn. Contagious things.

'What now?' Liz put the iPad away.

It was after eight.

'Terry is going to post a roster of sorts. Make sure everyone gets a break and sleep. We've stopped door knocking until morning but quite honesty I think we've exhausted that line of enquiry.'

Nosing the car into the steep driveway, Andy opened his window to tap his access card. The door open, he drove down several floors to his spot.

Liz was quiet again. Thoughtful. As they waited for the elevator she finally spoke. 'I'd like to keep going through the files.'

'Or you could observe the discussion Terry started a few minutes ago with Darryl. His lawyer finally fronted and I for one am keen to watch.'

She hit the button. 'Best offer I've had in hours.'

With a coffee each thanks to one of the constables, Liz and Andy settled onto seats in the observation room. The lights made an eery glow through the one-way window, periodically shadowed as Terry wandered from one side of the interview room to the other. A lawyer sat to one side with a notepad and Darryl slumped behind the table.

'He looks terrible,' Liz said.

'Well, he was offered a change of clothes and has eaten and

had a rest in one of the cells while waiting for his legal counsel. Does he ever look much better than this?'

Liz shot him a look of surprise.

'You've said he rarely changes out of his singlet and shorts... and by shorts I hadn't realised you meant boxers until we picked him up.'

'He has a certain style, doesn't he?'

Andy increased the volume from the other room.

'Can you see our problem, mate?' Terry stopped pacing and stood, arms crossed and legs apart, almost directly in front of the table. 'This video footage is clear as day.'

'Isn't me.'

'It isn't?' Terry leaned forward and tapped an iPad on the table. 'Can you tell me who it is then? I'd swear it was you. Same clothes as we found you in this afternoon, including the hoodie —which is being forensically inspected as we speak. Oh, look at that bit. You look straight at the camera, Darryl. Reckon if we run this through our facial recognition software it'll confirm with what we can all see.'

Darryl turned to his lawyer. 'Can they do that? The software thing?'

The man nodded.

'Do it then. Waste your time and mine because I said it isn't me.' Eyes back on Terry, Darryl almost smirked.

Liz's hands curled into fists. Andy got it. He'd like to pummel the truth out of the little shit but it was a knee-jerk response and nothing Andy would act on. McNamara? Well, if nobody was watching Pete would likely have a different approach to the interrogation but getting away with it was another matter.

Terry pulled out a chair and sat, his body language open. Darryl's smirk vanished and after a minute or two of silence, he relaxed and sat back.

'Never understood why Terry chose to chase rank when he's

this good,' Liz said. 'He's never done anything covert or undercover yet is a masterclass in interviewing a suspect.'

'Not everyone has the stomach for covert. And even the ones who do are hardly ever tapped on the shoulder. Makes McNamara a rare bird in recent times. Would you do it? If you had an offer?'

She didn't reply.

'Must have been a hell of a shock, Darryl. Someone knocks on your door and all of a sudden there's a dozen cops and you've got the call up to visit us here.' Terry shook his head. 'I'm going to be straight with you. A search of your apartment hasn't given us a whole lot.'

Darryl's eyes flicked back and forth, lawyer to Terry.

'Mind you, I'm only talking about the initial search. We did find some weed but seriously, who doesn't have a bit now and then?'

'Yeah, exactly.'

'Mr Tompsett.' That was his lawyer who'd finally paid some attention. 'We can call a halt to this anytime you want.'

'He's correct, Darryl. If you want a break, just say. Coffee. Food. A blanket,' Terry said. 'Couple of magazines.'

Liz sniggered.

'If you get tired we can get you back to that cell in minutes. That cold, bare cell with nothing but a crap mattress and thin pillow for the night.'

'He's uncertain. Look how much Darryl is fidgeting. I've not worked much with Terry like you have, Liz, but I tend to agree about his skillset.'

Terry was back on his feet, pacing. 'Your legal counsel wants you to keep quiet. Run every comment through them and you have the right to do so. The thing is, mate, it really is just a matter of time and our expertise before we turn something up. Your computer is in the hands of our forensic specialist and she eats passwords for breakfast. Anything on it will hit my desk first thing tomorrow.

'And Darryl?' Terry stopped again. 'I do mean anything. Illegal gambling. Porn. Dodgy looking emails. One way or another you're in the shit. How much depends on how helpful you are tonight.'

'I done nothing wrong.'

'Then you have nothing to worry about.' Terry sank onto the chair, this time leaning his arms on the table. 'Talk me through it, Darryl. How did the shoe get into your pocket?'

The lawyer cleared his throat. 'I'd like to speak to my client alone.'

'Sure. Just tap on the door when you're ready.'

On his way out, Terry turned off the recording and the sound disappeared. A minute later, he stuck his head into the observation room. 'Good, hoped you'd both be here. Any suggestions?'

'From the look of it, he wants to talk.' Andy nodded at the interview room.

Darryl and the lawyer stood face to face. Waving his arms around, Darryl's face was red as he tried to get some point across but the lawyer kept shaking his head.

Liz updated Terry with the new information from Maureen.

'Was that widely known, Liz? The press, for example?'

'No. That as well as the man doing up Ellen's shoelaces were kept quiet, which makes this a compelling argument for the same person taking both children. I've started to build a profile.'

'We'll need to bring someone in, Terry,' Andy said. 'With Liz providing a brief for an expert then Meg will have something solid to go on as far as narrowing the parameters once they've done their bit. In the morning can we go through some options?'

The lawyer tapped on the interview room door.

'My cue. Are you going home, Lizzie?'

'I'm still going through the files about Ellen.'

Her tone left no doubt that she'd argue the point if need be and Andy couldn't restrain a small smile when Terry rolled his eyes when his back was facing Liz.

'Don't take bets on the outcome of this interview.'

Door closed again, Liz raised her eyebrows at Andy. 'He rolled his eyes, didn't he?'

'You've known Terry a long time, right?'

She smiled and turned her attention to the window.

Back at his desk, Andy sent a text message.

Guess you've heard about the missing child? Need a favour. Names of who you'd have considered to work on the profile of the perp. Prefer to keep it local. TY.

His former boss, Ben Rossi, was a Melbourne lad through and through until his move along the coast and Andy had seen him pull contacts from his head more than once. Andy was a blow-in. A transplant from Sydney a year after graduating from university thanks to a relationship which almost immediately fractured. But he'd already begun his career in the Victorian Police Force and had fallen in love with the laneways and coffee houses of his adopted city. He just lacked the built-in contacts that a born-and-bred Melbournian such as Ben had to call upon at will.

The floor was quieter than when he'd left to pick up food. Half the officers had left for the night and those who remained had gravitated to the area around the whiteboards. Some of the lights were off, creating a wall of darkness around them.

His phone beeped.

I've sent a few names to your email. Poor kid. How's Liz holding up?

Andy had forgotten Ben had known Liz for a long time. He stared into the dark. For as long as he could remember, Andy wanted to work in Homicide. All of his higher education leaned that way. But so far he'd been overlooked for the rare vacancies.

Toughest person I think I've met. And thanks. How's life?

His position in Missing Persons was thanks to Ben leaving. He knew it. But he still grabbed the opportunity in both hands. Ben had a new life. He'd found love and family and decided it meant more than working on endless and often heartbreaking cases.

Loving my life, dude. Come and visit—there's always a spare surfboard.

He chuckled. His life was the polar opposite of Ben's. Career was everything. Ambition was his keyword to life. And he worked hard. He loved his job in Missing Persons and thrived on solving a case.

But this one?

So many moving parts. If Liz wasn't involved it would be simpler in some respects but his initial plan to ask for her to be removed from the investigation was no longer a consideration. Finding Eliza might lead to what happened all those years ago to Ellen. Or, if new information rose about Ellen, then Eliza might be found before it was too late.

Terry wandered in and glanced around until he found Andy. 'Done all I can tonight.' He dropped into the chair opposite with a grunt. 'Damned lawyer insisted Darryl get some sleep.'

'Why doesn't he want what's best for his client? By morning we're likely to have something solid to charge him with so he should be co-operating tonight. While there might still be time to find Eliza before…'

Running his hands through what was left of his hair, Terry muttered an expletive.

'I've got a couple of names to put forward to help Liz with this profile,' Andy said. 'She's working by lamp light at her desk going through those boxes.'

'Might drop in on her on my way out. You're okay with her now?'

'If you'd seen her with Maureen… took some nasty comments on the chin and then comforted the woman. Got back in the car and began making a plan to find the bastard.' Andy shook his head. 'How does she do it? I mean, she's being confronted with a repeat most likely of the worst day of her life yet apart from the early wobble, she's solid.'

'Most likely you'll only see what she wants you to—at least now she's taken stock of the information. Liz doesn't let anyone down, least of all herself except those few minutes all those years ago. Last winter she had to choose between stopping a murderer kill her oldest friend and ensuring a little kid was safe.'

Andy leaned forward. 'Are you talking about Vince Carter?'

'I am. She must have been torn but trusted another cop to protect Vince while she went after the kid.'

He remembered this. Well, the details as presented by the press as well as the official channels. Liz's name had hardly been featured.

'Trusted cop? Pete McNamara?'

With a laugh, Terry pushed himself to his feet. 'Never underestimate Liz. She can read people and she sees what most of us miss. Like Pete's good side. Night, mate. I'll be back at dawn.'

It went against everything Andy felt about McNamara. What he knew about him, to believe he'd been trusted with protecting a man who had once reported him for questionable ethics. But Vince Carter was alive and McNamara had been instrumental in that. Andy wasn't about to become his best friend, but he might have to ease up on Pete a bit. Maybe.

FIFTEEN
~DAY TWO~

Midnight had ticked over unnoticed.

This floor had no movement at all, not unless Liz stood and stretched or refilled her water bottle.

Elevators went by periodically and the street sounds intruded now and then. Terry had stopped by long enough to give her the crap news about Darryl. That was ages ago. One box was closed again, nothing left to look at. Nothing which wouldn't make her cry if she spent too long on it.

And crying was a waste of time and energy.

Her computer hummed in the background with several open tabs. Official channels and a couple of sites which were media driven but worth keeping an eye on.

On the desk she had an open A4 size notepad with several pages already filled. Words which stuck out. One page dedicated to a diagram of the park which she'd sketched tonight. One colour for Eliza and one for Ellen. Both overlapped. Names of witnesses, people interviewed. But nothing which immediately solved this. Nothing which assured her she would find a way to Ellen. And Eliza.

She opened another file.

Each was dedicated to different aspects of the case and this one contained the sum of the forensic evidence which was precious little.

Several reports covered samples taken from the area around the bridge. Bark, soil, fingerprints. There'd been nothing indicating a struggle. No trace from Ellen other than hair strands. Liz frowned, not recalling these. There was a photograph. A dozen or so short hairs from the scalp end. White hairs.

'That can't be right.'

Liz opened the other box and dug around until she found the evidence bag with the hairs. She held them close to the lamp. Definitely white. There must have been an error because Ellen's hair was golden blonde with not a trace of silver or white. She'd plaited her hair often enough to be certain.

She reread the report.

Sample located in the underside of the bridge. Position is in line with someone brushing the top of their head against the roughness of the beam. Due to the height, the sample is likely to have come from the child standing upon one of the painted stumps. Match is close to Ellen's DNA. Evidence potentially tainted by exposure to the elements prior to bagging.

'But this isn't right.'

She checked through the rest of the file on the forensic evidence. She took a photo of a technical report. Liz had a basic understanding of genetics and how DNA worked but so much depended upon external factors and that is where she was stuck. At the very least, this sample needed to be rerun because it couldn't belong to Ellen.

'Then who?'

Liz didn't recall ever standing beneath the bridge, let alone brushing against the slats. Her own hair had started like Ellen's but gradually changed to dark blonde—brown in some lights—but no greys that she'd found so far and besides, these strands looked thicker than her hair. And definitely thicker than Ellen's, which was very fine. Neither of Ellen's parents fitted either, with her mother dyeing her hair red forever and her father a sandy colour.

Phone still in her palm, Liz scrolled through her contacts, stopping on Anna's.

She'd not heard her sister's voice for years. Not seen her smile. Anna blamed Liz for Ellen's disappearance and over time the relationship deteriorated to the point where they couldn't bear being close to each other.

But they'd have to talk again because it was better if Anna heard about the similarities of this case from her rather than the media's version.

Using the phone, Liz took more photographs. The strands of hair under the lamplight and then under the bright fluorescents in the ladies bathroom. All of the forensics file. She couldn't take anything home from the boxes but at least this way she'd be able to do a bit of research away from the office. After packing the boxes up she carried them to the evidence lock up and checked them in for the night.

She had somewhere else to be.

Even now, at close to two in the morning, there were curious onlookers. The park was taped up and several officers patrolled the boundaries. At the largest entry, the police caravan was lit up but only had a skeleton staff who reported nothing new from the public in the past hour. One of the officers, clearly bored sitting behind a table, accompanied Liz to the playground.

'Is there something in particular you want to look at, Ma'am?'

'Under the bridge. Did the Crime Scene team finish up?'

'With the playground, yes. They are returning to the bench and fountain, I think. But we were told we can reopen the park once they do that first thing in the morning.'

Nevertheless, Liz donned a pair of slips over her shoes. 'I'm fine to work alone.'

She turned on a powerful torch and ducked beneath the bridge.

A chill ran up her spine as she flashed the light here and there. Nobody was in sight other than the officer, who leaned against a nearby tree. In the past she'd felt this on occasion and almost always it was from being watched. She doubted that was the case now. More likely it was a response to being where Eliza once was. Where Ellen once was.

She stood in a dry river bed of sorts. Lots of stones, from pebbles to small boulders, made up the bottom. Every so often were tree stumps at different heights, broad and solid and all colourfully painted. Scattered around were hardy, small shade-loving plants, mostly succulents gentle on little hands. In daylight it would make for an interesting and safe play space. At night it was a bit creepy.

There was plenty to indicate the earlier presence of crime scene officers with fingerprint dust over every trunk and the larger rocks as well as the half dozen upright posts. At least the weather had held with no expectations of rain for another day or two.

Liz worked her way from one end of the underside of the bridge to the other, taking her time to peer closely at the rough timber beams. All were above her height so she stepped onto the lowest of the stumps. That only raised her enough to be able to touch the beam without fully stretching her arm. She worked her way to the third in height before her head came close to the underside. Only one stump was higher.

But how on earth had those hairs—labelled as belonging to Ellen—got there? The child would have had to be on someone's shoulders. Liz stepped down and sat on the stump. Might that be the answer? A kid given a boost on someone's shoulders. A 'nice man' who was sad because his own little girl had died.

Somewhere in the forensic report should be a photograph or

drawing marked up with where the hair was located. Even standing on her toes on the tallest of the stumps, Ellen's head would have been nowhere near the bridge.

She called to the officer. 'Could I borrow you for a minute?'

He jogged over. 'Everything okay?'

'What is your height?'

'One hundred and ninety four centimetres.'

'Is there any part of the bridge you'd need to duck to walk under?'

With a grin he removed his cap. 'One way to find out.'

'Try not to brush the timber above you.'

The officer was cautious and thorough and found one place where he'd had to avoid touching the top. It was on the bank of the dry river bed where the ground rose a little. Liz took a few photos both with the officer in place and then when he stepped away.

'Do you happen to know if any hairs were recovered?'

'Sorry, no. Should I ask the others?'

'No. I'll chase it up. Thanks though.'

They returned to the caravan and the officer immediately went to attend to someone waiting for attention.

Liz crossed the road. As she headed home her eyes darted from one side of the road to the other pinpointing external security cameras. So many shops, and above them, apartments, all overlooking the streets where Eliza and Maureen walked less than a day earlier with nothing in mind other than a trip to the park. Somebody had to have seen them. Perhaps even noticed them being followed.

Once she reached the corner across from her apartment building she stopped and gazed at it. Most of the windows were darkened. But Brian Bisley's apartment was lit up like a beacon. His was on the top floor at the end with the working elevator. Figured. It was rent free as part of his role as building manager and was larger than most, even with a balcony which many others lacked. There was a slight movement out there and a cigarette was lit. Why was he awake so late?

Why am I?

She had to be back in the office at first light and standing here wasn't accomplishing anything. Liz dragged herself up the three flights of stairs. Darryl's apartment was closed up with no external indicators it had been searched earlier. Locking herself in she leaned against the door for a moment. Fifteen or so hours ago she'd got the news about Eliza and her life had changed. Again.

But this time was different. This time she was going to catch the bastard.

―――

Liz grabbed a tram in, using the time to read through the pages she'd photographed from the forensics file. There was a diagram of where the hairs were located and it looked roughly in the same area as the officer had indicated. Until she could put it all side by side she wasn't prepared to hope this was a key clue.

Arriving with a few minutes to spare before a meeting with Terry, Liz bought a decent coffee and a breakfast burrito and demolished the latter on her way upstairs. Earlier she'd woken up on her sofa, an empty wine glass on the coffee table, and with an intense longing for more sleep. But sleep would wait.

The meeting was again in Missing Persons, run by Terry and Andy, who both looked exhausted. The detectives who'd slept were there for briefing while most of those who'd worked overnight left. Several whiteboards were in different stages of development depending upon the focus of whichever small team managed them. The two which interested Liz were the forensics updates and one dedicated to the park and its immediate surrounds.

'We have Darryl Tompsett in custody—well, being held for

questioning. Despite clear video footage which identifies him placing one of Eliza's shoes where the dogs subsequently found it, he's denying it is him. Further, his lawyer is doing everything he can to keep his client from answering the questions he seems inclined to consider.' Terry shook his head. 'I'm going back into an interview later but we're getting to the point of needing to charge or release.'

'Happy to take that task from you, boss,' Pete said. 'Give you a chance to enjoy a decent breakfast out of the building. And no need to waste power on recording anything.'

A ripple of laughter lightened the atmosphere. Even the corners of Andy's mouth lifted for a moment.

'Half tempted, mate. Half tempted.' Terry gestured at one of the whiteboards. 'Let's run through the best of the calls we've had from the public.'

Liz zoned out. If there was anything she needed to know, there'd be alerts sent. Her eyes moved to the whiteboard about the park. There were several parts to it. An aerial photograph was in the centre and several areas were highlighted with markers. The playground, the bench where Maureen had sat, the entry she and Eliza used to come in to the park, and the spot where the shoe was found by the police dog. There was a list. Distance to the apartment building and route taken by Maureen. Several lines had ticks beside them presumably where there'd been surveillance proof of them passing. Everything else was too small to decipher from this distance.

Notes about the forensics to date was mostly in Meg's neat hand. Liz glanced around. She wasn't present so had she worked all night?

There were two columns. The first was titled 'Meg' and the other 'CSS' and each had a long list beneath them. As a forensic analyst, Meg's list covered data extracted from a number of sources including PTV who had a relationship and system with the police when it came to needing footage from their vehicles—buses, trams, trains—or their stations and stops. It was a massive exercise to manage so many cameras but more than once had provided useful evidence against criminal activity, or helped locate a missing person.

Crime Scene Services were the outstanding but overworked unit who dealt with the practical side of forensic science. Anything from trace taken from an accident or crime scene such as blood or paint particles, right through to DNA and reconstructing an old skeleton. The unit worked with groundbreaking technology and was vital to the solving of many crimes.

The list beneath CSS included fingerprints, photographic evidence, footprints, Eliza's shoe—with a query about the tying of the shoelaces—and a number of items taken from Darryl's apartment, including a laptop.

Nothing about hairs.

The briefing wrapped up with a quick pep talk from Andy and then most of the detectives dispersed, some to keep sifting through data in the office and others to return to the park or similar places.

Pete moved across the room and dropped into a seat beside Liz. 'Did you sleep at all?'

'Enough.'

'Yeah, sure. I'd say I got eight hours but if I subtracted how often I woke trying to puzzle things together it might amount to half of that.'

'I went back to the park.'

Liz filled Pete in on the important bits.

'You don't remember the hairs from Ellen?'

'Nope. I'll take a deeper look this morning.'

Terry beckoned to them both before following Andy into his office. When Liz and Pete joined them, Andy waved them to chairs. He smiled briefly at Liz before opening a file.

'Meg worked all night and has finally gone home to sleep. She accessed Darryl's laptop thanks to the warrant extending to anything found in the flat. Most of it is crap. Garden variety porn —nothing with kids. Email is filled with spam. Doubt he ever deletes anything but that proved helpful.' Andy dropped the file and leaned his elbows on the desk. 'There are half a dozen reoccurring contacts but only two which jump out as warranting our attention. One is Brian Bisley. Sometimes several emails a day and all worded in a way which indicates some type of code being used. Numbers followed by names. Nothing which makes sense.'

'Yet,' Terry said.

'Exactly. The other email address has so far eluded discovery. Meg has given the job to someone while she sleeps. But the emails themselves are bizarre. Nothing in the body other than an image of a newspaper clipping. All different. And sometimes a photograph of a place.'

'Anything in common?' Pete asked.

'Too soon to tell. There's a randomness to it all which has my spidey senses on high alert,' Andy frowned. 'I'm getting everything printed off and would appreciate you taking a look, Liz.'

Pete shot her a glance which she ignored.

'Of course. I need to tell you all something.'

She had their immediate attention. Part of her felt bad she'd not filled Pete in on more but time was her enemy.

'I came across an anomaly around Ellen.'

'Anomaly, how?' Terry asked.

'There are hairs—including follicles from the scalp—which are marked up as belonging to Ellen. I've not yet discovered when these were found but they are linked to her by DNA as a close match. Close enough, apparently.'

'Apparently?'

'Terry, there's something odd. The hairs are white and thick. Not golden blonde and fine like Ellen's hair was. I understand the weather might have affected them but there's a visible difference.'

'We can have them run again,' Andy said.

'Thank you. And yes. But there's more. I returned to the park last night… this morning. Anyway, there is no way Ellen's head could have brushed the underside of the bridge. Not unless she was on someone's shoulders. Or…'

Pete hadn't taken his eyes off her. She'd felt them boring into her. 'Something isn't right. Is it?'

She shook her head. 'I had the officer who'd accompanied me stand beneath the bridge. He's one-ninety-four centimetres in height and there was only one narrow spot where his hair might have been close enough to touch. But no chance in hell Ellen could have reached that height.'

'You think the hairs might be from whoever took her,' Pete said.

'I don't know. There might be several more logical answers.'

Her eyes met Andy's. Only a matter of hours ago she wouldn't have brought this information to him. Not directly. But there'd been a shift in his approach to her and one for the better. His expression was thoughtful.

'Liz, put together a list of any relative of Ellen's please. But don't prioritise it because we need to build that profile first.' Terry shuffled in his chair. 'The sooner we hand over a document to a third party the better. Which reminds me, Andy, you said you had some names?'

'I do, courtesy of Ben Rossi.'

Everyone nodded. Ben had been popular.

'Flick them across and I'll start making calls. I think we've got a good case to steal some of the budget for barbeques on yachts from the higher-ups.' Terry grinned.

'Better you than me.'

He might be happy to palm the job off, but Andy was equally capable of getting what he needed for his team… at least under these circumstances. Liz admired his focus and ambition even if occasionally it did misdirect back to Homicide. His time would come but when it did, would the young man have the stomach for this job of hers?

'What am I doing, Terry?' Pete crossed his arms.

'Actually, if nobody minds, I would like to borrow you, Pete,'

Andy said. 'Wouldn't mind running through some background on a couple of people who were named in some of the hotline phone calls.'

'You know that's just morons trying to offload their enemies?'

'Rather be certain and you know these people better than most.' Andy didn't back down. His voice was firm without being bossy and Liz had to hand it to him. If he was trying to get on Pete's good side—at least, his useful side—then he was doing a good job.

'Sure. But if Liz needs me. Or Terry.'

'Then you go and help them. There's a whiteboard freshly written up downstairs.'

Terry glanced at his watch. 'I'm gonna grab breakfast then resume the interview. Anyone else?'

Nobody followed him, each heading to their areas.

SIXTEEN

After collecting the boxes from the evidence lock-up, Liz got back into the files.

She printed the diagrams of where the hair was found as well as her photos and set them beside each other. The officer stood exactly where the hair had been located eighteen years ago, give or take a few centimetres.

Why hadn't she known about the discovery of the hairs and their testing? One look at them was enough to raise a dozen questions and had she been shown them back then... but she hadn't. For some reason this vital piece of evidence was overlooked. The fingers of each hand gripped a pencil until it snapped.

'Liz?'

She'd forgotten Pete was at the whiteboard a few metres away.

'Oops.' She tossed the two pieces away.

'We can't afford to lose pencils,' he said. 'Isn't Terry trying to increase our budget for resources?'

'Funny. Pete, take a look at this, would you? Give me your take on it.'

He was happy to walk away from his designated job and

looked over her shoulder. 'Any idea if there was previously one of those stumps in that spot? Something much taller?'

'None. And anything too tall would have been dangerous for younger kids.'

'Which means there might have been one which subsequently was removed.'

Liz made a note to check with whoever managed the park. Somewhere in all of this were the contact details. It was a possibility which she hadn't considered.

'Assuming you are wrong—' She started.

'Impossible.'

'How else would those hairs have become stuck in the underside of the bridge?' She swung around to look at him and he leaned on the edge of a cupboard. 'Quite apart from me knowing the hairs don't belong to a young child, what are ways they got there?'

Pete might joke around to the point of being annoying but right now, he was deadly serious. 'Not a lot of ways. I'm going to assume a bit here but nothing which we can't verify. I doubt they originated from above the timber. I spent a fair bit of time under and on that bridge yesterday and the slats are not open. There's barely room between them for dust let alone hairs magically shedding from someone and slipping through, not to mention grabbing onto the roughness underneath.'

And this is why I tolerate everything else about you, mate.

'The hairs were ripped from the scalp and that only gives me two conclusions. Somebody's head brushed against the timber which is rough enough to have latched onto the hairs. Or—' he leaned over to remove another pencil which had made its way to Liz's hands. 'Some person planted them.'

'If it was the latter, then why?'

Pete returned the pencil to its container. 'So hard to do without it being obvious to a forensics expert but answer that and you may well find who was involved in taking Ellen. Is there nothing more substantial in the report about it?'

Liz opened the file and flicked through a couple of pages. 'All I've found is a brief comment about hairs being located two days after Ellen was reported missing. Two frigging days.' She looked at him. 'With Eliza, the park was immediately closed off. A team swooped in to conduct a proper investigation on the day she disappeared. That is nothing like I experienced, Pete. Nothing.'

About to reach for the pencil she stopped herself. 'Happy for you to take a look. Actually, I'd appreciate it.'

'What if we do an interview?'

'Can you explain?'

He nodded. 'What if you and I go into an interview room and have a conversation. If you trust me, I'll go back to that day with you and see if there is anything forgotten or overlooked.'

A little part of Liz was crushed into a million pieces. She'd been interviewed after Ellen was taken and most of it was implications that she'd neglected her duty of care.

But the rest of her spiralled up into something like hope.

'Promise you won't turn the cameras off?'

With the biggest grin, Pete wandered back to his whiteboard. 'Never gonna promise something I can't keep, Lizzie.'

―――

Terry agreed to the interview but not until Liz had finished compiling the brief. He'd managed to source one of Ben Rossi's contacts who'd agreed to come in during the afternoon and left Liz in no doubt she had to have the information ready as possible.

She knuckled down on the remaining files and made copious notes, forcing herself to ignore the itch to track down everyone who had been involved in overlooking such a mix of compelling evidence about Ellen's disappearance and rip their heads off. It would keep. If anything, she had to find a way to manage the anger and be able to question some of them herself and that wouldn't happen if she showed her fury to anyone. Not even Pete. And he'd removed all of her pencils bar one.

Around her the room bustled with conversations and phone calls. Detectives, a few uniforms, and support staff moved between floors as different information came to light. Somebody shoved a coffee in front of her at one point and the atmosphere was intense.

Everybody wanted to find Eliza.

As her stomach began to protest its empty state, she finished compiling the brief. Several pages of cross-referencing data between the two disappearances were printed out. More were copied from Ellen's case. She'd created one page which highlighted the similarities which were compelling enough to warrant inclusion. And another—the most important page—everything pertaining to what they knew of the criminal. It wasn't much but it was more than they'd had.

There was nothing more she could do. Not yet.

After printing several copies of the brief and putting them into their own folders, she tapped on Terry's door. He was absent. Rather than leaving them on his desk, Liz went to Missing Persons and found him with Andy.

She hesitated to interrupt. Through the glass door it was obvious how involved both men were with a phone call they were on. But Andy noticed her and waved her in and she entered and closed the door quietly.

'Surely this is better handled by our media department,' Terry said. 'Taking me or Andy away from our teams is a waste of time. With respect, sir.'

The voice on the other end of the conference call was Terry's boss. Liz knew him as a by-the-books man who took a dim view of the media and a hard line on crime. 'And normally I'd agree. But you did well yesterday and having a familiar face to speak to the public now and then is better than leaving them to speculate or listen to some of the nonsense which is being spread. Make yourself available at the park at two.'

Terry's eyes gazed at the ceiling. 'Yes, sir.'

The conversation ended, Terry mumbled something unflattering.

'What's happening at the park?' Liz asked.

'There's going to be a reconstruction of Maureen and Eliza's movements yesterday morning. Filmed and subtitled. The route they took from near the apartment and then some at the park using actors. Terry will then front a short media release to ask for more assistance from the public and answer questions,' Andy said.

'The only question is why do this now.' Terry pushed his chair back. 'All of us are at capacity and it's something normally done when interest wanes. When there's less information coming in. But I just do as I'm told.'

Liz passed him the folders. 'Five copies of the brief.'

Terry dropped three onto the desk, handed one to Andy and opened the last. Both men skimmed.

'This is good work, Liz,' Andy said. 'Clear and concise. Good use of the information from both cases and solid connections. It will help.' He put the folder down. 'Terry told me you're doing an interview to revisit Ellen's disappearance. Would you rather I do that with you, than McNamara?'

About to tell Andy that his experience wasn't even close to Pete's, Liz paused to think about it. Because he barely knew her, it would allow him to press her on areas Pete might not. There'd be a benefit. But Pete—who might joke about his interrogation style being unfit for cameras—was a better choice for one important reason. She trusted him. Even though Andy was warming to her, Liz had no idea what he might do with anything which came of the interview.

'Let's see how it goes as is but I'll keep your offer in mind.'

Andy nodded.

Terry was on his feet. 'Liz, can you be available for when Doctor Carroll comes in? I might be stuck at the park at the same time.'

She glanced at her watch. 'Of course. Are you going back to Darryl?'

'Want to watch?'

'As long as I can eat and watch at the same time.'

'Won't give you indigestion?' Andy grinned.

'I'll take the risk. Anyway, wouldn't be the first time Darryl's made me feel ill. Being drunk and naked apart from boxer shorts and knee-high socks running down the hallway at home isn't something for those with weak stomachs to see.'

Just as well she was starving and ate quickly because Darryl wasn't being helpful.

'I want to go home.'

'Then answer my questions honestly and without going off on tangents,' Terry said.

His lawyer went to speak and Terry cast the man a dark look which shut him up.

Darryl had showered and wore a T-shirt and tracksuit pants. He looked rested and more certain of himself than Liz remembered. Ever. Cocky yes, he'd always been a bit like that, always keen to have the scoop on local gossip or brag about his illustrious career as a paramedic so tragically cut short. But the way he held himself and had a smirk on his lips every time he looked at Terry was disturbing. He knew something.

Terry opened a file and turned it for Darryl to look at.

'Your laptop computer has been the subject of forensic scrutiny which is ongoing. What I'm showing you is a print out of email addresses which I'd like you to identify.'

Darryl didn't even look.

'No?' Terry slid the top page aside. 'We're taking guesses in the office about these. Quite a selection of newspaper reports, all carefully curated for you. Would you explain their meaning?'

With a shrug, Darryl took a cursory look. 'Dunno. These

appear all the time. Figured I must have accidentally subscribed to a news channel.'

'From the past?'

And there was that smirk again.

'Because, some of these go back more than eighteen years, Darryl. What I think is that someone sent these as a kind of message—directions of where you should go or even where these are. Or were. So far we've identified a few.' Terry leaned forward to touch the paper. 'This one, from eighteen years and four days ago, is a story on one of the buildings near the park.'

'If you say so.'

'I do. And this one is about transport. Trams and trains. All which are within easy walk from your apartment and the park.'

'So they are. Very strange.'

Terry got to his feet and walked away. Liz knew he would like nothing more than to grab Darryl and throttle him... except Terry didn't do things like that. He was frustrated and stared at the window as if telling her something.

'Do you want me to call Pete, boss?' She grinned, knowing full well he could neither hear nor see her.

'And what about the emails from Brian Bisley?'

'He's the building manager.'

Terry returned to his seat and slid across another page. 'Numbers and words. What do they mean?'

'Gibberish. Never understood why he sent them.'

'Never thought to ask?'

Darryl feigned surprise. 'Yeah. That's an idea.'

Terry stared at him. Not a word, just a long gaze which did its job. Darryl's stupid expression disappeared and he looked away.

'Detective Senior Sergeant Hall, my client needs to be released.'

'Does he now?'

The lawyer nodded. 'There's no reason to hold him.'

'Tell you what. You suggest to your client that he has a frank and proper conversation with me about the shoe he placed onto the road and I will consider the charges to bring. There's already grounds for a whole range of them. Perverting the cause of justice. Interfering with a criminal investigation. Potentially, abduction of a minor. And so on. I'm going to make a coffee so you and your client take a few minutes to discuss the right way to do this.'

He'd almost reached the door when Darryl spoke.

'Yeah, okay. I'll tell you.'

'Mr Tompsett I must caution you against—'

'Nope. No more cautioning me. If anything, you can f off.' Darryl glared at his lawyer.

Well, well. What are you up to now, Darryl?

The lawyer pleaded with Darryl to reconsider but after a few sharp words had his briefcase packed and was stalking out of the room.

Terry wandered back to the table and dropped into the seat without a word.

SEVENTEEN

'This changes things.' Terry was at the whiteboard with the map of the park, surrounded by a group of detectives.

Liz perched on a desk at the back. She itched to be on the road. Out looking. Talking to potential witnesses. Talking to Bisley. Anything other than sit and wait but Terry had to go to the park soon and it was pointless her going too far in case he wasn't back to meet with the psychologist, Doctor Carroll.

'Our mate Darryl has admitted to putting Eliza's shoe onto the road. He's admitted to having the shoe in his possession. But he denies any part of her abduction.'

'Then how did he get her shoe?' A detective asked and others murmured in agreement.

'He claims he received an email instructing him to be at a certain place at a certain time. Here—' Terry used a red marker to make an 'X' on the whiteboard. 'He was told to collect the item of clothing he found. The shoe was underneath a bush, pushed back out of easy view. He picked it up, shoved it into the pocket at the front of the hoodie and completed the job.'

The 'X' was along the side of the park closest to the play area.

'Did you say 'item of clothing', boss? Not shoe.' Another detective.

'Those were his words and I asked him twice to clarify. He had no idea what to expect until he arrived. Crime Scene Services are taking another look in that general area and we will double down on finding any imagery—whether from a security camera or dashcam or passing taxi—covering that part of the footpath and park.'

Terry checked his watch and frowned. 'Meg is working on the email side of this information because Darryl had deleted it and cleared his cache.'

'So much for saying he knows nothing about computers,' Liz said. Everyone turned to look at her as if they'd forgotten she was there. 'He's always whined about not understanding technology since he was injured at work. Told me it was from the trauma but clearly he knows enough to remove an incriminating communication.'

'He says it was an anonymous sender.' Terry rolled his eyes. 'I asked why he would follow the instructions of someone he didn't know and he said… wait for it. He felt frightened.'

The laughter that erupted was far from amused. Everyone was at the stage of questioning each and any snippet of information and wanting a resolution. Patience was thin.

'What are we doing next?' Somebody asked.

'The same as before. Field calls. Scour footage. Identify people who need to be interviewed or re-interviewed. I'm heading out now but Andy will touch base with each of you if he has a specific need and Liz is your go-to person otherwise. Okay?'

Liz got to her feet as the detectives dispersed. Terry met her halfway.

'I'm sorry to leave you to manage things. Didn't expect to be dragged back to the park for a media show.'

'Will you take a look where the shoe was?'

'First thing I'll do.'

'I don't understand though, Terry. Darryl got an email telling him where and when to pick up an item of clothing. Assuming that's true, the perp didn't know what item of clothing he'd leave so it was sent before he took Eliza. But he had planned a way to misdirect us and chose a loser like Darryl to do the task.' Liz shook her head. 'There is more to this. We need to find who sent that email.'

'Go and talk to Meg. Darryl isn't going anywhere for now. And if you run into any issues with Doctor Carroll, call me.'

After he'd gone, Liz went in search of Pete. He'd not attended the briefing nor answered her phone call. She asked people on both active floors but got nothing but shrugs.

If you're doing your own version of investigating then bring me into it, dude.

Just once she'd love to be the one to step just outside the line and have a path into the underworld of the city.

Just once.

———

Liz ordered two decent coffees and Danish scrolls from a café up the road. She needed to leave the building before meeting with the doctor. Walk away from the organised chaos created by a full-on investigation. As always there was a wait. The place was popular thanks to the proximity of the huge police station which also housed several floors of administrative staff and around the building were plenty of other local businesses.

Waiting around forced her to take a brief break. Short of checking for any updates on her phone there was nothing to do other than people-watch and think.

A tram trundled past. Passengers stared at their phones or gazed through windows, their expressions blank. That was a big part of the challenge of finding witnesses to Eliza's abduction. And Ellen's. People were bored on public transport. Many turned to a phone or read a book. Others just waited to be at their stop. But there had to be some who watched the scenery and passing people with interest, even if only to pass the time.

Her name was called and she collected the tray and bag.

On the way back her phone beeped but she ignored it until she reached Meg's office. Meg was on the phone so Liz put down the coffees and scrolls and stepped to the end of the long space. The message was from Vince.

Have some thoughts. Better in person. Shall I come to you?

It was better he did, but when? Who knows how long she'd be tied up this afternoon and he had his granddaughter to think about after school hours.

Have a meeting soon. Can I drive out later?

The extra time to his place was a pain but another hour or two wasn't going to make much difference and could change everything if his 'thoughts' led to Eliza.

I'll be here.

She sent back a thumbs up. Seeing him, and maybe Melanie, was suddenly very important. It had been too long.

'Are these for me, Liz?'

Meg grinned broadly and held up a scroll.

'I figured if I needed coffee and sweet carbs then you might.' Liz helped herself to the other tasty morsel. 'I'm sure you're sick of people looking for updates every five minutes.'

'No, but I am a bit tired of dealing with liars and this Darryl is about as dumb as they get while still being irritatingly smart.' Meg took a big bite and tapped on her keyboard with her spare hand, talking through the mouthful. 'Mumuved debeted memails-'

'Cannot understand a word. You're allowed to eat. I'll talk,' Liz said. 'I know you specialise in cyber stuff but I found something odd. In Ellen's file. My niece?'

Meg swallowed, nodded, and took a sip of coffee, eyes never leaving Liz.

'There were hairs recovered from the underside of the bridge at the park after Ellen was taken. DNA testing led to them being labelled as hers but they aren't. Meg, these are adult hairs, thick. Wrong colour. And unless she was on someone's shoulders her head couldn't have reached that spot.'

'Run them again. We have new tech which will give better information.'

'Takes time and Eliza doesn't have it.'

'There's a private company which is getting some incredible results with much smaller samples than normally required and they are fast but Liz, the cost is prohibitive for us.'

'Can I pay?' All the money sitting in her bank account had to be good for something.

'Oh, I wouldn't even offer. That's the quickest way to have evidence discredited if it goes to court. I'll make a call and get a cost and timeframe and you clear it with Terry.'

'If I did it from a civil standpoint?'

Meg sighed. 'Only if you want to leave the force. At least, that's my opinion.'

'Appreciate it.' It was a longshot. Terry wouldn't go for it. Liz finally bit into her scroll.

'Now, as I was saying earlier, we've recovered the deleted emails. It isn't quite as straightforward as handing over the names because the sender is clever. Give me a couple more hours and I might have something to share.'

'But you're confident that you'll find the source?'

With a grin, Meg shoved scroll into her mouth and waved Liz away.

Doctor Candace Carroll was intense, abrupt, and drop-dead gorgeous.

Outside of her usual observation of people, Liz wasn't one to pay particular attention to looks unless it had a direct bearing on a case. People were people. But the fifty-something psychiatrist with her pixie-cut silver hair, piercing green eyes, and Helen Mirren features was arresting.

Am I turning in my old age?

Liz pushed that away. She had no interest in a relationship no matter how desirable the partner. Love sucked. It took everything a person had, crushed it into a million pieces, and threw it back like shards of razor-sharp glass.

'Detective?'

The doctor's low voice pulled Liz back from whatever stupid thoughts had rushed in. They sat opposite each other in a conference room with Liz's report laid out between them.

'Doctor Carroll, as mentioned earlier, Detective Senior Sergeant Hall apologises for not being here. There were some developments in the case requiring his attendance at a press conference. I am able to speak on his behalf to a degree.'

'You are also uniquely placed to present this information.'

'Perhaps. Some people believe I'm too close.'

'Call me Candace.' She leaned back in her seat, one hand resting on the table. Her fingers were lean and long. Elegant, with no rings. Short nails but perfect. 'Being close is unique. You see things nobody else sees. What might be a hunch for another officer is a truth for you. I've read the report. It is well written and offers compelling reasons to profile a person who has taken not one but at least two children. But Liz, what do *you* think?'

This was unexpected and threw Liz. What if the doctor was evaluating her ability to present a rational argument? But when Liz looked at Candace, at her piercing stare which cut to her soul, there was no malice.

'I'm not sure. There are aspects of my niece's case which aren't sitting right now that I've re-examined them and I have a… feeling, intuition, call it what you will, that whoever took these kids…'

She couldn't say it.

Candice leaned forward.

'I'm seeing things which aren't real. Making connections with no evidence which is provable… at least not unless there's a way to revisit a DNA sample and quickly.'

'Anything is possible if there are compelling reasons. What connections are you seeing?'

At the worst, Candace would tell Terry that his senior officer had lost the plot and she'd be removed from the case. It would make Andy happy. But what if there was even the smallest thread of truth in what had played in the back of her mind for hours?

'I'm here because I want to help, Liz. Not to judge you although if I did…'

Liz narrowed her eyes.

'You are quite sane. You work too hard and battle your demons with grace and courage. Ben Rossi thinks the world of you and I'm not about to speak out of turn to anyone, no matter what you trust me with.'

I trusted myself to look after my niece. My sister trusted me to keep her safe.

'What if this is about me?' The words burst from Liz. 'There is nothing coincidental about two girls being taken from the same park under almost identical circumstances. Both girls are close in age and looks. Both were playing in the same area and their adults were distracted. And both little girls have a strong connection to the same building.'

'Which might mean something or nothing at all,' Candace said. 'But all that tells us is that whoever targeted them had knowledge of the building or the park. Perhaps they live in view of either and have a particular type when it comes to children.'

A shiver ran down Liz's spine.

'There's more to it. Two girls whose names begin with E. Two girls living—or in Ellen's case—staying with a woman on her own. There's more. I am certain if I drill down further then I'll find more similarities.'

Candace nodded. 'I agree with you. But what compels you to

believe that these crimes are about you, other than Ellen being one of the stolen children?'

'The hairs.' Liz reached over and turned the pages in the file to the photograph of the sample. 'I was never privy to this until now but the hairs in the image were collected from the underside of the play bridge. These are *not* Ellen's and it was sloppy work by whoever dealt with this at the time. DNA connects her to me and they've accepted that the hair must then belong to Ellen.'

'You have never been beneath the bridge?'

'Not until last night when I went searching.'

'Then it makes sense you would question any connections. Does that thought process lead you to a suspect?'

Liz felt her shoulders drop. This was her dead-end.

'There's too much going on in my head. At the moment I have a dozen things needing my attention.'

Candace regarded Liz for a moment. It was unsettling.

'One of the detectives, someone I'm comfortable with, is going to interview me. Go over Ellen's disappearance again and see if he can extract anything new.'

'Be cautious. Comfortable is one thing but expertise is another.'

Liz smiled for a second. 'Pete has expertise. I trust him.'

There was a moment, an unspoken exchange which was gone just as fast but Liz was convinced Candace had wanted to offer *her* expertise in place of Pete's. Or possibly, alongside him.

'In that case I shall spend some time going back over your brief and arrange a time to meet with Terry.' Candace took out a business card and wrote on the back of it. 'If you need to talk, anytime, call me on this number. It's private.'

Although she had no intention of using the number, Liz accepted the card and stood. 'Please use the room for as long as you wish. I'll speak with Terry once he's finished the press conference. And thank you.'

'For what, Liz?' Candace tilted her head.

'For believing me.'

Another long stare and then Candace turned the file to the beginning. Her attention moved to the brief and Liz let herself out.

EIGHTEEN

Andy longed to find a sofa and close his eyes. Just for half an hour.

Except it will turn into half a day if nobody disturbs me.

He opened the top drawer in his desk and selected a chocolate bar from half a dozen assorted varieties. Tearing it open, he held it to his nose and savoured the aroma before biting into it. These were not average chocolates. He had a friend who part owned one of the country's best boutique chocolatiers and there was an endless supply sent to his home. He didn't do much in return. Just the odd favour when his friend occasionally messed up.

Outside of his office was a hive of activity. Busy bees, each and every one of the officers and support staff. And they needed to work at capacity because somewhere, a terrified little girl needed them. All it would take was one decent clue. A discovery which would lead to whichever creep had her.

When his landline rang he almost jumped out of his skin.

'Montebello.'

The line was silent.

'Speak or hang up.'

A moment. Breathing.

Who had put this call through?

'You're in charge?'

The voice was male. Older. Educated – private school.

'One of several. How may I help?'

'I want the person in charge.'

Rolling his eyes, Andy grabbed a pen and wrote on a notepad. *Nut job.*

'You want her back? Eliza? You talk to me.'

Straightening, Andy threw his pen at the window. When nobody responded he picked up a cup—long since empty from a coffee drunk cold hours ago—and tossed it after the pen. It smashed. Several heads lifted. Andy beckoned like crazy.

'I'm talking to you.'

The door opened. Andy pointed to the phone and mouthed 'trace it'.

It was probably impossible because most likely it came through the main switchboard but that officer was gone and others gathered in his place.

Andy grabbed his mobile and began to record, holding the phones close together. 'I'm listening.'

'But you are not taking me seriously.'

'I am. My name is Andy. What shall I call you?'

'Irrelevant. There's something you need to do for me if you want the child back.'

'Did *you* take the child?'

'Irrelevant. You have one chance so listen carefully, Andy. There's a place I'm going to describe, an address. Before it is light tomorrow morning I want to meet with one of your officers. With the woman.'

'Which woman?'

Andy's stomach churned. It could only be one.

'The detective who left her child alone in the park.'

'Why do you want to meet with her?'

There was a silence. Andy concentrated on the background sounds but could only hear the breathing of the caller.

'Is Eliza alive?'

'There'd be no point me speaking with you if she wasn't. She misses her mother.'

Andy's eyes closed for a moment. It sounded genuine.

'Tell Elizabeth Moorland to be at the location half an hour before dawn. I know you're recording this so I'll only say the address once.'

He rattled it off and Andy rapidly wrote.

'Eliza's mum is desperate. Please drop her somewhere safe. Don't make her wait.'

The man had gone.

Liz wasn't in the building and for that, Andy was grateful. She could stay out of the loop until he'd spoken with Terry and probably some of the higher-ups. But Candace Carroll was still here and she was listening to the recording in another room.

'I want McNamara so track him down please.' He got off the phone for what felt like the fiftieth time since the man had called.

The *perp* had called.

Andy couldn't spend the time yet to drill down into the conversation. He'd sent the recording to Meg along with his own recollections of anything from the brief encounter. That had been the first thing he'd done, even before he'd answered the dozen questions from the officers who poured in as soon as he indicated the call was over.

Somebody cleaned up the mess he'd made. There'd been shards of mug all over the carpet and now there was a crack in the window.

He barked a few orders. People from his team who he needed here right now. Even if they were having a break or not on duty.

Terry was on his way back and for once, all Andy wanted was to see the head of Homicide. They'd always got on okay but having to share responsibility for this case had got Andy's back up and it was only from working closely with Terry that he'd taken note of how much he still had to learn.

This was a breakthrough. Or a complete waste of time.

Meg tapped on his door. 'Boss, no way to trace the phone call. I have some notes on the emails Darryl Tompsett had received, the ones with newspaper clippings and the like? It isn't great.'

'Meaning?'

'The sender did a good job hiding their identity and uses one of the most notorious service providers who don't log anything. Quite illegal but not Aussie based so we can't do a thing but having said all that, I'd love a warrant to try if we could? I've just emailed you the notes if you can request one, please.'

'I'll get that done. How long, once you have it?'

'A bit. Also, I'm running the phone call through a voice recognition program. Low chance of a match but worth trying. Where's Liz?'

'I think she was driving out to meet with Vince Carter. Do you need her?'

Meg shook her head. 'I'm running a program cross-referencing aspects of Liz's brief. The similarities. And we got a lead on some footage from a car cam. Dude doesn't know how to download it so I've sent someone to grab it.'

'What kind of footage?'

'He was near the park at the right time and had a vague recollection of seeing an older man with a little kid. She was holding the man's hand and chatting as they crossed a street. He thought it was cute being a grandfather and grandkid.'

Andy was on his feet in a second. 'What street? How long until we can view it?'

'Chill. I've sent that info as well. Check your emails every so often, huh?' With a grin, Meg was gone.

'Check my emails. What do you think I do every two minutes?' He mumbled to himself, sinking back in the chair and refreshing the inbox.

. . .

'You want to see me?' Pete didn't knock but stalked in, closing the door behind himself, and slumping into a chair. 'Anything new?'

'You look like shit.'

'And proud of it.'

Pete must have been awake all night from the look of him. Clothes were crumpled. Hair was messier than normal. But his eyes were sharp and expectant.

'I had a phone call from a man implying he has Eliza.'

'You could have led with that.'

'Yeah, well the reason I called you in is about Brian Bisley. A warrant is being executed about now to seize his devices and search both his office and apartment. Meg is narrowing down the source of the anonymous emails sent to Darryl and in the interim we want some answers about Bisley's relationship to him.'

'So is he here?' Pete asked. 'You want me to do the interview?'

'Not with him. The one with Liz as soon as she's back. And what I'm telling you is in confidence, Pete. The caller wants Liz to meet with him tomorrow morning.'

'To do what?'

'I'll give you access to the recording of the call but he basically demanded to see her, alone of course, if we want Eliza back.'

'Then she's alive.'

'He said as much.'

Pete ran both hands through his hair and swore under his breath.

'I'd like you to see if Liz remembers anything else about Ellen's disappearance before I decide what happens tomorrow.'

'Liz shouldn't go,' Pete said.

'I agree.' Terry had opened the door and closed it in his wake with a firm click, his expression grim. 'We have nothing to convince us this isn't a past perp she's dealt with using the abduction to get access to her. Until we have better intel I don't want her knowing about the phone call.' He pulled up another chair. 'The re-creation of the events went well using actors. Media are distributing the finished product to all the usual channels and I did a live broadcast. On the way here I've heard there are a couple of promising leads.'

'Meg is following up one from someone with possible footage of a man and little girl near the park.' Andy tapped on his keyboard. 'I've just sent you the information she has so far. The best thing for everyone is finding Eliza today.'

Pete got to his feet. 'Liz will be a while. What if I have a quiet chat with Bisley?'

'Read the transcript of the last interview first. He's not under arrest yet and I would prefer he doesn't get a lawyer,' Andy said.

'I'll be nice.'

'Pete, push him a bit about the emails. There's already people looking at his computers and time isn't his friend,' Terry said.

With a grin, Pete got to his feet. 'Nor am I, boss.'

Andy took his first food of the day—apart from the chocolate bar hours ago—to where he could watch the Bisley interview. The way he was eating was appalling. Not regularly and carb-loaded. Neither suited him. At least the kebab was hot.

There'd been a standoff in Bisley's office until he was threatened with arrest for obstruction. Apparently he'd sworn and stubbed out his cigarette and left without another word. If McNamara could make him talk without a lawyer being called it would be a miracle.

I should have done this.

Leaving this to a man who had a dubious reputation was poor judgement. Terry's poor judgement. He had been a good cop. Now, he should retire.

'It takes a lot of smarts to handle such a big job, Bing. What got you into management?'

Pete sat with an ankle over a knee, relaxed, sipping on a coffee. He'd been in there for half an hour and had brought a coffee for the man opposite. And a few doughnuts.

'This building isn't my first. Nah, I started off small, doing the accounts at a place over in Geelong. Manager got caught with his hand in the pot and as reward for uncovering his theft, the job became mine. Stayed there for almost ten years and then a change of ownership and they turned the place into serviced apartments. Was going to take a year refurbishing and I wasn't getting paid to sit around.'

'Big change from Geelong lifestyle to crap-urbia.'

Bisley rolled his eyes. 'Don't I know. Gotta say though, my apartment is a step above anywhere I've lived before.'

Andy almost spat out a piece of tomato. What kind of standards did this man have?

'Nice, is it?'

'Best in the building. Top floor. Corner with a wraparound balcony. View of the park.'

He turned bright red and clamped his lips shut.

Come on, McNamara. That was dropped in your lap.

'My place is the opposite. No balcony. No nice views.'

What the heck? Is this compare the homes or something?

'Sucks, man.'

'Yup. Mind you, I'm rarely there to complain. Did you know I've spent most of my career undercover?' Pete dropped his ankle off his knee and leaned forward to put both elbows on the table. 'Best job ever. I get to be someone else. Dress up. Cosy up to criminals. Even smack a few heads together and you know what? I love it. I love the freedom of being *untouchable*.'

Andy finished his kebab. This might be why Liz had so much time for McNamara.

Bisley slid a finger between collar of his shirt and his neck.

'I'm not undercover now so interrogations aren't nearly as

much fun. But here's the thing. *Bing.*' He leaned as far across the table as he could without standing. Bisley didn't move. Bit like a deer in the headlights. 'I have contacts. Lots of them. And today I've been hanging around with some of those who are nastiest types you'd hope not to meet. See, I'm going to find Eliza Singleton—alive and well— and anyone who gets in my way isn't going to have a happy life.'

Looking like he was about to have a heart attack, Bisley recoiled.

'So, Bing. Let's chat about the view to the park. And the emails you've been sending Darryl Tompsett for about eighteen years.'

NINETEEN

The drive to Vince's place gave Liz time to think. Too much time in some respects with her mind replaying the moment she'd realised Ellen was missing. It would never leave her. The jolt of shock. Disbelief. Panic.

Days and nights of searching. Answering questions. Asking them.

And then the anger. Blaming herself. Anna blaming her. Strangers blaming her.

Stop it, Liz.

She'd thought the toxic cycle of rehashing this was buried but then Eliza happened.

What she needed to do now was sift through Vince's memories of that time and knowing him, he'd been doing exactly that himself.

As she turned onto the road to his house, she glanced at a car in her rear-vision mirror. It had been behind her on the freeway but she didn't remember when she'd first noticed it and white Toyota sedans were common. Slowing on the other side of a bend gave her the chance to get the rego number as the car caught up. She called the number in.

The car dropped right back and turned into a driveway.

Liz cancelled the request. She was jumping at shadows.

Vince lived miles from nowhere—or so it felt—beyond Bacchus Marsh where properties in varying acreages backed onto a long ridge. Last year his old cottage had been burned to the ground. Despite the horrendous experience, Vince had rebuilt and lived there again with the only family he had left, his grandchild, Melanie.

The driveway was still rough and basic but the new house was cute as anything, a weatherboard cottage with a grey roof and verandahs all the way around. She pulled up outside and had barely climbed out when a whirlwind of a child flew at her.

'Liz! Liz! You're really here.'

Liz cuddled Melanie. 'I really am. Let me get a look at you.' She released her and straightened with a grin. 'Have you grown six inches taller?'

'I grow in centimetres. Grandad is digging up a garden for vegetables. Come and see.'

Melanie sprinted around the side of the cottage and Liz followed, more sedately.

Vince was shovelling manure from a wheelbarrow to a raised garden bed while a woman around his age raked it in.

'Grandad, Lyndall! Look.'

Both raised their heads as Melanie came to a stop near the wheelbarrow, wrinkling her nose. 'Ew.'

'Ew indeed, young lady. That's the finest mix from my donkeys and your pony and it will make anything grow.' Lyndall put down her rake and tossed gardening gloves onto the grass. 'Liz. So good to see you, darlin'.'

Lyndall owned the property next door where she slaved over her rescued donkeys and maintained a stunning home and garden. She'd taken Vince and Melanie in after the fire and more than that, she'd been every bit as responsible for saving Vince's life as Pete had. Their bullets hit the killer at the same time. She was a crack shot. And oddly, she had a panic room in her house.

One day I want to hear your story.

Liz returned the firm hug from Lyndall and when she stepped back, Vince hugged her even more tightly. She held on, fighting back tears which came from nowhere, needing to draw on his strength for a while.

'It'll be okay, Lizzie,' he muttered.

'Now, Melanie and I are taking the wheelbarrow back to my paddock to collect more of the donkey dung,' Lyndall said.

'But I want to talk to Liz,' Melanie said with a pout. 'I've missed her.'

'I've missed you as well, Mel. But if you don't mind too much, I'd like to borrow your grandfather for a few minutes. Boring adult stuff.'

'Hm. But don't go home without saying goodbye.'

'Promise I won't.'

Melanie tried to lift the wheelbarrow on her own and with a smile, Lyndall took over. 'You open the gate, little miss.'

'Donkey dung. Donkey dung.' Skipping ahead, Melanie sang the words.

Vince poured two tall glasses of water. 'Are you staying for dinner? I can start it a bit early.'

'I wish. Soon though?' Liz accepted the glass and followed Vince back outside.

They sat on the back verandah overlooking the pony paddock, which currently was empty. The old pony who normally occupied it often spent time with the donkeys for company. Melanie and Lyndall were just visible in a paddock partway up the hill to her big house.

'It's nice to see the three of you together.'

'We're not together, together. Lyndall and me. Both a bit set in our ways for that but she matters to us both. Melanie loves her.'

So do you.

'Vince, you said you've had some thoughts when you messaged me. If there's anything at all it might help.'

'Have you read your own diary notes?'

'I have. And yours.'

'Anything jump out at you?'

Liz shook her head. 'Nothing which wasn't already on my radar. I thought I'd locked it away but a lot of it is as clear as the day Ellen disappeared.'

'Clear memories or feelings?' He sipped some water and put the glass onto a table. 'The feelings won't find Eliza but your instincts might. And somehow you need to separate them.'

He was right. The sharp memories were tainted with terrible dread.

'Yeah. Both. Which is why I'm here. I need to hear your version of what happened that day. Those days,' she said.

'As best as I can.' Vince nodded. 'You phoned me a few minutes after midday. I was working. You said 'Ellen's been taken'. I found out where you were and called my superior officer and was there less than half an hour later. There were two cops in the park both looking for Ellen. You were frantic. Searching and calling. I made you stop and take a minute in the shade while I called for more officers.'

Liz tried to drink some of the water but her throat was tight.

'You told me Ellen had been playing around the bridge and you'd been on a phone call and taken your eyes off her. When you got off the call you went to tell her it was time for an ice cream but she wasn't there. You searched the park and reported her missing and then rang me. More police came but not enough. I sent you to look at the apartment.'

'She wasn't there.'

'I know, Lizzie.' Vince sighed. 'It took three hours to get a detective on the scene. Three hours. I was pulled off the search and for that I never forgave them. The early theory was that Ellen had been collected by a relative or friend and too much time was wasted on that than anything else. But that's speculation on my part. Not facts.'

'There was some confusion from my sister. Ellen was going

home that evening and I'd planned to drop her. But Anna had some idea that it was Sav, her husband, who was picking her up. Sav thought Anna was. The police phoned both and each had different stories. It did waste time but it was a mistake.'

So much yelling and finger pointing had followed.

'Either way, this happened mid-morning, not early evening when Ellen was expected home.'

From up the hill came shrieks of laughter. One of the donkeys was chasing Melanie around the wheelbarrow.

'And that is the girl who was terrified of the old pony when she first moved here,' Vince said, his voice soft.

'She's lucky to have you.'

'Goes both ways, Liz.'

Vince had been through so much and survived it. Not gracefully by any means. But if he could overcome all the loss in his life then Liz certainly could hold it together while searching for a stolen child. She gave herself a mental shake.

'Anything else relevant? Any observation about Ellen's case which isn't in the diary?'

'A couple of things bothered me at the time but were too vague to do follow up. One was the lack of investigation into Ellen's family. I recall her parents being in for interviews. Do you know who else?'

'There was nobody else in the state at the time. Sav's side of the family all live in Queensland. Anna and I have nobody at all now. Mum died twenty plus years ago.'

'And your father?'

Liz's stomach churned.

'I haven't seen him since I was a child. Nor has Anna.'

'Is he alive?'

She shrugged. 'No idea. My parent's divorce was traumatic. He was violent. We were good without him.'

Vince stared at her, his eyes giving nothing away.

'Grandad! Liz! I played with one of the donkeys.'

Melanie was skipping in their direction.

'Thanks, Vince. Talking to you helps.'

'I didn't tell you the other thing that bothered me. That building manager. Only met him a couple of times but I reckon there's more to him.'

'He's being questioned again right now and I agree.'

Melanie reached the verandah and launched herself at Liz, ending up sitting on her lap. 'Do I smell of donkey dung?'

'You do. And donkeys.'

With a giggle, Melanie slid her arms around Liz's neck and cuddled her. 'And you do as well now.'

Liz stopped at home long enough to freshen up after deciding it best she didn't go back to work reeking of farm smells. Darryl's apartment now had police tape across the door. Brian's office had forensic work continuing inside and she didn't go in.

Nothing like last time.

Vince had been every bit as frustrated back then at the poor handling of Ellen's disappearance. It was true that the majority of missing children turned up quickly. How many parents had lost sight of their kid in a shopping centre? Daily. Everywhere, it was a regular occurrence. But Ellen hadn't been taken from a building. She'd wandered off from a park and would be found nearby—that was what officers told Liz on the day. The real search hadn't begun for almost two days and there'd been a half-heartedness about it by then because it was assumed it was a search for a body.

Back in the car she returned a missed call from Pete.

'What's your ETA?'

'Twenty tops. Why?' she asked.

'Had a fun chat with our mate Bisley.'

'You did what? Who let *you* loose with him?' Liz chuckled. 'And more to the point, is the man still standing?'

'Ha. Ha. Andy did. Do you know anything about his history? Bisley's. Before the gig at your apartment building.'

Liz waved someone through an intersection.

'We've never been friends, Pete. He was there before I moved in. Oh, he did once go on about how much nicer the tenants in his last building were. I was probably complaining about the lifts again.'

'Turns out he began life as an accountant. Got fired twice under shady circumstances which we are following up. Landed a job in a Geelong apartment building doing bookkeeping and ended up manager.'

'Geelong?'

'What about it?' Pete asked.

'Dunno. Something. Nothing. Go on.'

It isn't nothing. But why does it matter?

'He got the current job thanks to a recommendation by the old owner of the Geelong place. Reckons he doesn't remember his name but they had an arrangement and here's what matters. Old boss had some gig going which Bisley is still part of. Haven't got my head round it yet but there are chains of emails bouncing around and he both receives and sends them. Says it is some gambling business the other dude runs. Nothing more. He admits Darryl is a recipient but denies any knowledge of abduction.'

Liz's heart sank. If that was all it was the emails on Darryl's computer from Bisley might be nothing to do with stealing children.

'What about the emails Darryl gets with the newspaper clippings.'

'Meg's almost got an address.'

That was good. Something had to be good today.

'Lizzie? Let's get that interview done. I'll bring coffee and probably something stronger to add.'

Pete rang off leaving Liz with a racing heart.

She wanted this interview. No, that was a lie. She *needed* it. Between Vince and Pete's latest information there was stuff just out of her reach and if Eliza was to be found today, this might be the way.

TWENTY

'The camera is off. The sound is off. Nobody can see in.'

This was surreal. Liz had interviewed hundreds of witnesses. Interrogated as many perps. Many in this room.

But I've never been on this side of the table.

It didn't matter that this wasn't a real interview.

It didn't matter that the purpose was simply to extract any long-forgotten memories.

It was terrifying.

'I feel guilty.'

Pete laughed at her.

'No, really. Do you think this is what everyone feels no matter whether they've killed someone or simply run a red light?'

She didn't know what to do with her hands. On the table. Off the table. In the end she leaned back in her seat, crossed her legs, and folded her arms.

'Now you do look guilty. Relax, Liz.'

'Easy for you to say. Have you ever been on this side?'

Something crossed his face. A shadow of… anger? Contempt?

'Try your coffee.'

Pete finally sat and he put both hands around his cup.

'Truth serum?' Liz asked.

'Have you been watching too much American television? But sure. Truth serum.'

She took a tentative sip. There was brandy in the java. Well, why the hell not? She took a longer sip. Truth serum indeed.

'Is there somewhere you'd like to start, Detective?' Pete asked, his eyes on his coffee.

So this is it.

'My five-year-old niece was abducted and nobody took it seriously for two days. Two. Full. Days.'

'You were watching her. Weren't you?'

'Not closely enough as history has proved. Parks are meant to be safe places for kids. For families.'

'Is anywhere safe when you're a little kid on your own? What were you doing while she was being taken?'

Liz gasped.

'Put the emotions aside, Liz. What took your attention away from her?'

'A phone call. But I was still sitting on the bench in view of the play area.'

'Talk me through it. Everything from the moment you got to the park.'

Ellen's hair needed braiding again on one side after she'd accidentally pulled off the elastic band. Liz sat on the bench to plait while Ellen stood, chatting about what flavour ice cream she'd like later. This was the third day in a row they'd been to the park.

'Do you think Mummy and Daddy are home yet?'

'Their plane landed a bit earlier this morning and your mum was going to go home to unpack and do some grocery shopping. I think your daddy was going to work for a while. Are you excited to be going home tonight?'

'I miss them lots. And I know they'll have a present for me because they always do.'

'A new doll?'

'I'd like a bracelet.'

The braid was done and Liz dropped a kiss on Ellen's cheek. 'Well I hope you get a bracelet and I'm going to miss you hanging out with me.'

Ellen threw her arms around Liz's neck. 'Not goodbye. Just 'til next time.'

Liz laughed. She always said that to Ellen and it was cute hearing it back. She loved having her niece visit when Anna and Sav took one of their long weekends, usually to visit his family in Queensland. 'Here's your bag.' She held out the pink, shiny kids handbag and Ellen checked inside before slinging the long handle over her shoulder.

'Hanky. Purse with fifty cents. And yours and Mummy's name and phone number for mergies.' She screwed up her face at the word.

'Emergencies. Go on, I'm going to sit here in the sun for a while.'

Ellen skipped across the grass and went straight under the bridge. Liz could see her and hear her singing to herself. After a bit she played on the top of the bridge and was in and out of the fort-like structures.

Liz dug around in her bag for the bottle of coke she'd hidden. Ellen wasn't allowed soft drinks and Liz rarely drank them, but now and then it was a guilty pleasure. When she opened it, bubbles erupted, covering her hands with sticky sweetness. She had nothing to clean her hands with and for a moment stood by the bench with coke dripping from her fingers, already attracting the attention of a fly. The fountain was only a few steps away and she quickly sploshed some water over her skin.

'Auntie Liz?'

'I'm here.'

Ellen had returned to the bench and was eyeing what was left of the bottle of coke. 'I'm thirsty.'

'There's some water in the bag, honey. My hands are a bit wet so can you get the bottle out?'

'Can I have some of that?'

'Not a chance. It doesn't taste nice.'

The look Ellen gave her was comical. She didn't believe a word. But she helped herself to the water and took a few long sips before returning the bottle.

'My shoelace came undone.'

'I can... oh, did you tie it?'

Ellen had put the offending foot forward and the laces were tied differently from how Liz did them. Re-laced completely.

'Nice man did.'

'What nice man?' Liz gazed around. The park looked empty. 'Can you show me?'

Ellen took her hand and they walked around for a while. On the bridge, around the swings, along the perimeter. 'He was sad.'

'How so?'

'His little girl died.'

'Oh, that's awful. And he was kind to tie your shoelace but Ellen, you have me here to do things for you. I don't want you talking to any strangers.' Liz squatted in front of the little girl, who was frowning. 'Promise me you won't.'

'Promise. Can I go back under the bridge now?'

'Sure.'

Ellen ran off in the direction of the bridge.

'I'm going to grab our stuff and come and sit closer, okay?' Liz called.

The little girl turned and waved. ''til next time, Auntie.'

Liz was almost at the bench when her phone rang.

'Who was on the phone, Liz?'

'Brian Bisley. How did I forget? He was going on about one of the residents stealing his office supplies or something and wanted me to investigate. He went on and on and I had sat on the bench to put the lid back on the coke while he was ranting.' Liz touched her face. There were tears pouring down her cheeks.

Pete pushed a box of tissues her way. 'And then you went to find Ellen. Could you see her at all from the bench?'

'Yes. But when I hung up I had my back turned for a few seconds while I picked everything up. And that's all it took, Pete. A few precious seconds.'

'til next time, Auntie.

Liz gulped, forcing down a lump in her chest.

'We'd done the same thing for three days in a row, Pete. Mid-morning we'd leave the apartment and walk to the park. Same way each time. Ellen would play on her own then I'd push her on the swing and she'd often want to splash in the bottom of the fountain. After a half hour or so we'd visit the ice-cream shop on the next road across. Someone was watching us.'

'Did Vince have anything to add?'

Her hands were shaking and she shoved them under the table, then remembered the coffee and finished it in a few mouthfuls. There wasn't much brandy in there but it was taking a sliver of the edge off the pain.

'Vince said he was worried about Brian. He barely met him but you know how good his judgement is when it comes to spotting criminals.'

'I don't. He thinks I'm crooked.'

That made Liz smile for a second. 'And you're not?'

'Not even close. What about Bisley is his issue?'

'Gut feeling that there's something illegal going on in the background.'

'Anything else?'

'About Ellen's family. He doesn't understand why there wasn't more probing into a relative being behind her abduction. Sav's family all live in Queensland. They did then and they do now. I'm Anna's only relative.' She dropped her head for a moment, then met his eyes again. 'Apart from our father. But he's been out of our lives since I was a little kid.'

'Where do I find him?'

'He disappeared, Pete. Not like Ellen. But from our lives and it was for the best because Kyle Moorland wasn't a good father. Or a good husband to my mother.'

And I don't want to go down that path. It leads nowhere.

'You know I'm going to go looking for him, Liz. What do I need to know?'

Pete's gaze was unwavering.

Pity any perps wanting to hide stuff from him.

'I haven't thought about him in years. Decades. The thing is that I was too young to remember what went on apart from seeing my mother hit a few times. There was yelling and doors slamming and then one day he was gone.'

'Sorry, Liz. What about your sister? She's older, right?'

Pushing back her seat, Liz stood. 'By ten years. And I have to talk to her sometime before she realises how similar the two cases are. But she hates me, Pete. My own sister. Anna blamed me and I lost her as well. So whoever took Ellen, and took Eliza, also took my family away. Are we done?'

Pete nodded and Liz rushed past.

She made it as far as a cubicle in the ladies room before the choking sobs overwhelmed her.

Face washed, minimal makeup reapplied, Liz swallowed a full bottle of water before seeking out Terry. The brandy might have relaxed her enough for Pete to get past her defences but it was unprofessional and messed with her self-control.

Terry was in his office with Candace, Andy, and Pete.

They stopped talking when she stepped into the room.

'I feel like I'm here for an interview to join some prestigious board,' she said, only half joking. 'Did I miss a memo?'

'Take a seat, Liz. Pete just ran us through a couple of things which came out of your chat.'

That I'm over emotional and need to step down?

Andy had an open file on his lap. 'Meg is continuing to work on the emails with images from Tompsett's computer but it isn't looking good. The email provider is notorious for illegally not keeping logs. Anyway, this line of enquiry may be pointless.'

'Pointless?' Pete muttered more than asked.

'Tompsett has shut up again and has a new lawyer. For someone with no money he's found a hotshot who knows her stuff. We have another couple of hours to charge or release. Him picking up a shoe and dropping it again isn't enough to make charges stick. And we are no further along understanding the cryptic nature of the emails.'

Terry stirred. 'We know there's a connection between Bisley and Tompsett and Eliza but *what* connection is where we're stuck.'

'Boss, it was Brian who stopped me returning to Ellen that day. His phone call which distracted me.'

'Do you think it was deliberate?' Andy raised his eyebrows. 'How would he know to call at that precise moment?'

'How did Darryl know to pick up the shoe? Didn't he say it was one of those emails? How do you know Brian didn't get an email back then? Or a phone call because if they are working together, he might well be higher up the chain than Darryl.' Liz forced her tone to stay neutral. It was Andy's job to question everything.

Mine as well. I just didn't know the right questions back then.

'Ellen and I followed the same pattern for three days. Eliza and Maureen follow the same pattern several times a week. That falls nicely into the hands of a perp who needs to plan. And although I've never been in his apartment, I think it is high enough to see the park. Pair of binoculars and he could be a lookout without leaving home.'

Although she felt sick to her soul, Liz had to lay it all out.

'After I couldn't find the man who tied Ellen's shoelaces I wasn't going to leave her alone in that area and she wasn't ready to go home. Pete helped me remember something. We were close to the playground and Ellen ran back to go under the bridge. I called to her.'

Liz stopped, licking dry lips. Her eyes found Candace's and the other woman nodded ever so slightly in silent encouragement.

'I called out that I was getting our stuff from the bench and would be right back.' Her fingers curled into her palms on her lap and she slowly inhaled.

'And then you got the phone call?' Andy seemed unaware of her struggle to talk about this. 'You were on the phone for how long, Liz?'

'It was eighteen years ago. Maybe four or five minutes.'

'If the person intending to take Eliza overheard you say you'd be right back, they knew they had limited time to do it. Bisley was a distraction. It fits, doesn't it.' Andy looked from one person to another. 'Eliza already knew the man from him tying her shoelaces and talking about his daughter dying. Not hard to get her to go with him.'

'I had just reminded her not to talk to strangers.' The break in her voice was obvious. 'She wouldn't have forgotten already.'

For the first time Candace spoke, softly. 'He wasn't a stranger anymore. Not in the eyes of a five year old.'

Nobody spoke. If anyone wanted to, they reconsidered it. But all three watched Liz. And she wasn't giving away a thing.

She lifted her chin. 'What now.'

TWENTY-ONE

'Gather around. Everyone, thanks.'

Terry had pushed a whiteboard to near the windows where there was more space for bodies to stand or sit. Candace Carroll was writing on it as detectives and other officers moved closer. Andy said something to Terry, who shook his head and then both looked straight at Liz.

She was sitting on the corner of a table and gazed back at them.

'There's things they're not telling you.' Pete perched beside her. 'You're doing great, Liz but watch your back. Don't give them reasons to exclude you further.'

Andy took a phone call, swore, and conferred with Terry. And then he was walking their way.

'Exclude me from what, Pete?'

'Information.'

'Liz, once the briefing is done will you come and find me please.' Andy didn't even stop as he strode past.

'Sure thing.'

Even if just to find out what was being withheld.

'I might need to go home soon. Sleep,' Pete said.

'What are you, a toddler?' Liz tried to make it sound funny but it fell flat. 'Sorry, I don't have much humour in me.'

'You don't have any. Nothing will happen this side of midnight. I reckon not. Better if I'm alert early tomorrow.'

He gave Liz the oddest look and she was about to ask him what the hell he was going on about when Candace spoke.

'Thank you for your time. I'm Doctor Candace Carroll. My background is psychology, criminology, and forensics. I'm in private practice and for the purpose of this brief I'm acting as what some might call a profiler. Over the past few hours I've compiled an early outline of the person responsible for the abduction of Eliza Singleton yesterday morning.'

Using a marker, she pointed to the whiteboard.

'The information I'm drawing upon comes from many sources and as we speak, more data is being analysed and considered by other members of the greater team. We are in a unique position and I am here for that reason. Although many years apart, there are striking similarities between Eliza's disappearance and that of Ellen Georgiou.'

Several heads shot around to look at Liz. She didn't move or respond, keeping her eyes on Candace.

'As such, I've made some educated conclusions about the person who is responsible.'

She tapped the whiteboard.

'Almost without doubt this is a male aged sixty to seventy years. He is well educated. He has avoided trouble with the law. This does not mean he has not offended, only that he hasn't been caught. He is patient. He plans. He uses a small network of carefully curated helpers.'

'People like Bisley and Tompsett?' One of the detectives asked.

'There are indications toward them. Yes.'

'Then why can't we lean on them more?'

Terry answered. 'We're all fed up with the time this is taking. Trust the process. Meg and her team are getting valuable data.'

He glanced at Candace. 'What else do we know? What is driving him?'

'Despair.'

Liz blinked. Despair?

'This man was profoundly changed by loss. There are two accounts of him telling five-year-old children that his own daughter died. On the surface it is a way to gain sympathy, after all, a child that age understands death to a degree. What tells me there is more to it than a simple lie, is his choice of target… and here is something else to consider. Has there been another missing child, or children, matching the two we know about?'

'You're saying he's a serial killer?' Someone asked.

Liz began to rise and Pete's hand shot out and steadied her.

'There is no evidence either child is deceased and it would serve us all well to believe them well and alive until proved otherwise.' Candace's voice hadn't changed but she met Liz's eyes for an instant.

A curious calm settled her nerves and she glanced at Pete with a tight smile.

'Let me get this straight, Doctor Carroll.' The first detective spoke. 'We have a man who is aging, educated, and patient. That tells us next to nothing. But the loss aspect? What kind of loss. Did his daughter really die or is he saying that based upon a different loss?'

'Excellent question. While searching for the deaths of young girls over a substantial period of time may bring a list of possibilities, I fear it may not lead to this person. The loss may well be from divorce, separation, or even a young sister gone too soon. But I do believe by looking at the two girls in question that we have a chance of narrowing down this search.'

She turned and wrote more on the board, talking as she did.

'Five years of age.'

'Blonde. More than that, long, golden blonde hair.'

'Blue eyes.'

'Independent. As in, they are both confident little girls who will talk to strangers. Let them do up a shoe lace.'

Candace stopped and regarded the officers in the room.

'This man lost someone who fits that description. It was at least eighteen years ago but I believe it was much longer than that.'

'What is the significance of that park?'

'Perhaps not the park. That is where it has proved possible for him to take a child. I believe the only connection is that both children visited there. No, where attention needs more focus is the apartment building where both children were living or visiting,' Candace said.

Terry spoke. 'Someone in the building?'

'It is the sensible place to search because if not the perpetrator, then an accomplice lives there. Of this I have no doubt.' She stepped away from the whiteboard in order to look at it from a distance. 'There's more. Something has triggered him taking Eliza. I doubt she has any connection to him. Assuming the disappearance of these two girls are his doing then the second child is in response to the first.'

'Not sure we're following, Doctor,' Terry said, followed by a murmur of agreement.

For the first time since Liz had met her, Candace had an air of discomfort as she returned to the whiteboard. She wrote "Ellen" and circled it. 'Let's assume this child was the first taken, that there'd been no others before her. The person responsible didn't simply grab her and run through an opportunity presenting itself, and then return eighteen years later to do the same. He had a connection to Ellen, either through her appearance and age, or an actual family tie.'

More murmuring and a few heads turned toward Liz.

'Hold it together,' Pete's voice was so quiet Liz struggled to hear the words.

'Something significant happened to send him searching for another Ellen. It could be an important birthday. An anniversary of some kind.'

'Did he kill Ellen and want to replace her?'

Whoever called that out was shushed by other detectives.

'Ellen would be twenty-three now.' Liz stood. 'Why would he kill someone of that age? Why would she not now have her own life?'

'Perhaps she does, Liz,' Candace nodded. 'Perhaps she had her own child. She was no longer the little girl this man has a pathological need for in his life so he found another.'

Ellen might still be alive. She might have grown up remembering nothing of her family.

Liz had never believed Ellen was dead but for the first time, she had a proper glimmer of hope.

As the briefing with Candace continued, Liz slipped out. It was pointless speculating any further until more facts were known.

She tapped on Andy's door and he jumped. He might have been dozing.

'Sorry, boss. You want to see me?'

He rubbed his eyes as she closed the door.

'Grab a seat, Liz. What did you get out of the briefing?'

Liz gave him the short version.

'If only Ellen's disappearance was taken seriously from the beginning. I've felt for ages this was something to do with me, rather than the park or the building.'

'Your father?'

'What? No.'

'How long since you've seen him, Liz?'

'Not since I was a small child and while I understand why you are thinking about him, he doesn't fit Candace's profile, not apart from the age group. He was a reckless, violent man rather than educated. No patience. He had no interest at all in seeing me or my sister after the divorce and I believe he didn't even pay child support. That is a man who wiped his hands of his children rather than tried to replace them by stealing his own grandchild.'

Andy listened, head nodding.

'And why wait until she was with me rather than any number of opportunities around kinder, or playdates, or her local park?'

'It doesn't add up,' Andy said.

Liz slowly exhaled. Everyone needed to stop wasting precious time on theories.

'If anything it would be a perp. Someone I've arrested.'

'We're already looking at that possibility.' Andy stretched. 'You've been here for too many hours. Go home.'

'What's happening with Brian and Darryl? I can talk to them.'

'No, you can't. The reason I left the briefing was Bisley who had troubling breathing and pain in his left arm.'

'He had a heart attack?'

'He's in hospital. And we hadn't arrested him so all I've been able to do is post a general duties officer to keep half an eye on him. Tompsett is being released.'

'What, no!'

'We have nowhere near enough to charge him yet. And don't go knocking on his door.'

Sure. Why would I dream of doing such a thing?

'Are you doing okay, Liz? Couldn't have been fun have McNamara doing his bad cop thing on you.'

Liz smiled. 'He only knows one way. But I'm alright. If you really don't want me here I might visit Anna. My sister.' The smile faded. 'She must be joining the dots and have questions.'

'How long since you saw each other?'

'Been a while.'

And she'll probably shut the door in my face.

Anna still lived in Keilor in the home she and Sav bought thirty years ago. Back then they'd both worked in aviation, Sav on the ground and Anna in the air. When Ellen came along, Anna wasn't prepared to be away from her child for any length of time and retrained as a travel agent. Like Liz, she hadn't been able to move away from the home Ellen knew. Just in case.

Liz parked several houses down and spent a few minutes getting her nerve up.

The last time she'd seen her sister was at Sav's funeral.

He'd never got over losing Ellen and drank until his liver gave up on him. That was four years ago. Until the funeral the sisters had kept in touch—not often—but enough for Liz to believe she might be forgiven one day. The funeral was a tipping point for Anna and the words she used were scorched into Liz's mind. Not the least being not to ever contact her again, not unless she was bringing Ellen home.

At the risk of a repeat tirade, Liz rang the doorbell.

The woman who opened the door bore little resemblance to the sister Liz remembered. Her once glossy red hair was dull and grey and pulled back with a hair band. The body Anna used to pride herself on keeping lean and fit was lumpy and weighted with kilos. Her face was lined and drawn without a shred of makeup.

'I wondered when you'd get here.'

'You've heard?'

Anna shrugged. 'Bit hard not to. Come in.'

Liz took her shoes off and left them just inside the door. Anna was heading toward the kitchen. Along the wide hallway were the familiar framed photographs of decades past. One wedding photo. Anna pregnant. Baby Ellen. A family portrait. Liz hurried past.

'Have you eaten?'

With a shake of her head, Liz took in the decline of the room Anna had always called the 'life of the house'. No bowl of fresh fruit. No flowers on the table. A stack of dirty dishes were in the sink. Anna stared into the fridge.

'I'm fine if you've eaten already,' Liz said.

'Can't remember when. Should have something. Just can't

work out what. Never got used to cooking for one.'

Liz joined Anna at the fridge. 'Eggs? What if I make an omelette?'

Anna stepped aside. 'Be my guest. Wine?'

'Sure.'

They ate at the kitchen bench, omelettes with toast and wine.

'More breakfast than dinner. Not that I drink wine in the morning,' Liz said.

'The eggs are good. No idea of the last time anyone cooked for me. How about you? Anyone cooking for you?'

'Does it count that one of my bosses shared takeaway Thai with me last night?'

'Nope. Why did they do that.'

'Everyone is tiptoeing around me at work. Andy probably thought I'd starve if nobody took pity on me while I sorted through… well, through a box.'

Anna held the wine glass but didn't drink. 'Andy.'

'Thirties. Ambitious. Not my type.'

'Whatever that means.' Anna put the glass down. 'Is it the same person, Liz. The one who took our Ellen?'

Our Ellen. Our little one.

'There's a strong possibility. Yes.'

'And you're going to find them? Bring home Eliza Singleton. And my baby?'

The waver in her voice ripped at Liz's heart.

'There is a huge team of detectives and forensic scientists and a profiler working non-stop. We have leads this time.'

Now, Anna took a mouthful of wine and replaced the glass, her eyes wide.

'Can we talk about some stuff?' Liz asked.

'Stuff?'

'About our father.'

As if she'd been stung by something Anna jumped off her stool and it crashed to the ground. She looked at it, puzzled, and began clearing the plates.

Liz righted the stool and helped.

'I haven't washed up for a while. No idea why not.' Anna began filling the sink and piling plates into size order to one side. 'You should know. I'm on anti-depressants. The dose isn't right yet and I forget to do things. They make me too hungry. And then I stop eating for days. Bit of mess, Lizzie.'

And totally understandable.

'Shall I wash or dry?'

'You choose.'

Scrubbing the dishes seemed to help Anna focus on the conversation. 'Our father was a terrible man. You must remember?'

'Not much. A bit. He wasn't nice to Mum. Lots of yelling.'

'He hit us. Mum. Me. Not you.'

'What? He hit you? Oh, Anna.'

'Don't fuss. Too long ago to care now.'

'Why not me?' Liz ventured.

Anna laughed shortly. 'You were his perfect child. Took after him with your blue eyes and blonde hair and always saying no as if you were in charge of everyone. Bossy little thing then and you still are.'

A shiver ran up Liz's spine. 'I don't even have a photo of him. Or me back then.'

'Good. Nothing but misery our childhoods. Best thing was when Mum divorced him and she had to fight tooth and nail to keep you. He didn't want me but little Elizabeth? Made every threat under the sun until we moved and he couldn't find us.'

Liz finished the last dish and hung the tea towel on a hook to dry. Her hands shook as she did and her heart raced. Was Candace right and Ellen's own grandfather had taken her?

'Just be glad about one thing, Liz.' Anna went to the counter and picked up the bottle of wine. 'He can't hurt anyone now.'

'I don't understand.'

'But you must know. Our father died years ago.'

TWENTY-TWO

Night was the best time of all. Perhaps not so much to pursue his great love— surfing—but almost everything else. Families were usually safe inside the walls of their homes. As evening stretched into the small hours there'd be less traffic. Fewer people wandering. More criminals roaming. This was his world.

Pete followed a short, burly man down a shadowed alley in the city.

He'd had enough of waiting around for the higher-ups to make decisions and would find the mongrel who took the kids himself. Liz was out of the picture for a few hours and didn't even know she'd be getting a wake-up call at three tomorrow morning. At least, that was Montebello's plan and one which Pete was determined to prevent going ahead. After Liz left and the doctor left, there'd been a heated argument between him, Montebello, and Terry. He'd backed down. Best to let them think he'd gone home to sleep off his temper.

The man Pete was following tapped on a door partway along the alley and by the time it opened, music blaring through it, Pete was right behind him. The man jumped and reached under his jacket before he recognised Pete.

'Of all things holy… good way to get shot sneaking up on a man. You coming in?'

'Not if I can help it. A minute, Tony?'

'One.'

They stepped to the other side of the alley and the door closed, muffling the music.

'Don't owe you money, do I?' Tony lit a cigarette.

'I wish. Just a favour. Looking for Kyle Moorland. Know him?'

Tony's face was easy to read. Always. And it gave away that he did.

'Excellent. Where do I find him?'

'According to the obituary I once read, he's in Keilor Cemetery along with half the underbelly of the city.'

'According?'

'Doesn't pay to believe the papers, mate. You should know that. Look at the rubbish being said about the little girl. Her daddy is a crim and I reckon there's something there behind it.'

A group of loud women and louder men staggered down the alley then found their way back out.

'That's your minute up.'

'Obituary aside, where do I look?'

Tony tossed his cigarette onto the ground. 'Ask his daughter.'

'She hasn't seen him in decades.'

'Not the cop. The kid he had with his second wife. Geez, mate. Do I need to do your work for you?'

'Wait. What kid. How old?'

Tony was getting frustrated. Probably had a fix waiting for him on the other side of the door.

Pete held up a bunch of notes. 'Age. Name. *Anything*.'

Tony reached out and took the notes, counted them and shoved them into a pocket. 'Look upstairs at Maisie's in Geelong. We done?'

He wasn't waiting around and Pete wasn't stopping him. Another cop might drag the man in for questioning but as difficult as it was to track him down, Tony was one of his reliable ears on the street and Pete was keeping things that way.

He started to dial Liz's number and stopped. It was a lead on Ellen. Nothing more.

The drive to Geelong took under an hour and Pete ignored the second and third calls from Andy in that time. He'd answered the first as he'd left the city and wished he hadn't.

'Where are you, McNamara?'

'Home. Sleeping.'

'Cut the crap.'

'Ditto.'

'Don't even think about taking this into your own hands.'

'Did you need me for something, *boss*?'

The silence went on longer than five seconds and Pete disconnected the call.

Terry would ring if he was really needed but Pete was off duty. If he ever was off duty.

Maisie's was in an industrial area outside the main streets of Geelong. Pete parked and ran a search on the place. One owner. Maisie Baker. He visited the website for the premises and looked at the girls on offer. Plenty of blue eyed blondes alongside a selection of races and body sizes.

He did a search on Kyle Moorland. Dead and buried at Keilor Cemetery.

'Might be time for exhumation.'

Cause of death was drowning. The man was found in an almost unrecognisable state after apparently falling off a boat. He'd died twenty-one years ago.

When did Liz say her mum died? Twenty-plus years?

Pete made himself some notes on his phone using the code he'd created for himself decades ago. He sent a copy to the cloud.

Before leaving the car he checked the mirror and then pulled his hair back into a ponytail. This kind of place was his least favourite. Some people chose this path. Men and women, but more of the latter. Choosing was one thing, if they knew what they were getting into and were able to separate selling sex from living a life. Spend five years making as much money as possible then walk away before it destroyed them. But more people found themselves there in often grimy rooms with little say over the men who visited or what was done to their bodies. Drugs. Other dependencies. Pay for those and later, often not very much later, pay the real price.

At the front door Pete pressed the buzzer.

Some of the Melbourne brothels were class acts. The women —men as well—had every protection and got the point of having their own client lists. This wasn't Melbourne. It was more cloak and dagger, wham bam thank you ma'am… not often a thank you, just a hundred dollar note.

The door opened and Pete stepped inside.

There was a staircase leading straight up. No signage. Nothing to encourage him to keep going except he knew what this place was and thanks to word of mouth, so would the seedy men of the region.

The lights were low. The carpet on the stairs was a deep red colour which matched the walls.

He reached a landing with a door at either end. One was plain and had a padlock. The other was glass, and on Pete's side was a thickset man, bald, gold chains around his neck, tatts. A cliché of a bouncer.

He sized up Pete.

Pete offered nothing.

The gatekeeper opened the door.

On his way past, Pete slipped a fifty dollar note into the man's pocket.

Everything changed on the other side.

There was the rich scent of sandalwood and soft music played. The room was lush. Velvet sofas in dark green. Even darker green walls and carpet. A coffee station with a machine and selection of finger food. And a coffee table with an open book of photographs.

Women.

Women to choose from.

Pete wanted to throw up. If this was where Ellen worked, how the hell would he tell Liz?

There was a small counter and beside it, a narrow open doorway.

After minute or two, a woman appeared.

She was in her early twenties and had the bluest eyes Pete had ever seen.

Apart from one person.

Liz.

TWENTY-THREE

During the day Keilor Cemetery was solemn enough with its endless rows of headstones dating back to the mid-1800s. Every so often there were small gardens where mourners could sit and reflect. Toward the Western Ring Road boundary, a huge mausoleum loomed, surrounded by crypts and more gardens.

Under a cloudy night sky with only occasional glimpses of the moon, the place was positively unsettling.

Liz had been here a few times and was well aware of the final resting places of some of Victoria's most notorious criminals—underworld figures among others. She'd attended some of their funerals as part of the police presence which accompanied high profile gatherings.

After leaving Anna's, she'd sat in the car for a while writing notes about their conversations. They'd talked for a while before her sister needed to sleep and they'd hugged. Liz hadn't wanted to let go. Losing Anna from her life was almost as bad as the disappearance of Ellen and all she could do was her best to finally solve the mystery which had hung over their heads for so long.

She'd looked up their father's name on the cemetery's

website and knew exactly what paths to take to find his final resting place.

His headstone was small and to the point.

Kyle Moorland.

His date of birth and of his death.

That was it.

Anna had had no idea Liz didn't know about the death and had only found out herself after the funeral. There'd been nothing left. No will. No earthly goods to dispense. One of Anna's neighbours had seen an obituary in the paper and came to offer condolences. It was strange and yet somehow fitting that no family attended the funeral of a man who'd walked away from them.

'I barely remember you, Dad,' Liz whispered.

She glanced around. Nobody else was silly enough to be here in the middle of the night talking to the dead. *She* wasn't supposed to be here. A security guard was the most likely person to find her.

Liz squatted. 'You hurt my mum and my sister. What kind of man does that? And what was so special about me that you never laid a hand on me? Was I too young to trigger your temper?'

Anna had said it was Liz's blue eyes and her cheeky attitude.

'People think you had something to do with Ellen disappearing except it is impossible. Unless it isn't you in there.'

She straightened and stepped back.

Was that even a possibility?

Faking one's own death was difficult but far from impossible.

From the direction of the mausoleum a flashlight moved from side to side. After a last glance at the grave, Liz retraced her steps but this time kept close to the shadows.

The apartment building was quiet.

Bisley's office was in darkness so the job of the team who'd been in there was done. Liz checked her phone for any updates but there was nothing new.

The television blared in Darryl's apartment and it took all of Liz's self-control to keep walking. With every fibre she wanted to knock on his door and then knock some sense into him. Or a confession out of him. Instead, she put down her head and rushed past.

Her front door locked behind her, Liz stripped off all of her clothes. She left them on the floor with her shoes and didn't bother with a light. In the bedroom she dragged a men's T-shirt—about ten sizes too big—over her head. From beside her bed her feet found slippers. One little luxury with their soft interiors.

Liz opened her laptop on the kitchen counter and poured a glass of wine as it booted. She glanced at the clock on the oven. Before long it would be midnight and another day gone without finding Eliza.

She pulled up a stool and searched for information about her father. Every detail she could recall, which was precious little. But she had his date of birth and death. The date of his wedding to her mother. And Anna had given her another morsel of information. Kyle had gone to one of Victoria's most prestigious boys schools and then qualified as a data analyst.

That was hugely interesting.

Despite many attempts in the past day or so to remember his voice, Liz couldn't. She had a memory of him yelling. Throwing things. Slamming doors. Slapping her mum so hard she fell and both Anna and Liz ran to comfort her. But his voice was distorted by fury and madness and chaos. Candace speaking of an educated man didn't marry with the person Liz knew. Not from that memory. And for whatever reason it was the one which dominated.

There were reports of the accident which killed him. He'd been onboard a cruise ship just off an island. It was night. He'd fallen from a railing he'd decided he could walk along. There was a witness. They'd made friends on the cruise and were both from Victoria. There was an evening of cards and drinking. A few men. And things got stupid. The witness was so distraught he'd needed medical attention. There'd been no chance to save Kyle and his badly decomposed body was recovered months later on a remote beach.

Liz dug around a bit more and found the name of the witness but it was such a common name that searching the usual places led to dead ends. With the length of time that had passed, the witness might well be deceased or living outside the state.

She sighed and finished her wine.

There was a tapping in the hallway. Someone else's door, not hers. Persistent.

Liz grabbed jeans and shoved her feet into runners before peeking out.

Bisley was at Darryl's door. He faced away from Liz, knocking then stopping. The television still blared. Bisley knocked harder then slammed the palm of his hand against the door. A few seconds later it swung open.

'Watcha want?'

Darryl stumbled into the hallway wearing his trademark boxers and knee-high socks.

'What kind of idiot are you?' Bisley poked at Darryl's chest.

Seriously.

She'd intervene only if she had to.

'Same goes for you. They found all the emails you sent me and now they think I took that kid.'

'Well, didn't you?' The back of Bisley's neck was beet-red. 'Tell me where you stashed her.'

'Didn't touch her.' Darryl whined and leaned against the wall. 'Was told to look under a bush and take whatever clothing was there and put onto the road. There was a map with x's and everything.'

'But why? Who sent it?'

'Dunno.'

'You must know. Someone must have paid you to do it.'

Bisley's voice raised. 'I can't have you living here. You've brought the cops in and everyone is talking and upset. Pack your stuff and get out.'

'Not going nowhere.' Darryl tried to go back inside but Bisley blocked the doorway. Darryl took a swing and it was all on. Bisley side-stepped and his fist shot out, straight into the wall. He was howling, and doors began opening along the hallway.

'Okay that's enough. Both of you stop.' Liz waved at the other residents to go back inside. 'Brian, stop yelling. Darryl, go inside and lock your door. I'll be there shortly to speak to you.'

'My hand's broken.'

'Self-inflicted, mate. We'll get some ice on it in a minute.'

Bisley swayed.

'Sit down. Why are you out of hospital?'

'You were in hospital?' Darryl did nothing to help Bisley as he slid to the floor and sat with a bump. 'Thought you looked like crap.'

'Told you to go inside, Darryl. Go and call an ambulance. Now, right?' Liz squatted beside Bisley. Darryl disappeared, hopefully to do as he was told. 'Why didn't they keep you in?'

'I got tired of waiting. Building owner kept messaging to tell me to get Tompsett out.'

Bisley's colour had drained to a sickly tone which alarmed Liz.

'Sit tight for a minute and I'll get my phone.'

She dashed into her apartment for her bag and phone and locked the door behind herself on the way back out. Bisley looked ill and he leaned his head back against the wall. Liz phoned for an ambulance. Darryl's door was shut and the television blared again. He was next on her to-do list.

'Brian? Ambos are coming. Breathing okay?'

'Yeah. Just tight. My chest.'

Liz glanced around. The other residents had done what she'd said and she and Bisley were the only people in sight.

'Why did you phone me all those years ago? The day Ellen

was taken. This is important.' Liz knelt beside the man. 'Who told you to phone me at that moment and distract me?'

He shook his head.

'Don't pretend. I can help you avoid jail time but it has to be now, Brian. Tell me, please.'

His lips looked off. Blueish. Sweat poured down his face. But his beady eyes were as hard as nails. 'Thought you were a crack detective. You must know who took them both.'

'I don't. I really don't. Please help me find them.'

Bisley began to cough.

'Don't you dare die on me, Bing. Help is coming.'

'Hurts.' He waved a hand around, the one which was bloody from hitting the wall. Then he found the top of her arm and gripped it painfully, pulling her near him. 'Close to home, Elizabeth. Close to home.' His fingers bit into her skin. 'Right under your nose.'

His hand dropped and he fell onto his side.

'Get up! Don't you die, you bastard!' Liz screamed at him, using all her strength to pull him upright but his weight was too much and his eyes were closed.

Darryl opened his door, beer in hand.

'Help me.'

'You're kidding, right?'

'Help me sit him up. Damn you, Darryl, help me.'

For a moment Darryl wavered. He gazed at Bisley and then without a word turned and shut himself in his apartment.

There was no point Liz going to the hospital. The paramedics had worked on Bisley for excruciatingly long minutes before stabilising him enough to move. Liz had led them to the far end of the building to use the working elevator. She'd stood there watching the lights indicate when they reached the ground floor and even then she didn't move.

She longed to phone Pete. But he was off duty.

Instead, she dialled Terry.

He answered after two rings and asked what was wrong.

Everything. It is worse than wrong.

Liz managed a reasonably cohesive explanation for why she'd called. Bisley was likely to die in hospital if he made it that far.

'How on earth?'

'He was trying to evict Darryl. They got into a fight and I stopped it.'

'And his heart packed up.'

'Yeah. Darryl refused to help me. He was a bloody paramedic and he turned his back on me when I asked him to help.'

'Where are you, Liz?'

Staring at an elevator door.

'Home.'

'I was going to ring you in an hour or two and ask you to come in.'

'To work? Why? Do you have a new lead?' Liz began walking toward her apartment.

'Something happened earlier. Nothing that we could action at the time. No new sightings or information.'

'But you planned to phone me at what… two in the morning?'

He laughed shortly. 'A bit after. Look, Liz, I know you've walked in on conversations which stopped today and I'm sorry. Pete and I had hoped against hope to avoid this and he is still adamant it shouldn't go ahead.'

She unlocked her door and went inside, almost tripping over the shoes and clothes she'd dumped there earlier. She scooped them up with her spare arm.

'Andy received a phone call from someone claiming to have Eliza.'

Liz stopped dead, dropping the clothes and shoes. 'I'm only hearing this now?'

There was a pause. An annoying pause while Terry obviously tried to filter what he had to say.

'The person wants a meeting before dawn this morning.'

The irritating ringing in her ears returned.

'He wants to speak with you, and only you.'

'Terry?'

'I know. Thing is, he says Eliza is fine and he'll return her unharmed. But only if you meet him. And I hate this because every bone in my body screams that this is the most dangerous thing imaginable.'

'And it is the only thing to do.'

'Are you sure, Lizzie?'

Liz turned on a light and gazed into the mirror in the living room. She looked so serious staring back. And so ready.

'I am.'

TWENTY-FOUR

'Where is it happening? The meeting?'

Liz and Terry sat at a small table in his office with steaming coffees and some kind of nutty slice on a plate between them. Since his divorce he'd begun using the team as taste-testers for a myriad of cooking attempts and some were more successful than others.

'Brimbank Park. Just about no cameras once you get off the main track. Kilometres of paths. Hundreds of hectares of land.'

'So he's not planning on handing himself in.'

Terry shook his head. 'We have a chopper standing by at Essendon Airport. Couple of minutes flying time from there. Special Ops are already setting up some vantage points. But you'll be on your own some of the time.'

'Why me?'

'I'd like to play the recording and see if you recognise the voice. It is less than perfect as Andy used his mobile to record the landline but it might help.'

They moved to Terry's desk where he clicked around on his computer.

'Montebello.'

The line crackled and there was a long pause.

'Speak or hang up.'

'You're in charge?'

'One of several. How may I help?

'I want the person in charge.'

'You want her back? Eliza? You talk to me.'

'I'm talking to you.'

'But you are not taking me seriously.'

'I am. My name is Andy. What shall I call you?'

'Irrelevant. There's something you need to do for me if you want the child back.'

'Did *you* take the child?'

'Irrelevant. You have one chance so listen carefully, Andy. There's a place I'm going to describe. Before it is light tomorrow morning I want to meet with one of your officers. With the woman.'

'Which woman.'

'The detective who left her child alone in the park.'

'Why do you want to meet with her?'

Another long pause.

'Is Eliza alive?'

'There'd be no point me speaking with you if she wasn't. She misses her mother.'

And another.

'Tell Elizabeth Moorland to be at the location half an hour before dawn. I know you're recording this so I'll only say the address once.'

'Eliza's mum is desperate. Please drop her somewhere safe. Don't make her wait.'

Liz motioned for Terry to replay it, closing her eyes to listen. There was something about the way the man spoke. His voice was more white collar than blue.

And the word 'irrelevant' was odd. Few people used it let alone twice in a short conversation.

'Anything, Liz?'

She opened her eyes. 'Bisley called me Elizabeth tonight. He told me I had to look close to home and that the person who took Ellen was right under my nose. I don't know if he meant someone I know or someone living close by. But everyone calls me Liz or Lizzie. Always have apart from… anyway, that is impossible.'

'Your father?'

'Who is buried in Keilor Cemetery. I saw his grave a few hours ago and have read everything I can find on his death, which was years before Ellen was taken. Who the hell actually knows?' Liz stalked to her seat. 'Maybe he had a secret brother or something who has a grudge against me. With our mother long gone, Anna and I are working off our memories as kids and we were always told there was nobody on his side of the family.'

'We've checked. Your memories are right.'

'Oh.'

Why be surprised they'd look?

'Andy and Pete will be here in the next hour. We'll go over a map and make a plan. You'll wear a protective vest and be miked up.'

'But he's got Eliza. Why would he hurt me when he must see me as an easy way to surrender her?'

Terry leaned his elbows on the desk. His face was as tired as Liz had ever seen but his eyes were still focused and alert.

'Interesting you say that. Dr Carroll was of a similar opinion, or at least that was one of them. Because you went through the experience of Ellen being taken and are a police officer, he might believe he's less likely to be shot if things get tense. Question is why he doesn't just drop her somewhere?'

'What other opinions did Dr Carroll have?'

After hesitating for a moment, Terry sighed and leaned back. 'Until we confirmed the death of your father, he was top of her list as the perp. She still believes there's a personal element here but so far we can't find anyone in your history who matches enough of the profile—or the couple which do—are in prison.'

'This isn't a grudge, Terry. Nobody takes a child from their family just to prove a point. Okay, it does happen but they don't then repeat the offense almost two decades later.'

Terry's internal line rang and he answered, listened then grabbed a remote and turned on a television in the corner. As he hung up without saying a word, the screen came on and he tapped a couple of times.

The station was the one hosting *Tonight at Six* and Teresa Scarcella was live, somewhere in the dark.

He put the sound up.

'This special report comes to you from outside Keilor Cemetery.'

Liz's heart thumped.

Teresa's face was sincere, intense, as she gazed into the camera.

'Strange scenes earlier tonight as a senior homicide detective was observed visiting the cemetery long after the gates closed. Detective Sergeant Liz Moorland is in the centre of the case of missing child Eliza Singleton and is best known for the disappearance, eighteen years ago, of her own niece, Ellen Georgiou. Many experts believe the cases are connected and all eyes are watching the behaviour of this officer.'

'Load of bullshit,' Terry muttered.

'This footage was recorded only a short time ago.'

The woman's face was replaced by a long distance video which was grainy and at first showed nothing other than trees. Then, after a bit of going in and out of focus, it settled on a figure near a grave.

Teresa's voice continued.

'The detective spent a few minutes at the grave. She appeared angry, our person on the ground reported. Almost ready to tear the grave apart. But why would she do so? This was the grave of her own father, Kyle Moorland, a man long gone from her life.'

Tear it apart? What have you been snorting?

The video changed and on it, Liz was hurrying away from the grave in the direction of the camera. It was obvious that there was a flashlight moving behind her and at one point, she glanced over her shoulder, then looked directly at whoever was filming.

The image paused.

A woman hiding in the shadows.

A woman who was being filmed.

'Where were they? How did they know I was there?'

That image reduced to a corner of the screen and Teresa again dominated. 'So many questions. Why was the detective at Keilor Cemetery in the dead of the night? Why was she acting as if she was hiding. Or afraid? And what, exactly, is her part in the disappearance of two young girls, eighteen years apart? I am Teresa Scarcella and this is *At Six Tonight*. Call our hotline, email, or message and we will always take you, our beloved viewers, seriously.'

Terry clicked the television off and tossed the remote onto the desk. His eyes met Liz's. And his phone began to ring.

Andy stormed into Terry's office. 'How on earth has that woman got footage of Liz?' He noticed Liz, who was studying a map of Brimbank Park at the small table. 'And what the hell were you doing there at that time?'

'Grave robbing.'

He stopped in his tracks and blinked. Terry sniggered from behind his desk.

'That's about the only thing she didn't accuse me of.' Liz wasn't about to let Andy have a go at her and she kept her gaze level. 'The real question is who was following me. And why.'

'Obviously it was one of Scarcella's creepy reporters.'

'Not obviously, Andy,' Terry said. 'Just because she used the term reported means nothing. That show encourages its followers to send in random rubbish so they're bound to get something useful now and then.'

'Are you saying someone is following Liz?'

Like near Vince's?

'I called in a rego yesterday,' Liz said. 'White Toyota sedan was behind me along the freeway and almost all the way to Vince's house. Turned off when I slowed and didn't reappear.'

Andy sat opposite Terry but his attention was on Liz. 'Who owns it?'

'I cancelled the check when it turned off.'

'Might see if it was logged.' Andy got on his phone and spoke for a few minutes. 'I'll get a call back. I want to do something about Teresa Scarcella. She's intrusive as it is and this kind of irresponsible reporting is side-tracking the public from what matters.'

'Good luck trying,' Terry said. 'At least Liz is going into Brimbank Park from an entrance away from the cemetery. If the film crew are still nosing around we'll need to be careful going past.' He checked his watch. 'Anyone heard from Pete?'

A kind of grunt emanated from Andy.

'He knows when to be here?' Liz asked.

'He does but if you hadn't noticed, McNamara sucks at following orders.' Andy dialled and held the phone up so that everyone could hear. 'Leave a message. Unless you're Andy.'

Terry burst into laughter and even Andy had a wry smile.

'I thought you two were getting on okay.' Liz wished they would. The angst made it harder for her to focus on the next few hours. 'He'll just have been sleeping, if he knew this was on.'

'I spoke to him a few hours ago and he was on his way to Geelong.'

'What?' The word came out louder than Liz expected.

'He's been digging around about some aspects of this case and took himself off after a lead. Why?'

Both of them were staring at her with odd expressions.

Laughter. Playing hide and seek with Anna. A big tree out the back. Big enough to hide behind. Hot summer days splashing in a wading pool. And regular trips to the beach down the road.

'29 Collaroy Street, Geelong.'

Terry wrote it down, both eyebrows raised.

'I think I lived there as a little kid. Before Dad left.'

How did I not remember this?

'Geelong is huge. It's just a coincidence or else a red herring.' Nevertheless, Andy nodded to Terry. 'Who can we get to chase up a history of the property? Can we send someone around?'

Eyebrows still not back in place, Terry made another note. 'Not at this time of the morning, mate. Let's not go frightening innocent residents.'

'Wasn't suggesting forced entry. My name isn't McNamara.' Andy mumbled the last bit but it was clear enough.

Liz got to her feet. 'I'm going for a walk. It's either that or explain some stuff about Pete you might not want to hear but either way I'm actually a bit over the crap about him. Everyone thinks it funny to talk about him as if he's a perp and would act illegally. Ask yourself why he'd still be a cop—a *Homicide* detective—if that were true.'

On that note, Liz grabbed one of the nutty slices and stalked out but not before she'd seen Andy pick up on her emphasis that Pete was in the place he wanted to be.

Liz wandered the hallway of the floor without seeing another soul. Homicide was deserted and she found herself standing at a window looking onto the street.

She dialled Pete.

'Leave a message. Unless you're Andy.'

'It's me. Are you on your way? I don't want to do this alone.' She rolled her eyes at herself. 'What I mean is that with you there I know who to trust apart from Terry.' Not much better. 'Just phone, okay?'

If he was following a lead from one of his shady contacts then it was serious. Particularly knowing he had to be back in the city for this… whatever it was. He wouldn't let her down and him staying out of contact was worrying her. This whole thing was worrying her and Liz wanted to process the information from the past few hours but there wasn't time.

She leaned her forehead against the glass.

Was the caller really the person who had Eliza?

'Will you be back in your mother's arms by breakfast, Eliza?' Her voice was a whisper. It didn't feel like it was real. The search for the little girl hadn't eased with police and other agencies from around the country involved and there couldn't be a person in the state who was unaware of her photograph. 'You are clever, whoever you are.'

If only Eliza was alive and well.

If only Liz could get through the next couple of hours and arrest the perp.

If only she could then find Ellen.

TWENTY-FIVE

She called herself Lena and was one of the working girls.

She'd asked Pete to wait while she located Maisie. 'She's on the roof having a ciggie.'

'I just want some of your time, if that's possible.'

Lena smiled knowingly. 'Whatever you want, honey. But I'll need Maisie to manage the transaction so take a seat and we'll be right back.'

Even the way she talked sounded like Liz. Not the words or the suggestive tone but the timbre of her voice. He waited, unable to sit because all he wanted was to scoop her up and take her to her aunt. End the nightmare which had haunted Liz from before he'd met her.

No amount of training could prepare a cop for this. He couldn't arrest her for being abducted as a kid. He couldn't force her to go to the station. And he probably shouldn't even be talking to her without having sought Terry's advice. But alerting anyone until he was certain this was Ellen Georgiou was risking heartbreak for the people who had loved her as a child. He had to be certain.

Maisie was closer to seventy than sixty and had the jaded

expression, the world-weariness that Pete had observed with so many workers in the trade.

'Have you had a look at our services, sugar? Lena is available for any on the first two pages but if your tastes are more on the er, adventurous side then I have some other beautiful young women to introduce to you.'

'Not really after anything other than a friendly chat. Feeling a bit lonely. If that's okay?'

'Sugar, you can spend your money however you want. What if we put you in the Garden Room? There's a nice sofa to sit on and the package includes a bottle of our finest champagne.'

About to say no to the wine, Pete changed his mind. Alcohol might help the conversation. So he paid a ridiculous amount extra and in a moment was following Maisie while Lena collected the bottle. The room was awful. Painted in lime green, it had some sad pot plants and a painting of a flower.

'There you are. Your hour begins when Lena steps inside and she'll let you know when the time is up. But until then, enjoy her company.'

This was heartbreaking. Little Ellen stolen from her family to end up here in a room with a lumpy bed and worse sofa, expected to accept whatever foul men came her way.

'Here we go, champagne and lovely company.' Lena carried an open bottle and two flutes to a small table. 'Would you care to pour and I'll close the door.'

Pete obliged. The 'champagne' was one of the cheap and nasty sparkling wines on the market worth a tenth of what he'd been charged. But none of that mattered.

Lena accepted the glass he offered and tapped it against his. 'Cheers. I don't know your name, honey.'

'Pete. Shall we sit?'

He waited until Lena settled on one end of the sofa, her legs crossed in his direction, to join her, deliberately keeping his body language relaxed. He needed to draw on his best questioning skills. He took a tiny sip of his drink to encourage her and she did the same.

'So, Pete, tell me about yourself.'

'I work at night a lot. Bit like you, I guess,' he said. 'More money to be made at night.'

'What line of work?'

Lena looked interested. Really interested, as if his words meant something.

'Bit of security. Just came from outside a Melbourne club where things can get a bit rough.'

'Is it dangerous?'

'Can be. But I can handle myself so it is a fool who takes me on.'

A flicker of uncertainty crossed the young woman's face. He might have gone too far.

With a laugh, Pete gestured around the room. 'My job isn't nearly as dangerous as yours. I bet you get all kinds in here.'

'My clients are lovely. And you would have gone past our own security guard at the top of the stairs. He makes sure we are safe.' She took another sip. 'The funny thing is that I often feel safer here, at work, than outside. If it wasn't for my little one, I'd probably only leave the house to get the bus here and back.'

A kid. Holy crap.

'Bit harder with kids, huh? They like to be out and about. Visit the grandparents. Go to the park and stuff.'

He held his breath, watching her intently.

She put her glass onto the table, her eyes anywhere but on him and nothing to say.

He tried again. 'Me? No family. No kids to take to the park.'

'My boy is just a toddler so he is happy to play in the back garden. Best at the moment until they catch that creep who took the little girl.'

Now she looked at Pete and for the first time he saw her for who she really was as a person. The mask of bravado was replaced by honesty. She was scared.

He redirected the conversation. 'I take my hat off to women who work and have kids. Even married, I reckon most of it falls on the mum. It was like that with my parents. Mum worked full time, raised me—which wasn't the easiest because I learned to say the word no early and practiced it often—and cared for my dad who had MS.'

Lena drew her legs up onto the sofa, cuddling them as she listened.

'She was always tired and never complained. Well, she did, but not often.'

'Your mother sounds wonderful.' There was a wistfulness in her voice.

'Still is. Going on eighty and fusses after the residents of the residential care home she now lives in. What's your mum like?'

Her face fell. 'I barely remember her. She died when I was little.'

'Sorry. That's crap.'

In more ways than one.

'Pop told me about her though. How she looked just like me and had bright blue eyes and she used to take me to the park all the time.' Lena suddenly grabbed her glass and finished the wine in a few gulps and when she replaced it, there were tears in her eyes. 'The thing is that I remember someone like that but she wasn't Mummy.'

'An auntie?'

Her eyes widened. 'Maybe. My mum had red hair and went in airplanes a lot.' She giggled. 'Here I am going on. I'm sorry, Pete. You wanted to talk and I've taken over with memories I had almost forgotten.'

Pete's heart was pounding and his mind raced. This *was* Ellen.

'You mentioned your pop. Did he raise you?'

'You've barely tasted the champagne, Pete.' She unfolded her legs. 'Maisie will wonder what we are doing in here.'

Lena leaned closer and extended her fingers to touch his face.

Pete pretended not to notice, collecting the bottle and refilling her glass.

'I like listening to you, Lena. Hearing about your family is nice. Please tell me about your pop.'

'Sure, if you want. He was great. Took me in when I was about five and raised me like his own child even though he must have been heartbroken about my mum dying, being his only daughter. Only kid. Sometimes I'd be teased about having such an old dad and he'd just laugh and tell me he was fitter and stronger than most younger men. And he was, I guess. Went to the gym a lot. Ran. Oh, how he loved running!' She smiled, her mind away somewhere. 'He won a seniors race only a few years ago. One of the around-the-bay ones.'

Pete was itching to get on the phone and start a search.

'Sounds like a good man. But you speak as if he died?'

'No. But he might as well have.' The wine glass was back in her hand and Lena sipped again. Something had changed and it seemed that she genuinely wanted to talk. 'I finished high school as dux. Had offers from three universities to do either law or criminology, both of which I find fascinating. But I came home late one night to find all of my stuff outside in boxes.'

'Why?'

'Broke his rules. I was just with friends but he called me names and said I'd disappointed him and I had no idea what he gave up for me. He cut me off financially, took my keys, and said never to come back. Told me I was dead to him.'

Lena's—Ellen's—voice never wavered.

'I was shattered. Fell in with the wrong types rather than lift myself up and follow my dreams. Ended up here. Told Pop when I was pregnant and he called me more names. But Maisie? She looked after me. So did the other ladies. We're friends now and we all share the cost of child care and babysitting. Most of us are mums.' She smiled. A warm, beautiful smile which was as perfect as the ones Liz occasionally bestowed on the world.

'You are an incredible young woman,' Pete said. 'I imagine what I need to tell you is going to rattle your world but if you hear me out, you'll finally have some truth in your life. So will you? Hear me out?'

TWENTY-SIX
~DAY THREE~

The drive to Brimbank Park took less time than Liz expected. Almost no traffic on the freeway helped and as they passed Keilor Cemetery there was thankfully no sign of a film crew.

Dawn was approaching and already the sky was changing.

Liz wore a protective vest, an ear piece, mike, taser, and a gun. Her head was clear now on what she had to do and how to do it. The plan had been gone over ad nauseum until every person knew their part and the risk of human error was as low as possible. They weren't the only police out there but Special Ops would be well out of sight and manage their own actions.

Terry was driving. Andy was beside him. Liz had the backseat.

'You're sure Pete is behind us?'

'He is. We won't leave the car until he's in place.' Terry glanced at her in the rear vision mirror. 'He knows what to do.'

Liz had doubts, not about Pete's abilities but the lack of transparency.

Pete had arrived only a few minutes before they left and was immediately in a huddle with Terry and Andy behind a closed door. Liz was being kitted up and could see but not hear a heated conversation. It made her stomach turn. She was still being kept out of discussions and having information withheld gave her a sense of insecurity. All it would take was one wrong move to destroy the chance of getting Eliza back.

He'd come out of the office fuming, hands clenched and barely glanced at Liz. It was only when she exited the ladies room just before leaving that he appeared and uncharacteristically hugged her. 'Everything is fine, Lizzie. Everything.' Then he released her and strode away. In some ways that settled her nerves. But her mind was working overtime. He had been in Geelong following a lead. He'd tried to get Andy and Terry on board with something and failed.

'This is our first stop,' Andy turned in his seat to look at Liz. 'We're out of sight of any of the public roads and half a kilometre from the meeting point. Unless the perp walks past we are invisible.'

'And I'm walking from here.'

'Yes. But before then Pete will move to his position and as soon as you leave the car, we'll move to ours.' Terry's voice was steady and reassuring. 'Everything you say will be heard by us. Do you want to run through your trigger words?'

'Sure. The most important being "baby" if Eliza is present.' She went over the others to cover eventualities such as the perp running, her belief it was a false alarm, imminent risk to her life, and so on. If she needed extraction then "chopper" was the word. But if she was under threat from this man then she'd do anything to keep him alive and not lose sight of him. No matter what it was she was supposed to do.

Terry checked a message. 'Right. Pete's in place. You good, Liz?'

Not even close.

'I'm ready.'

'Check your mike works before you start down. We'll leave once you are fifty metres away so do it before then,' Andy said. 'It will take us two minutes to get into place so walk slowly.'

His face was the most serious Liz had ever seen.

She nodded and climbed out.

The air was warm and humid. Storms were forecast for later in the day but for now the sky was clear and a half-moon gave some light. Liz got her bearings and headed for the edge of the small carpark.

'Testing. This had better work.'

The ear piece was clear as a bell. 'We're moving now, Liz.'

Behind her the car started and drove away.

She left the carpark and the descent was steep.

Brimbank Park was an easy place to get lost with its ravines and hideaways.

Liz followed a narrow and winding road by the light of the moon rather than use her flashlight. It helped her eyes to focus and her senses to adjust to the environment. She had excellent night vision and steady nerves. Usually. But here, at the most remote part of the sprawling grounds, she wasn't so sure.

When she was within site of the designated spot, she stopped for a moment. She could hear the river from here but not see it. Trees bunched around an information board and another fifty metres beyond that was her destination. From higher up, where Pete and the others were waiting, it would be almost impossible to get a decent look at the perp, let alone a sniper shot from one of the Ops team if it came to it.

This is it, Liz. Best chance to find those girls.

Ignoring the churning in her stomach, Liz moved closer, eyes slowing scanning the area ahead and to each side. Stepping under a canopy of trees, she almost turned back.

She was isolated and felt it keenly.

There was a small clearing in the middle of the trees and she forced herself to stand there. It was so quiet.

Except there was a crunch of a footstep, a crack of a twig.

Her heart began racing and adrenaline surged through her body.

And then he was there.

. . .

Whatever Liz had planned to do and say at this moment was cast aside. She had a carefully rehearsed script which Terry and Andy had worked on with her, designed to keep her at an emotional distance and ask the most appropriate questions.

But at this moment, a surge of rage flared and it took every ounce of her fortitude to keep her feet planted rather than attack the man with her fists. Or take out her gun and force him to reveal the truth.

He stood a few metres away.

Half a head taller than Liz, he was lean and wore black, body hugging pants and long top, black running shoes, and black gloves. He was muscular but like a runner rather than a body builder.

She couldn't see his face. He had on a black mask of the disposable type widely available for the past few years. And sunglasses. How he could clearly see wearing them was curious, but it might work to her advantage if he took off and stumbled about in the dark. His hair was white and very short. Clever to cover himself up but terrifying because he obviously had no intention of revealing his identity.

'So you did what I said.'

His voice gave away his age. This wasn't a young man, nor even middle aged.

'Where is Eliza?'

'Irrelevant.'

The word, delivered in person, made the hairs stand up on her arms.

'At least tell me how she is. Please.'

He took one step forward. 'Eliza is asleep. Safe.'

As reassuring as the words were on the surface, they sent a chill through Liz. Asleep and safe might have other meanings. Grim ones. She waited for him to speak next. His agenda needed revealing before she could decide what to do with him.

'You need to stop looking for Ellen,' he said.

'What do you know about her? You *did* abduct her as well?'

He made a tsking sound. 'Abduct is a harsh word. Regardless, the time for searching is long past. You failed her, Elizabeth. Too busy to properly care for your own child. What if someone meant her harm?'

'She is my niece, not my daughter. And taking her from her family and her life was the act of someone who wanted to cause harm so don't pretend you were saving her.'

'Easy, Liz.' Pete's warning in her ear almost made her jump.

The man crossed his arms. 'It would benefit you to manage your temper.'

Liz knew his voice. Some long lost memories tapped away in the back of her mind but as much as she tried to draw them out, they taunted her.

'We're talking about a little girl who didn't get to grow up with her parents.' Liz was back under control. 'Telling me not to search for her raises questions. I'm sure you must understand that. I have relived that day in the park endlessly. I've dreamed about Ellen. Lived in the same crappy apartment in case she came looking for me and her mother has done the same. Did you know her father died recently?'

He shrugged. 'A weak personality.'

'Tell him you'll stop looking for Ellen.' It was Andy. 'Bring it back to Eliza.'

Liz wished she could remove the earpiece.

'I'll stop searching for Ellen.'

Now, the man laughed. 'Good girl. Not that I believe you but it is a step closer to what I want from you.' He walked a few feet forward. 'Sometimes a terrible situation happens to a person through no fault of theirs.'

Like being stolen?

'A decent person. A good, caring father has his entire world ripped away. One day he is watching his daughter grow up, her laughter and cheekiness bringing such joy to his heart that he believes he has everything a man could ever want. When she smiles at him he feels like a god, because she idolises him.' He dropped his head and sighed deeply. 'And then she is gone from his life forever.'

'Say nothing, Lizzie.' Pete knew her so well. 'I promised you everything is okay and it is. Play his stupid game.'

A bit more information would be helpful because his cryptic comments had her mind darting from Ellen to Eliza and back again. He knew something important and that angry exchange with Terry and Andy had been about it. They'd stopped him from talking to her.

Have you found Ellen?

'It messes with a man's head, Elizabeth. At first there's doubt. Was I a bad person? Did I fail my family? I knew I hadn't. But I had made a mistake by marrying the woman I did. A woman who was below me in every way and particularly without Aryan genes.'

Liz blood ran cold. What monster was this man? She dug deep. 'But you wouldn't have had that child without her.'

That seemed to give him pause and he stared at her—if that was what he was doing behind the sunglasses. He removed the mask, crumpling it into a ball in one hand.

She pressed gently. 'Marriages break down all the time. Horrible but true. I will never marry because I couldn't bear to live through divorce again after that of my parents.'

The effect of her words was immediate. He strode toward her until only an arm's length away. He said nothing for the longest time and she had no idea where to go with it. This was sensitive. One wrong word and Eliza might be lost forever. There was no unsolicited advice in her ear. It was all up to her.

'I am so sorry,' she said in the softest tone she could summon. 'You deserved better.'

The breath he drew was audible and his chest visibly raised and sank.

'Yes, Elizabeth. Yes, I did. And so did you. Growing up without your father ruined your life. Imagine how different you would be now, had that not happened.'

'You know an awful lot about me. Or are you speaking rhetorically?'

His head tilted.

'It is impossible to know without seeing your face. I think I know who you are... I feel I am connected to you... but it has been forever.'

If that doesn't do it, nothing will. Take off the damned sunglasses.

Instead, he shook his head and when he spoke, there was a heaviness about his words. 'I fear too much time has passed. Not your fault. Not entirely. But let me ask you this. If I asked you to come with me this minute, will you?'

'No, Liz.' The chorus was from Terry and Andy. Pete was silent.

'Will it mean I get to see Eliza?'

The man's hand rose to his sunglasses. And hesitated. Then he smiled. 'Know this, Elizabeth Moorland. Everything I've done has been for you. But now it is irrelevant because you made a choice. You are first and foremost a police officer. Not a daughter. You've lost that right.'

Before Liz could respond, his hand dropped to his waist and he was suddenly in her face and then something hit her stomach so hard that she fell to her knees. She couldn't make a sound or move from the pain and loss of breath and even as he ran away, Liz had no choice but to watch. And then she fell onto her side and the world turned black.

TWENTY-SEVEN

Andy began running the minute the perp said "Aryan". His gut screamed that Liz was in deep trouble and being under the trees gave the snipers no chance of stopping the man.

He reached Liz first, yelling for help as he slid onto his knees beside her.

She was on her side, barely conscious, and moaning. Despite that, she pointed in a direction and managed to get out the words, "get him".

'Liz!'

Pete flew in their direction.

'Keep going. He's gone toward the river,' Andy shouted.

As much as must have hurt Pete to obey, to his credit he changed direction with barely a loss of speed and disappeared into the dark.

Andy leaned down to check Liz. 'Are you shot?'

'Baton. Stomach. Go.'

He straightened and tapped on his radio. 'I need assistance at the meeting zone now. And an ambulance.'

It was Terry who appeared next, gesturing wildly for Andy to follow Pete as he stumbled through the trees in his haste to reach them.

'Terry's here. I'll catch that mongrel.' Andy told Liz, and then he began to run, unsure whether the mongrel was the perp or Pete. He was fit from years of gym and road work and in a minute caught sight of the Pete in the distance, racing alongside the river.

The terrain wasn't good for running, with no real path and dips and holes to avoid. What began as almost gorge-like conditions gradually opened up as the river widened. Andy's legs and lungs hurt as he closed the gap. It must have been a kilometre before he almost ran into Pete around a curve.

'Need a water unit on Maribyong River between Avondale Heights and Brimbank Park.'

Pete was almost doubled over to catch his breath and was gasping instructions into his phone.

'Black dinghy… with an outboard motor. Single occupant. Male. Sixty… to seventy. Five eleven. Lean build. Dressed… in black top, pants, footwear. Carrying a baton and possibly other weapons. Do not kill. He is the main suspect in the disappearance of Eliza Singleton. Do not kill him.'

He finished the call and slowly straightened.

Andy gazed down the river where in the far distance a small boat was chugging away.

'Why aren't you with Liz?' Pete demanded.

'Terry's there. She isn't shot and told me to chase the man down. But a damned boat?'

'Where's the helicopter?'

'Two minutes away. I'm going to follow the river in case he stops somewhere.' Andy set off at a jog alongside the water.

Pete caught up quickly, seemingly over his struggles to breath. They moved in silence until the heavy whirring of helicopter blades approached from behind and they stopped to watch as it swept over their heads and straight down the middle of the river, low and fast, leaving the water rippling and trees swaying along the sides. Huge spotlights moved from side to side as it flew, rising briefly to go above a bridge on one of the arterial roads.

'We need to stay close to it. Kyle Moorland might land somewhere or at least try to get under some cover.'

'You don't know he's Kyle Moorland.'

'Yeah. I do know.' Pete was off again, faster than a jog.

They had no chance of catching the helicopter but both kept going, slowing up the rises in the track then speeding again when it evened out. Sweat poured down Andy's back and neck and McNamara looked as bad. The sky was lightening a bit and he turned off the flashlight. When they reached a narrowing of the river, the track disappeared and they halted.

Somewhere further along the helicopter was hovering but there was a bend between it and them.

'Do you reckon he'd outrun the chopper in a dinghy?'

'Ever been in one, mate? Helicopters are damned fast,' Andy said.

'He was ahead. Had time to get out of the water.' Pete pulled out his phone and dialled. 'Terry. Yeah, nothing yet. How's Liz?'

'Ask about the helicopter,' Andy prompted.

Pete glared at him and turned away as he listened. 'Thanks. She's going to hospital? Okay. Oh, yeah, Detective Senior Sergeant Montebello requests an update on why the chopper is circling up ahead.' A moment later he put the phone away and faced Andy, crossing his arms. 'They got eyes on a dinghy for an instant. Looking for it now.'

'Slippery bastard.'

'He planned this as carefully as he planned the abductions of Ellen and Eliza. The issue is that we have almost no intel on him apart from the address in Geelong which Liz remembered.'

'That wasn't where you went? Not even a drive-by?' Andy could hear the snark in his voice and even in the poor light it was clear Pete was riled.

'Mate, the first I heard about it was in Terry's office this morning and I'd just come from Geelong. Focus on finding Eliza and stop sniping at me all the time.'

Had Liz said something to Pete about the earlier comments in the office? It was unhelpful if she had but at the same time, Andy hadn't meant to let his guard down and talk about Pete behind his back. Much better to do so to his face.

'If you don't want negative comments then stop making it so easy. I phoned you several times last night and you ignored me.'

'I was busy.'

'And I needed to speak with you. Instead of being irresponsible and making decisions outside the chain of command, why don't you try to be a team player?'

Pete moved fast. He didn't touch Andy but was suddenly right in his face and although Andy was a head taller, Pete's sheer presence was intimidating. 'You should have let me tell Lizzie about Ellen. What if she'd died just now instead of being hurt? What if she'd died without ever knowing her niece is alive? Can you live with that? Mate.'

He swung away and squatted on the edge of the river, splashing water on his face.

The helicopter was heading their way but slowly, floodlights pausing on a spot along the banks and then another.

'Look, we need to work together, Pete. Terry and I made the best decision on short notice. This woman, Lena? I want her to be Ellen. Good god, how much I want that but you know there's a long road ahead. DNA tests. A lot of stuff before her identity is proved yet you wanted Liz unsettled going into that meet.'

Pete shook his head as he got up. Water dripped down his face and his hair. 'You don't know her. There isn't a stronger cop on the force but she needs information and to know the status of things. If you imagine she is unaware that something big has happened then you're not a very good detective.'

The helicopter was close enough to drown out conversation now and as the floodlight settled on them, Andy gave it a thumbs up. It turned and headed back the way it came. 'Shall we keep going for a bit? I can cross over and check the other bank.'

'You? Nah. I'll wade over. That way you know I am a team player.' Pete removed his shoes, tied the laces, and slung them over a shoulder. He dropped his pants with a huge grin. 'You can turn away if you don't want to see something to make you envious for life.'

A chuckle escaped before Andy could stop it. 'Dream on, sunshine.'

Of course it was Pete who found the dinghy. Less than ten minutes since Andy's eyes were scarred for life by watching Pete's jock-clad backside disappear into the river, a triumphant shout was followed by a text message. 'Team player wins.'

'Best that I appeal to your competitive side more,' Andy muttered to himself.

Not far up ahead was a bridge and he ran across and backtracked to Pete's location, talking to Terry on the radio as he moved. Pete was back in his clothes and anxious to get going.

'Need to track him. Do we have a dog unit coming?'

'On its way. Chopper is sweeping this side inwards. Have you checked the dinghy?'

Pete ignored him and led the way to the small craft which was pulled all the way out of the water and covered in a camo sheet. 'See, he plans everything. And before you ask, he's not under the cover and the boat looks clean *and* I haven't interfered with any trace.'

'Leave it then.'

Andy scanned the area around them. Although there were a few trees it wasn't as dense an area as the one where Liz met the man. Within a few metres there was a steep ascent with no visible trails.

'That's where he expects us to look.' Pete kept his voice low.

'I saw no evidence of him from the direction I came which leaves a couple of options.'

'The way I came, the river, or he has taken the obvious route.'

'Which is it then?'

Flicking his flashlight back on, Andy focused on the trees but not even a bird was in them. And that on its own was useful. He'd heard nothing of agitated birds and there were none here.

'He is at least five minutes or more ahead of us,' Andy said.

'Fifteen. Think of his speed. I reckon he planned to leave the boat here and for all we know had scuba gear ready.'

'Crap.' Andy tapped his radio. 'Terry?'

'Anything?'

'Is there a way to monitor the river? Not only boats but someone in the water? Under the water?'

There was a moment's silence and then Terry swore. 'Kyle Moorland had his scuba licence. Got it on the cruise before he died. Allegedly died. Leave it with me.'

Pete sank onto the ground, head in his hands for a minute. Then he inhaled deeply and looked at Andy. 'Why didn't we know this earlier?' He wasn't angry. If anything, he was at a loss, sad, unaccepting. 'Our team gets results but we've put one of our best into danger and she's hurt. We've allowed a serial child abductor to outsmart us. How?'

Andy dropped onto the grass beside him.

'You want the company line? Over stretched. Not enough officers to cope with a situation so vast let alone delve into a mystery from the past.'

Pete looked at him.

'There's no excuse good enough, Pete. Ellen's disappearance should have been treated differently from the beginning. Eliza's has been—I feel. But there's a disconnect between the two cases and nobody can fix that now.'

'Liz needs to know about Ellen.'

'And she will. Where now? I'm not going to sit around and I doubt you are. Which way, Pete?'

. . .

Daylight had overtaken night by the time a scuba tank was found abandoned a few hundred metres away. From there it was a steep but doable scramble to a secluded carpark.

'No cameras in the area. Airwing is checking for footage which might show a vehicle there but at this point, the perp is gone.'

They were back in Missing Persons. Terry had taken lead to give Andy a chance to shower and change and eat. By the time he returned to the floor, there was a whiteboard with a map on it and circled areas in red. A dozen officers, most who'd just begun their shift, asked questions and made notes. Pete had his back to them all staring out of the window. He'd neither showered nor changed and was simmering with anger.

'We're exploring the strong possibility that the perp is Kyle Moorland, presumed dead and buried in Keilor Cemetery. What I need is information about the person who went overboard on the cruise—allegedly Kyle. Everything about the person who witnessed the so-called accident from their name to their first born.'

There was a murmur of agreement from the detectives.

Andy stepped up to the front. 'We've just had an update about Liz.'

Pete turned.

'She's being released shortly. Nothing broken or seriously injured. The blow with the baton was to soft flesh and avoided all organs.'

'Boss, did she know the perp? Have any intel?'

The question came from a detective Andy didn't know.

'Liz will come in to debrief and we'll have better information then. What I can share is that during the course of the conversation between the perp and Liz, he made several comments which lead us to believe he has personal knowledge of her life. More than ever it is important to look for the smallest of references in any communication which might lead us to him. The dinghy is heading to the Crime Scene garage for investigating.'

'He wore gloves. He planned ahead. There will be nothing,' Pete said.

'But he got the boat from somewhere and the scuba tank may be a good lead.' Terry tapped on the whiteboard. 'There's plenty of cameras once he got to a road and Meg is chasing down footage.'

'What about the Geelong address?'

Everyone looked at Pete.

'Where Liz lived as a kid. Be a good place to hide a child, I would think.'

Andy glanced at Terry. They'd already discussed this.

'Let's wrap this up for now,' Andy said. 'Pete, get some food and fresh clothes and meet us in my office in an hour.'

Without another word, Pete stalked out. A couple of the officers sneered and Andy glared at them until they shut up.

TWENTY-EIGHT

Everything hurt but none so much as her heart.

Liz had refused painkillers and the minute she was cleared of anything life-threatening had insisted on leaving the hospital. Rather than waste the resources of a patrol car, she called an Uber and went home first, desperate to shower and take a proper look at herself.

The bruising was still coming out but was scary enough with dark splotches around a central cluster. She touched the skin where the baton, end first, had hit with enough force to knock her to the ground but not enough to cause long-term harm. That on its own was curious but Liz had no desire to try and understand him.

My father.

She couldn't look at her eyes in the mirror.

He said he'd done this for her.

Stolen Ellen.

Stolen Eliza.

Destroyed so many lives.

For me.

If Eliza wasn't still somewhere out there needing her then she'd curl into bed and weep.

But there were no tears. No feelings, other than ones of inexplicable grief and sorrow. And only her promise to Eliza and Ellen to find them could keep her going. Later… once there was a resolution, she had to face a lot of truths and make some decisions. And the one which hammered away in the back of her mind was about her job.

They'd let her down.

Back with Ellen and now, with Eliza.

She'd gone to that clearing without full knowledge of what she was walking into and it didn't matter if it was to protect her or to stop her from backing out. Terry and Andy had no right to withhold information. And Pete was the only one on her side right now.

Dressed, she made coffee and phoned Vince. It went to voicemail. She didn't leave a message. There was a lump in her throat. She'd needed to hear his reassurance. His opinions. His no-nonsense advice. Without even drinking the coffee, she let herself out of the apartment.

Darryl's door was swinging open from inside and she caught a glimpse of him before it slammed shut and the security chain was locked.

She didn't have the energy for him right now and kept walking, aware he'd opened the door again as she'd passed. Liz slowly went down the stairs, wishing she'd gone the other way for the lift which she'd come up in.

Was Brian Bisley still alive? Thinking about the lift made her think about him and it was yet another part of the puzzle which was getting more complicated by the minute.

The only way she was going to get through this without losing her sanity was by removing the emotion and setting her mind on one thing. Catching her father and finding Eliza. Everything else would fall into place once she accomplished that.

At the bottom of the steps she stopped to catch her breath and from her bag she extracted a business card. She turned it in her fingers. Candace Carroll had said she was there for Liz. Any time. For any reason. And Liz had plenty of the latter.

Candace was a complication.

Liz wasn't ready to trust someone new.

Liz wasn't going to trust anyone.

The debriefing was tense and short and Liz was glad to leave Andy's office. He and Terry were still keeping something from her. It was obvious. She'd asked where Pete was and they'd looked at each other and Terry said something about him having a break to sleep. She wasn't convinced.

Liz went to find Meg.

Stepping into a room where a handful of people were all focused on their data was oddly comforting. There was a quiet buzz. Tapping. An occasional word. Chairs moving.

'Liz?'

Meg was out of her seat in an instant and almost threw her arms around Liz, stopping at the last second. 'You must hurt so much.'

'Only if I move. Breath. Talk. Otherwise I've never felt better.'

Serious eyes regarded her. 'We *are* going to find him. And Eliza.'

She should have felt relief. Hope. She didn't.

'Come and sit with me so I can show you what I'm doing.' Meg hurried back to her station and spoke to the uniformed officer sitting closest. 'Lou? Move, dude.'

It was the young officer who'd been so helpful to Liz at the apartment building, getting his head around an antiquated video security system at short notice. He glanced at Liz with a sympathetic smile and vacated his seat.

'Thank you.' Liz was happy to get off her feet and she carefully moved the chair a bit closer to Meg.

'Right, three searches happening.' Meg had three screens today and each was busy with information. 'While Lou hunts down the source of the scuba tank, I'm liaising with Water Police, and Parks about the river. Nobody just jumps into a strange waterway for the first time when they know their life will depend on it so our man has some history of diving there, or boating there, something, which will come to light.'

'And the dinghy?'

'Being looked at right now. One of thousands in the state so not hopeful at finding an owner but the outboard motor might help. Do you know how long he's been scuba diving?'

'Me?'

Meg kind of screwed up her face as if she shouldn't have spoken.

'You believe he is Kyle Moorland. My father.'

'Yup. I've heard the live feed of your conversation with him and I can't find a reason to believe otherwise. Do you?'

It wasn't something Liz could say aloud, so she shrugged. And regretted it. Even that small movement hurt.

'Over here I have a program running to find him. Kyle. It is weirdly simple for something sophisticated.' Meg gazed at the screen with a small smile.

'Are you in love with it?'

'Quite possibly. Software is less demanding than a person.'

You are singing my song.

Meg continued. 'I've gone all the way back to the day your mother had divorce papers served on him. I can't identify the day he left the house—unless you can?'

'Not me. I was little. But I could ask Anna. My sister. She is ten years my senior and remembers a lot more than I do.' And after their dinner last night, she might be willing to help.

'Would you ask her if she'd come and spend half an hour with me? Do you think she would?'

If she isn't drinking, spaced out from tablets, or sleeping, maybe.

'I'll phone her.'

'Cool. Any additional information will tighten the parameters. I'm looking for indicators of behaviour—things Kyle did before his alleged death. Where he lived and what he did each day. Where he worked. And then compare to the life of the man who is supposed to have witnessed Kyle fall overboard.' Meg shot a glance at Liz. 'Unsolicited this might be but my opinion is that Kyle killed the dude, making sure his features were destroyed, and then tossed him overboard and took his identity. And I'm really sorry how blunt I am today.'

'Blunt is fine. At least *you* are sharing with me.'

Meg shot her an odd look.

'You said three things?'

'I did?' Meg glanced at the furthest screen. 'I did. I'm working on Ellen's case.'

Liz's heart skipped a bit.

'As in…'

'Not supposed to talk about it but if those boys are being all closed-shop and protective then they need a wakeup call. I've been looking at some information which might have been overlooked in the past and before you get too excited, telling you the ins and outs will take an hour which I don't have.'

'Is it about the hairs? The DNA.'

Meg did a zipping gesture across her mouth.

Liz pushed herself to her feet and walked away without a word. She got as far as the hallway before Meg caught her, touching her arm. They both stopped.

Meg looked either way and waited until there was nobody in earshot.

'Can you trust me, please? I'm between the proverbial rock and hard place and dealing with bureaucracy and old-boys-club crap so cut me some slack. Please, Liz.'

It was true. Of everyone, Meg had the heart of the investigation on her plate. The nuts and bolts and far beyond that. And everyone wanted a piece of her and expected answers. Yesterday.

'I do trust you. You and Pete and that's about it in this building.'

'No, Liz. You can trust the others. They just have their own masters to appease and when it comes to Terry, he has a father-figure sense of wanting to look after you. Kinda old-fashioned but he's that kinda man.'

'But why will nobody tell me the truth? I know something has happened. Or is happening. Pete has disappeared.'

'He's asleep. Go see if you don't believe me.'

'Huh?'

'On the floor of one of the interview rooms, lights out, snoring.'

Unsure if that was sad or funny, Liz managed a smile.

'We good?'

'We are good, Meg. Sorry.'

'No need. You've been through hell these last few days and then your idiot father—sorry—thumps you with a baton. Phone Anna, okay? Sooner I can talk to her the better.'

Meg disappeared again and Liz leaned against the wall.

She wanted to cry and scream and throw things.

All responses alien to her. Tears now and then. But not stupid displays of temper and loss of control. Yet recently she'd fantasised about interrogating Brian and Darryl away from any legal boundaries. This wasn't her.

Or perhaps, Liz was changing into the person she was meant to be.

'I need to apologise.' Liz spoke aloud to herself and she wouldn't follow through because she hadn't shared the dark thoughts she'd had about Terry and Andy with them.

Pete lay on his side against the wall of the interview room, a blanket barely covering him and his arm cradling his head as a pillow. He wasn't snoring, but he was deeply asleep. His phone and wallet and gun and shield were in a pile on the table along with an empty water bottle.

She sat there for a while in the dark of the observation room.

There was no noise in here. No chaos. No man who had destroyed her world and that of her sister all in the name of a terrible belief.

Aryan. A white supremist.

A woman who was below me in every way and particularly without Aryan genes.

This monster had said that about her mother. A beautiful, kind, and intelligent woman who had been the best mother Liz could have asked for. Had she known who he was before marrying him? How could she? People so evil as Kyle could hide their intentions for as long as they needed… until they didn't.

Liz drew in a quick breath. And another.

Her own father had chosen her as worthy of proper treatment because she had blonde hair and blue eyes.

Monster.

She rocked back and forth in her seat.

Her mother wasn't good enough. Anna wasn't good enough. But Anna's child was. A carbon copy of Liz. Kyle's version of good genes. Had he taken Ellen to replace Elizabeth—the child he'd lost to divorce?

The room was spinning. Closing in on her.

Liz closed her eyes and tried to remember her father. What did he look like? Sound like? The voice earlier was familiar but she'd listened to the call he'd made to Andy so had no way of knowing if it was that she remembered.

A large shady tree in a big garden. An above ground swimming pool.

Laughter.

Yelling.

Screaming.

Crying.

She was on her feet somehow. At the window, banging for Pete to wake up. Make this go away.

Then she turned to run and fell over a chair. She stumbled to her feet, crying aloud at the pain.

She flung open the door.

The hallway was bright.

'Liz. Lizzie, I'm here.'

She screwed up her face as the tears came.

Vince.

He was running to her.

And then she was in his arms and he held her so tight that it hurt but she gripped him as though her soul depended upon it.

TWENTY-NINE

Thank goodness she hadn't woken Pete. That was all she could think about at first. He was so tired and there was not a shred of doubt that he'd done something good… something to do with Ellen, perhaps. Earlier he'd hugged her, reassured her that everything was okay and although he was obviously gagged by their superiors, it was a glimmer of hope in an otherwise dark place.

'Liz? At some point we need to find somewhere more private to talk.'

Vince was right. They still stood in the hallway and although she'd stopped clinging to him like a limpet, he kept a protective arm around her and had told interested officers to move along. Nothing to see.

He was a rock.

She dropped her forehead against his chest for a moment, then straightened with a sharp intake of breath as pain shot through her abdomen.

'Why the hell aren't you in hospital?' He growled. 'Or at home.'

'Can't bear home.'

'Then come back with me. There's a spare room and you can sleep and rest. Melanie will be thrilled.'

How she wanted to say yes. To crawl between fresh sheets knowing someone was watching out for her. To sleep without an eye open.

Liz looked at Vince. 'Thank you. I can't yet but thank you.'

He was so worried. Lines were etched in his face and he looked ready to pick her up and take her back to the cottage he shared with his grandchild. And if he did, she might just have to live with it.

'Not happy about it but I understand. So, somewhere private?'

'I know where.'

'Can't say I've ever been in here.' Vince wandered around the conference room. 'Doubt if many street cops would.'

Even when Liz had first been paired up with Vince in her first year, he'd called anyone in uniform a street cop or similar. At the time it was strange and she'd put forward her reasons why. All police were equal. They just had different jobs to do. And anyway, didn't detectives spend time on the streets?

He'd laughed and shaken his head and after a while she'd understood. A cop on the beat was his history. The streets were his to protect in his allocated area and he'd loved it. Eventually becoming a sergeant, he'd spent more time in an office than he liked but always remembered his roots.

'This is only about the fifth time I have, Vince, and yesterday was the fourth.' Liz cautiously lowered herself onto a chair. She might have refused painkillers at the hospital which would make her sleepy or stupid but she was ready to give in to taking some over the counter stuff.

Vince dug around in a small fridge at one end of the room and extracted two bottles of water. 'Do you know there is wine in here? Beer as well. What exactly is this room used for?'

He didn't seem to need an answer and pulled up a chair opposite.

Yesterday she'd sat in this seat and Candace had been in Vince's place. The woman had seen into her soul. It felt that way. Perceptive. Caring. Thoughtful. She pushed it away. Nobody could get close to her now. She was poison.

'Hey. Hey, Lizzie? What was that look?'

'Why did you come, Vince?' Her voice sounded sharp to her ears and his eyes narrowed. 'Why now?'

He took his phone from a pocket and placed it on the table. 'You phoned but didn't leave a message. You never do that.'

'Sorry. Did you call back? Have I missed a call from you?'

She knew she hadn't. God knows she'd checked her phone often enough in the last few hours.

'It *was* your father. What a dreadful shock.'

Liz couldn't speak. Her throat closed up like it seemed to a lot lately and the tide of nausea rose. She forced it all away by sheer will power. Being sentimental about this was pointless and a waste of time.

'So everyone keeps saying.'

His eyebrows lifted. 'You don't think it is?'

'You know me, Vince. I deal in facts and evidence and the man I met with isn't familiar. Not his voice nor his build or stance. Nothing other than words to the effect that he'd done everything for me. That he had taken Ellen and Eliza *for me*.' She almost spat the last two words. 'He certainly believes he's my father or wants me to believe it but wanting something doesn't make it so.'

'But why abduct two children? How is that remotely connected to you?'

Liz leaned her forearms on the table, fingers tapping against each other. 'Eliza was a mistake, I think. I feel he expected her to be the perfect replacement for Ellen who by now is either dead or an adult, but she wasn't a good fit and that scares me because he wants us to believe she's alive.'

'I don't understand.'

'What he said to me. Eliza is asleep. Safe. Which might be code for dead.'

'Or might be that she is safe. You just told me you deal in facts and evidence and you haven't seen a body.' Vince gazed at her. 'Cut through the crap, Liz. Father or not, this perp is out to mess with your head and you need to fight back. If he is your father, you'll deal with it. But none of this—' He leaned forward to lay his hand over hers. '*None* is your doing.'

'Then what do I do?' Her voice was nothing more than a pathetic whisper. 'How do I find him and more importantly, how do I find Eliza?'

'By doing what you do best. Logic. Instincts. Information. Go back to the basics you know. Trust your judgement because it is sound. And question those who are in your way.'

'Terry is in my way. So is Andy who was ready to throw me off this case at first. Only Meg and… Pete, believe in me.'

Vince's lips curled up. 'How is the shithead?'

That finally made Liz breath properly and almost smile. 'Last seen he was asleep in an interview room. And there's something else. Before I went to Brimbank Park he hugged me and said everything was okay. It was as if he knows something but can't share it and I have seen Terry and Andy talk about me.'

'Not being paranoid? I was.'

'Were you though? Vince, they looked at me while talking and still shut me out when I asked leading questions. Is that paranoia?'

Perhaps he'd say yes, just to keep her from spiralling into even more worry. Vince was kind at heart and he loved Liz. She had no doubt of the strength of their friendship. But he'd never lied to her. Not that she knew.

'No. That is not paranoia. I'd suggest it is some idiot idea about protecting you from information which will either hurt you or possibly get your hopes up. And they don't know enough yet to make an informed decision on which it is. What do you think that's about?'

She was going to sound ridiculous. A dreamer. But this was Vince and the worst he'd say was to be realistic.

'Ellen. Vince, I think there's news about her. Perhaps a sighting somewhere?'

Liz's phone beeped with message after message. Mostly from Pete wanting to know where she was. Two from Anna.

'My sister is here, Vince.'

'Go. I can see myself out.'

Vince had made a difference. His calm, no-nonsense suggestions helped Liz back from the proverbial edge. She had a plan now. Solid ideas on how to manage those in charge and her own emotions. Nobody was going to wear her down. Or push her out by pushing her buttons.

'Feel free to help yourself to anything in here,' Liz grinned. 'I'll wipe any footage of us using the room.'

'Liz Moorland, you shock me. And make me proud to know you.' Vince checked his phone. 'I'll come with. Do you want me to stay a while?'

'I wish you were here all the time. But can you do me a favour?'

'Sort out the shithead?'

'No, but if I send you some digital files, would you take a look? Things I can't get to yet or get my head around. I need a second opinion and yours matters.'

He nodded. 'Send whatever you want. I'll revisit my memories as well of that time.'

They went down in the lift and when it opened, a uniformed officer approached and caught her eye. 'Someone to see you. She's waiting near the interview rooms.' He gave Vince an odd look.

'I'll leave you to it.' Vince raised a hand and left.

Liz glowered at those who were curious and they all quickly got back to whatever they were doing. Some knew Vince personally and had their prejudices against him. Others were younger, newer, but were still as interested in the man who'd saved numerous lives one Anzac Day years ago, only to burn almost every one of his bridges when he left the force.

Is that what I'm going to do?

There'd never been a time in Liz's career that she'd felt like quitting. Not even in the weeks and months following Ellen's disappearance. Something kept her going, believing, and she'd blocked out the very things which now, were driving her away.

Being a police officer was all Liz had wanted since she was little.

On her way she checked the time, shocked to see it was almost six hours since she'd met with the perp at Brimbank Park. She hadn't even begun to write a statement yet.

Outside the interview rooms was a row of seats with only one person using them.

Anna. Her head was in her hands. There was a cup of takeaway coffee on the next seat. The picture was one of desolation.

Liz's heart broke a little.

'Please tell me everything he said. That you said. I need to know.'

Anna gripped Liz's hand. They were inside an observation room, the lights in the accompanying interview room turned off. It was more comfortable and private in here.

'I'm still processing a lot of it and some of stuff has nothing to do with Ellen.'

Liz had no idea what to filter. Her newfound closeness to her sister was fragile and Anna wasn't strong. Not these days.

'Well, what was about Ellen?'

'You failed her, Elizabeth.'

His voice was in her head and she lifted her spare hand to touch her stomach where he'd hit her.

'He said to stop looking for Ellen.'

'He what? That means he knows where she is or what happened to her? Doesn't it?' Anna's eyes were wide. 'Did you ask him?'

'Of course I did and he skirted around the question but didn't deny it.'

'But you didn't arrest him!' Anna's voice rose.

'Please be calm or else I can't continue. I haven't even written a report yet and shouldn't be talking about this.'

Tears filled Anna's eyes and she nodded, but withdrew her hand.

'He went on about losing his family through no fault of his own. About marrying the wrong woman.'

'It is Kyle. Our father.'

'I don't understand.'

Anna wiped the tears away with a tissue from her bag. 'Long after he left, Mum found a notebook with stuff about us. Me and Mum. It was pretty awful and I didn't get to read it but Mum said he only recognised you as his child. I had completely missed out on his genetic purity and received all of Mum's, which was inferior.'

'Good grief. He's insane.'

'He is a white supremist. Dad was kicked out of several religions for trying to introduce elements of some old heathen beliefs so he never had a platform or buddies. Not that Mum knew about. As a loner he turned his frustration back on his family.'

Screaming. Cries. Things being thrown. Memories deep in her mind were getting clearer and it hurt.

'He asked if I would go with him.'

'When? Today? Oh, Liz.'

'I am so sorry, Anna. He's a monster and I'm going to find him.' Liz touched Anna's face and wiped away another tear. 'We are going to find him. But right now, if you feel up to it, would you meet with Meg? She's the forensic analyst and is not only working on finding Eliza, but trying to get a lead on Ellen.'

Anna's eyes lit up. 'Ellen's alive?'

'We don't know. But Meg thinks it will help to talk to you about our father. If you don't mind.'

'Can we go now?'

THIRTY

Liz took a couple of painkillers, washing them down with water before putting some coins into a vending machine to get a chocolate bar. With the tablets she needed to eat something but had no appetite.

'If you want chocolate, help yourself to some in my desk. Better than that cardboard.'

Andy had walked past and turned to come back.

'How are you doing?'

At least he was talking to her rather than avoiding her.

'I just took my sister to talk to Meg. Anna confirmed our father was a white supremist and a loner. I should probably let Dr Carroll know to give her this new information.'

'Agree. But you didn't answer my question,' Andy said. His eyes were serious and if she didn't know better, Liz would think he actually cared. But what he cared about was adding to his impressive list of solved cases.

'Bit of residual pain but manageable. What do I need to catch up on, Andy?'

'Walk with me.'

They cut across a couple of open plan offices then took a lift up to Missing Persons. He chatted about nonsense while she forced the chocolate bar down. But when they stepped into his office, he dropped the act.

'Grab a seat, Liz. We've located the teenage boys who were at the park.'

'The ones who helped Maureen look for Eliza?'

'Yes. They did see a man a bit before locating the backpack. I've got them with artists but there's something else we're doing.' Andy pushed an open folder across the desk. 'These are photographs we've tracked down of your father and of the witness to his alleged death on the cruise ship.'

Liz picked the folder up and began to go through a dozen or so images. She'd not seen a picture of him past the time of the divorce – actually, earlier. These were a little more recent. 'Where is this one?' She showed Andy the image. This was Kyle, leaning against some kind of railing with a big smile. It made her breath catch. He looked happy and some old memory confirmed his identity.

'Cruise ship the day it left Melbourne. Go to the next image.'

Another man in a similar pose.

'He looks the same height and build. Same colour eyes. Is this the witness?' Liz looked up. 'You know the witness is the dead one.'

Andy nodded. 'There's some compelling evidence emerging. Meg has sent these to some expert she knows who is aging both photos. We'll get a pretty good idea of how they'd both look now and if the boys ID one of them…'

This was good.

'There's nothing new about the scuba gear or boat?'

'A team is working it right now. Liz, it is just a matter of when, not whether, we find him. I just wish I'd been faster this morning.' Andy ran a hand through his hair. He was frustrated with himself.

'You stopped to help me.'

'Thought he'd shot you.'

'He doesn't want me dead. He had the chance to kill me. The

baton was brought in case his fantasy of me turning back into his little girl was challenged.'

Andy snorted. 'Well and truly challenged. Do you want to go home and get some rest? There's little to do while we wait.'

'I have to find Pete. And Dr Carroll. But thanks.' Liz handed back the folder. 'Once you have the aged image of Kyle will you send me a copy?'

'We'll be circulating it soon enough but yes. And are you sure you don't want one of my secret chocolate stash?'

Candace Carroll was in Terry's office. When Liz tapped, Terry gestured for her to come in and like Andy, wanted to know how she was. She gave the same answers, aware of the doctor's eyes on her.

'We're preparing a new brief based on the additional information coming in,' Terry said. 'While this morning wasn't the success we hoped, it provided valuable data.'

'I might have more to add,' Liz said. 'My sister told me Kyle was thrown out of several religions or cults before the marriage ended. He'd attempted to introduce radical beliefs and ended up with no support. I'd imagine this would have shaped him in some way.'

'What way.' Candace spoke quietly. She was taking notes but her eyes kept flicking up to Liz.

'At some point when Anna and I were young, he began to hate his life. His supremist views hardened, if anything, certainly about my mother and sister. And I have to ask why he married a woman who lacked what he considered 'pure genes'.

He must have loved Mum at some point so what happened?

'I have some memories but nothing clear. Snippets of my childhood where there is laughter and Anna and I are playing in one of those above ground paddling pools. A big tree. And there are other memories which are not happy. Adults yelling. Things being thrown. Doors slamming. I remember my father but not his voice so much.'

Candace stopped writing and gave Liz her full attention. 'If you ever wish to explore those memories, there are techniques which help. Once the girls are found.'

Whatever it was about the other woman which exuded calmness and quiet confidence, Liz wanted some for herself. At no point was she being pressured into delving around in a history which no doubt was painful. And for that she was grateful.

'Liz, we have reason to believe your father is not only still alive, but murdered and then assumed the identity of another man. We want to start the process to exhume the body at Keilor Cemetery and you can help with that from a legal perspective.' Terry sighed deeply. 'For what it's worth, I'm so sorry this has happened. Ellen, Eliza, and then today.'

'I'm okay.'

'You were on the ground semi-conscious, Lizzie. Thought I would lose you.'

All of the anger about being kept out of whatever Terry and Andy and Pete were working on dissolved. She couldn't maintain it. Too exhausting. Terry was a good man. A good cop. If he was keeping her out of the loop then she had to believe there was a damned good reason.

Liz's phone beeped.

I'm getting lunch. What do you fancy?

She quickly replied to Pete.

Hot chips. Salty. Be there soon.

'Is there news about Brian Bisley?' Liz put the phone away. 'Last I heard he was critical.'

Terry looked grim. 'Touch and go. No chance of a conversation until he improves, if he improves. But… there's a link, a tenuous link, between Bisley and Garry Ford.'

'Who is that?'

'The witness from the cruise ship.'

'A connection to my father? That's what you mean though.'

Liz's mind raced. 'What link? The gambling or the apartment buildings?'

'Garry Ford owned the apartment building where Bisley worked in Geelong. When he sold it, Bisley was slotted nicely into his current job. Unsure about the gambling yet but it isn't the priority now.'

Liz stared at him. 'Do you know where he lives? Garry Ford?'

'We have multiple addresses and before you jump the gun, there are teams checking out each of them. Cautiously.'

'I need to help, Terry.'

'And you will once we have better intel. Go home for a bit. Eat. I bet you haven't.'

As she got to her feet, Liz tried not to show her discomfort but Candace saw. There was sympathy in her eyes but she said nothing.

'I'm meeting Pete to get some lunch and catch up on the last few hours but I can be back the minute you need me.'

Stop sounding so clingy.

Terry's phone rang and Liz waited long enough to be sure it wasn't about her father. Vince had said to listen to her instincts and they told her to stay vigilant. There was every chance Terry would keep her out of the loop about any raids on these addresses and she couldn't allow that to happen. Not while Eliza's life depended upon Liz looking for her.

Liz and Pete wandered along a path beside the Yarra River. Being outside, away from the station, was helping, and the walk down to Southbank had given her time to think.

The chips were hot and crunchy and her appetite was back.

Pete devoured a kebab and his own tub of chips.

It was only when they settled on a bench that they spoke of the past few hours. Pete gave a brief, and sometimes amusing, account of the chase along the river, clearly overstating his part and taking the opportunity to make a few more potshots at

Andy. But then he looked away, over the water to the bustling cafés and restaurants.

'I should have been closer. Taken him out before he hurt you.'

He was the third person to say as much and she had run out of ways to respond. The whole thing had been badly thought out and put her in extreme danger. Had the baton been a knife or gun, she might well be dead.

'Lizzie... once we find Eliza I'm gonna head off.'

'Head off? Take a holiday?'

Pete turned to look at her. His eyes were unreadable.

'Permanent holiday from being a cop. Done with it.'

'Done with the job or done with bureaucracy?'

'Kinda the same thing lately.'

Again she had no words to offer and she understood. Pete had gone as far as he would in the force having neither the drive nor the support from his superiors to advance.

'What will you do?'

He grinned. 'Work my way along every beach on the Surf Coast then head up to Queensland to try a bit of kite-surfing. And after that, if I'm bored, I might go private.'

'Pete McNamara, PI. I like the ring of that.'

'Liz Moorland, PI. We could start a detective agency. Trench coats. Art deco furniture. Bad coffee.'

'We already get bad coffee.'

'When you've had enough of the crap at work, come and find me.'

He was serious.

'What do you know about Garry Ford?' Liz stood and crumbled the empty chip tub in her hand. 'Shall we go back?'

'Much nicer here in the sun, but sure.'

Pete took her rubbish and his to a bin then caught up.

'Garry Ford?' she prompted.

'The alleged witness to your father's death.'

'Except?'

'It has to be Kyle. He's been living another man's life for

two decades right under everyone's nose. Has Terry told you he's got cops watching three properties which are owned by Ford?'

'Just found out. But you're not out there,' Liz said.

'Not yet. Not until they identify the most likely one as a residence and hopefully with Eliza inside. I've been told to be available later today. Warrants are being obtained and Special Ops are gearing up.'

Liz stopped. She was going to be left out again.

Pete doubled back. 'Am I going too fast? Do you want to rest?'

'No, Pete! I want everyone to stop wrapping me in cotton wool and for everyone to start telling me the truth!'

A few people stared and she bit her lip. It wasn't like her to raise her voice.

'Fair enough. Remember our recent conversation? About leaving the job?' He smiled, but there was understanding in his eyes. He never took anything personally. 'The time will come, Liz. Mine has.'

'You might be right. But first I need to find them. I need to bring the girls homes.'

Unwilling to go too far from the station, Liz wrote her report on the events at Brimbank Park. Terry's office wasn't far away and she kept half an eye on him. Between phone calls and people going in and out, he worked on his computer and got the occasional coffee. At one point he brought one to her desk.

'I'm going to put a sign up saying that I'm feeling fine and am fit for work,' she said with a forced smile. 'And I am.'

Terry's own smile was tired. 'Good. I won't ask in that case.'

'Sorry. I'm as frustrated as hell about not anticipating his attack. I could have stopped him. Made him talk.' Her hand reached for the remaining pencil. 'When Bisley was on the floor, clutching at his chest and lips blue, he said stuff about the person who took the girls. That they were close to home and right under my nose.'

'And if the connection between Bisley and Ford pans out, then he's told you the truth.'

'Pity he waited so long.' Liz snapped the pencil in two.

A raised eyebrow was the only response as Terry headed to his office.

Liz put both pieces back into the container. She could still use them. She put her head down to keep working.

When her phone rang a bit later, she jumped. Tiredness and nerves were getting the better of her.

'Detective Sergeant Moorland speaking.'

There was a pause.

'How can I help?'

'Call them off, Elizabeth.'

She was on her feet and moving to Terry's office.

'Why did you hurt me, Dad?'

Liz let herself into the office and when Terry's head shot up from his computer screen in surprise, she gestured at the phone.

'Hitting me with a baton and leaving me without knowing how badly injured I was is awful.'

'You were surrounded by police. Did they not come running to help?' he asked.

'Irrelevant.' The choice of word was deliberate and Liz heard her father draw in a sharp breath.

Then, he laughed.

Terry had rushed past her and was instructing someone, presumably to do something with her phone number.

'Please, Dad. Tell me where Eliza is. Let me come and get her.'

'The problem is, Elizabeth, that your police friends are nosing around my property. They think I can't see them and they are mistaken. It would be unfortunate if some tragedy should befall a detective. Or a child. Call them off.'

'Dad, wait a minute… crap, crap, crap.'

She dropped onto a chair as Terry rushed back in.

'He says he can see police around his property and it would be unfortunate if some tragedy should befall a detective. Or a child. Those were his words.' She held out her phone and Terry took it. 'But he said property. Not plural.'

'I'll get all the teams to fall back for now. Meg can look at this. Did a number come up?'

'Anonymous. Let me take it to her.'

'Or you can sit for a while. You've gone white, Liz.'

'Just shock. Sooner Meg looks the sooner I have it back. Is the warrant approved?' Getting to her feet, she took the phone again.

'Still waiting. Tell Meg to make this first on her list.'

The shaking didn't stop until Liz stepped out of the elevator on Meg's floor.

THIRTY-ONE

Andy looked up from his phone to the passing scenery through the passenger window. Passing fast. Sirens were on and the detective driving didn't mind putting his foot down.

'How long?'

'About twenty to the meet up.'

Thanks to footage from the helicopter this morning, a car was identified as belonging to Garry Ford. Spotted in a side street off the river, it matched the plates of the one Liz had called in the other day. How different things might be now had she not called off the check. She'd messed up by not noticing the tail was a serious one and then making it obvious to whoever followed when she did pay attention.

Eliza might be home by now.

Although Andy knew in his gut he was being unfair, he pushed it aside.

Liz banged on about wanting to find Eliza and yet hadn't done a thing about a suspicious vehicle on her tail even though she was heading in the direction of one of her old partners. She should have been paying closer attention.

He liked Liz. Had admired her as a detective for a long time. But he'd never worked so closely with her as on this case and was seeing cracks which were disturbing. Her obsession with her niece, with Ellen, was a weakness.

And she still didn't know that there was a high possibility that Ellen was alive and well.

He'd made sure of it.

Until Eliza was found it was a need-to-know situation. How he'd got Terry to agree was a miracle, but he'd come at it from the perspective of protecting Liz's mental health. What was the point of getting her hopes up until there were facts to back up Pete's claim that Lena Ford was Ellen?

You know she is.

Andy returned to his phone. Message after message were piling up. Communications from Terry, Meg, Pete. The latter's were sparse and disrespectful and once the dust settled on this case, Andy intended to begin an investigation into McNamara. Their occasional moments of agreement were a speck of dust compared to the detective's refusal to follow orders and insistence on debating every decision. It was time for him to go.

The speed decreased as the freeway changed to main roads. Geelong was an old industrial town which now sprawled both along the coast and inland, making it Victoria's second largest city behind Melbourne.

Meg needed to speak to him so he dialled her number.

'Only be a minute, boss,' she answered. 'Those images have been helpful. We have a good idea of how Kyle Moorland looks now and both the teenage boys have identified him as the man they saw at the park.'

'Brilliant news.'

'Even better though. Remember the caller who thought he'd got video of an older man and a young girl on his dashcam?'

'I thought nothing came of it.'

'No, but yes. The quality was awful but a few minutes later there is a couple of seconds of footage down the road. The driver was turning and he didn't know but had picked up Kyle and Eliza getting into Kyle's car. A white Toyota sedan.'

Andy closed his eyes for a moment. This was good and would further justify their actions.

'Still there?' Meg didn't wait for an answer. 'Everyone will get the new image of Kyle Moorland or whatever he calls himself.'

'Two minutes or so,' The detective driving said.

'Thanks. I have to go, Meg. Almost at my designated property.'

'Don't get killed.'

He laughed shortly. 'Thanks.'

Special Ops were the ones at risk and they had the expertise to stay safe while taking down the most dangerous of criminals. Kyle Moorland was one man and an older one at that.

Who outran you.

Terry sent another message.

Liz has gone to attend a disturbance at her apartment building. Uniforms on the scene. Darryl in the middle of it.

That would keep Liz out of his hair. He tapped back.

Probably knows his mate is about to be arrested. We're almost there.

News about Brian Bisley was a bit more encouraging with an update as he'd left the city indicating a more positive outcome. But still no chance of a discussion with the gentleman about his relationship with Kyle and possibly Darryl's involvement. If this operation was successful then they could keep. Just for a while.

The house was weatherboard, plain, in an ordinary street in one of the older suburbs of Geelong. At the front the curtains were drawn. The letterbox was overflowing with junk mail. There was an empty carport on the side.

'She's not here, mate,' Pete said.

He was annoyingly close to Andy and kept parroting on about his theories.

'If she ever was here, Kyle has moved her. She won't be in any of Garry Ford's houses.'

'Then why don't you tell me where she is?' Andy snapped.

'I have. Multiple times. He'd have been keeping her at the Collaroy Street address. Where Liz lived as a kid.'

Andy's radio crackled an alert and suddenly police were convening on the house. Special Ops, uniforms, and then he was running as well. There was yelling as police warned they were coming in and then the door was battered three times before being forced open. Around the back there were more officers climbing over the fences of the adjoining properties.

By the time he and Pete were at the front door, an officer was heading out, shaking their head. 'No one inside.'

'Told you,' Pete muttered, pushing ahead.

The house had no furniture. No pictures on the walls. Nothing in the kitchen or laundry. It was clean and well maintained. Likely a rental—in between tenants.

Back outside, Andy phoned Terry.

'All three were hit at the same time and all three are empty,' Terry said. 'Just got off the phone with head of Ops. Come back. Bring Pete.'

Pete stormed out of the house, straight to Andy, and waited while he finished the phone call.

'Terry wants you back.'

'We need to go to Collaroy Street.'

'Neither Kyle nor Garry own it.' Andy had just about had enough. 'There's no record of the Moorlands ever owning it and no grounds for a warrant.'

'Maybe they rented. Maybe Kyle owned it under another name. But I can tell you one thing you might not know. Lena grew up there. But sure, ignore anything I have to say in your pursuit of looking good.'

Andy turned and stalked toward the house. He glanced back. Pete was jogging in the direction of where their cars were parked.

'McNamara!'

Pete's middle finger came up but he didn't stop.

. . .

With two detectives following, Andy drove to 29 Collaroy Street. The best outcome was finding Eliza. The worst was another empty house, or upsetting the residents. Either of those would result in a report against McNamara so there was no downside.

Pete had parked a few houses up and was leaning against his car, arms crossed.

Andy directed the detectives to walk around the block to look for ways a perp might escape. He didn't believe for a minute anyone dangerous was inside but wasn't about to let McNamara hold anything against him.

At the other car, Pete smirked. 'Couldn't resist?'

'I told you we don't have a warrant.'

'No law says we can't knock on the door, mate. When we do, there might be a call for help. The smell of smoke from a house fire. Take your pick.'

If this was what it took to get into Homicide then it was sickening. Andy neither bent nor broke rules. They were there for good reason.

'I'm not endorsing this.'

'Good. Leave it to grown-ups.' Pete crossed the street, hands in his jeans pockets as if he had not a care in the world.

Andy spoke to the other detectives to give them the heads up then followed.

This house was nice, at least from the outside. Red brick, white fencing, a cottage garden. Behind the house was a big tree and Liz's memory of a paddling pool came to mind. The street was leafy. Middle income.

Andy hung back at the gate. Pete was carefully checking through the windows across the front. He glanced at Andy and shook his head.

The front door of the next house opened and an elderly lady pushed herself out using a frame. This was the last thing they needed. Andy hurried to meet her before she reached her own gate.

'Ma'am?' He flashed his badge. 'I'm Detective Senior Sergeant Montebello. Would you mind returning to your house?'

She was at least eighty and not at all fazed by his request. 'Not until I tell you what I saw, young man. The white car was here again and that horrible man put the poor little girl into it about a half hour ago.'

Pete was tapping on the door.

'I'm listening.'

'She's such a sweet little thing and I've called the number about a missing child twice, but nobody took me seriously.'

Andy's heart sank.

'I'm taking you seriously. May I just get my associate and come back to speak with you?'

'I will put the kettle on. Always wanted to make coffee for the police instead of that stuff you drink on television shows.' She turned the walking frame. 'Come right in when you are ready.'

Pete was at the front door knocking when Andy reached him. 'Hello! Anyone home?'

'Stop.'

'Sure I can hear someone calling.'

'If we'd been here thirty minutes ago, maybe.'

'What?'

'Old lady next door saw a little girl get into a white car with a man she called horrible.'

'Then tell Terry. Get everyone on this. I'll talk to her.'

Andy got in Pete's way. 'I will. You will observe. And then you can call it in.'

'You're wasting time. I'm letting Terry know now.'

'About what? We have no idea where the car is.'

'And we won't if nobody is searching.' Pete began to dial.

"Your approach of going off half-cocked at every clue, real or imagined, is unprofessional.'

Pete slid past as he put the phone to his ear. 'Nothing about me is half-cocked. *Boss*.'

Andy was feeling more invisible by the minute.

Expecting the elderly lady—who'd introduced herself as Mrs Marsden—to prefer to speak with him, she'd warmed to McNamara on sight. True to her word she had made coffee and it was among the best Andy had ever drunk. There was also a plate of tiny shortbreads which she mentioned she'd baked that morning.

After telling them to sit in an old-fashioned living room, she immediately directed her words to the long-haired lout who passed for a detective. Andy opened his notebook.

'At exactly four-seventeen I was watering my front garden. Not with the hose, but a watering can which contained my special mix of natural fertiliser to bring on the next bloom of flowers. He wouldn't have noticed me but I certainly saw him. He parked on the street rather than the driveway and went into the house through the front door. He had a key.'

Mrs Marsden paused to look at Andy.

'Are you writing this down, young man?'

'I am. What happened next?'

Her eyes narrowed as if making sure he was writing. 'It was exactly three minutes before he left the house. I know because the watering can takes three minutes to empty when I follow my routine.'

Andy wrote down *OCD?*

She was talking to McNamara again. 'I heard the front door click shut but then the little girl began to cry. Broke my heart. She is a dear thing and was clutching a toy which I couldn't see. He was carrying her and kept saying it was alright.'

'Mrs Marsden, in your opinion, was she afraid of him?'

'Oh no. She said something about wanting to see her mother. But she had her arms around his neck and it was only the fact that she seemed to care for him which stopped me running straight over there and confronting him.'

With a bit of effort, Andy avoided smiling. Mrs Marsden hadn't run anywhere for a long time.

'That is very helpful. You mentioned to my colleague that the man was horrible. Can you elaborate?'

Reaching for the plate of shortbread, Mrs Marsden offered them first to Pete, who took one, then Andy. He didn't want to eat but accepted one out of good manners.

'He *is* horrible. Mr Ford. His granddaughter is such a sweet and kind girl. Lena. But he threw her out when she needed him most. I ask you, what kind of man does such a thing?' She stared earnestly at Pete. 'After that happened, I didn't see him much until five days ago he returned. Parked in the driveway and carried four boxes inside. He dropped one and what fell out was strange.'

'Strange?'

'Toys. Stuff toys and dolls and stuff.'

Pete glanced at Andy. And that was when his stomach began to turn. This was ahead of the abduction. He was setting the house up to bring Eliza.

I was wrong. Idiot.

'Mrs Marsden, you have been so helpful. Did you notice when the child arrived at the house?'

'Well, not precisely. But it was three days ago and during the afternoon. I was watching the women's cricket on television and it was only when I got up to make a snack during the drinks break that I heard her little voice from the back garden. She wasn't there at the beginning of the game.'

Andy was writing fast to add notes to himself as well as record her words. He could find times of the start and drinks break of the cricket.

'These shortbreads are just like my mum's. Plenty of real butter.' Pete took a second one.

Mrs Marsden beamed. 'Old recipes are the best. I'll put some in a container for you to take.'

'That sounds lovely, Mrs M. Just a couple more questions and then we'll be out of your hair.'

Much as Andy wanted Pete out of *his* hair, he had to admire his way with people. The people it suited him to be nice to. It didn't change Andy's mind about taking steps against the other detective but for now, finding Eliza felt like it was slipping away and he needed every bit of intel to tighten the net.

THIRTY-TWO

'He will only speak with you, Detective Moorland.'

This was the second person to tell Liz what she already knew. Darryl had locked himself into his apartment after smashing her front door to pieces with a heavy mallet.

All the apartments on the floor had been cleared of residents and there were cops at either end of the hallway stopping access.

Liz stared at her front door. All that was left were the hinges and handle. Everything else was shards and chunks of wood both in the hallway and inside her apartment. She stepped through against the advice of the officer who'd just spoken to her. First she wanted more painkillers and a loo break. Then, she'd deal with Darryl.

She checked her phone for anything about the Geelong operation which was going down any minute. Being left off the team was hard to swallow and it irked her that Terry used her injury as an excuse but hadn't stopped her attending this incident.

I'm getting sick of this crap.

For now she had Darryl to sort out and she returned to the hallway.

'We should wait for some back up.' It was the same officer who didn't want her going into her own apartment.

'They are doing something far more important and Darryl isn't going to hurt me.'

They both turned to look at her front door and laughed.

'He left the mallet behind. I'm not going to put myself at risk.'

Liz placed herself against the wall and reached across to tap on the door. 'Darryl? This is Liz. Feel like having a chat?'

'Changed my mind.'

The words were yelled from a distance.

'See, I like being able to lock myself into my apartment, same as you are right now. But for that I need a door and something seems to have gone wrong with mine.'

There wasn't a response but it sounded as if Darryl was shuffling closer.

'Do you know if he's been drinking?' Liz whispered to the officer.

'One of the neighbours said he reeks of beer.'

She waited for a couple of minutes in the hope Darryl might unlock the door. A message came through from Pete that nobody was found at the properties and he was going to look elsewhere.

Elsewhere? Collaroy Street?

'Darryl, listen up, mate. Either you talk to me or I'm going. You demanded I come here so stop stuffing me around.'

'Nobody cares about me.'

Liz couldn't help rolling her eyes. 'Sure we do, Darryl. Why did you smash my door to smithereens?'

'Sorry. You wouldn't answer when I knocked.'

'So you knocked harder and with a bloody big mallet? I wasn't home,' she said.

'I needed to talk to you. Tell you about Tina.'

'What about Tina? Open the door, mate. Easier to talk face to face.'

The door handle turned then stopped.

'You'll arrest me again.'

'Where is Tina?'

'I think I hurt her again.'

Liz's stomach plummeted. She gestured for the officer to meet her a few feet away.

'Track down Tina Pollock. She's his ex and he's been violent to her in the past. Detective Senior Sergeant Hall knows how to contact her.'

The officer moved away to use comms.

'Liz? Liz, don't go.' Darryl wailed.

'Darryl, this is very important. How have you hurt Tina? Be specific.'

'We got into it. Argued about Eliza. And she said it's my fault if anything happens to her 'cos I haven't told you what I know. So I went to tell you but you weren't there.'

'Tell me now. But first, Darryl, have you harmed Tina?' Liz's voice sounded desperate to her ears. The officer was approaching, this time dialling a number on his phone.

'Might have killed her. I didn't mean to. She wouldn't shut up.' Darryl started sobbing.

From inside the apartment, a phone began to ring.

With Darryl no longer responding to Liz's demand to let her in, two of the officers broke his door open. They hauled a weeping Darryl out into the hallway while Liz and another officer rushed inside the apartment.

The ringing phone was on the kitchen counter inside a women's handbag.

Liz worked her way through the small apartment. No sign of blood or a disturbance other than a pile of empty beer bottles in the living room. She left the bedroom and stopped, sure she'd heard a thud.

'Tina?'

Another thud followed by a muffled cry. A female cry.

'Can I get some help?' Liz yelled as she dashed back into the bedroom.

There was a built-in wardrobe with an ironing board leaning against the door. Liz lifted it and dropped it again with a gasp as pain shot into her injured stomach. Another officer was there and removed it and Liz opened the door.

Tina was on the floor, hands and feet tied with bandages and blood trickling down her face. Her eyes were wide and distressed but focused on Liz.

'We're here now. Tina, where are you hurt?'

'Head. Hit me with a bottle. Get me up.'

'Best to assess you first,' Liz squatted beside her. 'There's an ambulance downstairs so someone will be here in a min.' She pushed a row of hanging clothing clear. 'Best to check the head injury.'

Another officer brought scissors and carefully cut the bandages to free Tina.

She rubbed her wrists and then touched her head. 'I should have known he'd resort to violence. Where is he?'

'Hallway and in handcuffs. We'll move him out of sight when you leave. What were you doing coming here?'

'Thought I could appeal to his real nature. The one which used to love kids and would put people's needs ahead of himself. I knew he was hiding something and I saw it in his eyes when I asked him to talk to you.'

The sound of footsteps approached.

'I'm going to go speak to him. Ambos are here.' Liz patted Tina's arm and straightened.

She waited until Tina was being attended to then went in search of Darryl.

He sat on the floor, hands cuffed behind himself, still crying. Liz caught the eye of the officer watching him.

'Bring him into my apartment. I don't want him anywhere near Tina.'

Darryl was yanked to his feet and marched through the remains of Liz's front door.

'Straight ahead to the kitchen and sit him in a chair. I'll be there soon.'

'Liz, I need the cuffs off.'

The officer with him said something too low to hear and Darryl stopped whining but the sound of his snivels followed Liz back to the hallway.

She phoned Terry and quickly filled him in on the events of the past few minutes. 'Tina is convinced he knows something and he wanted to talk to me. I just hope he still will.'

'Arrest him and get him processed,' Terry said.

'I'll do that. Is there anything from Geelong?'

'Pete and Andy are at Collaroy Street. There's nobody there but a neighbour is helping with information.'

Liz's heart lifted. 'About Eliza?'

'There was a sighting of small girl and man meeting Kyle's description but that's all I have until Andy updates me.'

'I should go there.'

'Nothing for you to do other than bring Darryl in for questioning. Okay?'

She drew in a small breath to steady her voice. 'Okay. I'll see you shortly.'

Liz had no intention of arresting Darryl until he'd explained himself. The minute he was cautioned, he'd ask for his lawyer and that not only meant wasting time, but potentially losing the information forever.

She asked the officer to check on Tina and leaned against the kitchen bench.

Darryl had regained control of himself although his bloodshot eyes still glistened. 'Please, Liz. The cuffs hurt.'

'I'll get them off but you need to tell me whatever it is that made you destroy my front door. Do that and I'll release you.'

His eyes flicked in the direction of the door.

'Tina will be okay. You didn't kill her or even come close. What do you know about Eliza?' Liz softened her voice and sat opposite. 'This is a chance to make a difference, mate.'

And if you don't help I really will beat you to a pulp.

A little bubble of hysteria threatened to turn into a laugh. The thought was comical, particularly when she couldn't even lift an ironing board. Liz took out a notebook and waited, her face as friendly and expectant as she could manage.

After fidgeting in his seat and looking at the ceiling, Darryl seemed to come to a decision and met her eyes. 'I'll tell you everything but I want you to understand I was coerced and blackmailed.'

'And I will take that on board, Darryl.'

'It started after I was attacked in my job.'

Darryl spoke coherently and at length about his hospital stay, recovery, and losing his relationship. Jail was where the descent really began and certain connections were made which led him to move to the apartment building. Liz wrote as he talked, letting him spill his guts about criminal activity, mostly as part of the illegal gambling ring.

'Bing had me doing stuff he didn't want to do. Same with Maureen. She wasn't part of the gambling but her old man was in prison and Bing used that against her. Had her delivering god knows what to undesirables.'

He wasted time complaining and twice Liz rejected calls from Terry. Pete rang as well and she had no choice but to ignore it.

'Did you know Eliza was going to be taken?'

His head shook. 'Never. Wouldn't have been party to it. Just got the directive to find and then leave the item of clothing. No idea it belonged to a kid until I picked it up and even then I figured it was part of a gambling event. There were a lot of those things… a race when people have to find stuff in different places?'

'Scavenger hunt?'

'Yeah that. Sometimes got nasty with people hurt in the process. Didn't like them.'

Liz longed to ask why he didn't stand up for himself. Why had he allowed one incident in his life—although horrific—to turn him from a lawful person to one who thought it was okay to move a child's shoe and then lie about.

'I asked Bing what the hell was going on. You know, I'd done what I was told and picked up and moved the shoe and it was clearly a kid's shoe. Felt wrong, Liz. The kid was from our own building. Her mum was doing everything she could to look after her and build a bit of a future.'

'And what did Bing say?'

Darryl's face reddened. He leaned forward and looked her in the eye. 'He told me to pull my head in and if I ever questioned him again, he'd make sure I was back in prison.' The tears returned, streaming down his cheeks. 'I can't go back, Liz. It almost killed me.'

'But I overheard him say that he knew you'd taken her. He asked where you'd stashed her. Before you both got into that stupid fight.'

'And it was all a show because he wanted me to take the blame for everything.'

Unsure if she'd actually learned anything new, other than confirming Brian Bisley's involvement, Liz sat back.

'Liz. Come on. You believe me, right?'

'I want to. But here's where things stand. Eliza is missing. Her abductor has disappeared, with her. He's clever and determined. And we are no further along knowing how to find a frightened little girl who just wants to see her mum.'

'Then write some notes because I know a place which most people don't. A place Garry pays rent on. And I might be the only person who knows, other than Bing, because I've been there. And you know what? I reckon that is where he'll run with the kid.'

THIRTY-THREE

Liz got the uniformed officer to arrest Darryl. With residents allowed back, she asked one of the few neighbours she knew to keep an eye on her apartment and had phoned a company to replace the door. There would be a cop around for a while anyway to finish up at Darryl's place and he'd had fun putting police tape across her doorway.

Tina was on her way to hospital to be checked but she had avoided serious injury. Although she'd put herself at risk, Tina's actions had resulted in the best lead since Eliza disappeared.

Brave, caring woman.

Back in her car, Liz tapped the address into her navigation screen and drove away from the police cars still parked around the apartment building. Terry's number came up.

'Boss, sorry. I meant to call straight back.'

'Where are you, Liz?'

'Just leaving the apartment. Darryl is coming in with the uniforms.'

'That wasn't what we agreed.'

'It wasn't? Well, he's under arrest and Tina is going to hospital but just to check her. Where are things with Eliza?'

Terry took a moment, talking to someone else but too quietly for her to hear. 'Sorry. Meg just let me know she's got back a new analysis on those hairs from Ellen's file.'

'How? I thought we couldn't do anything?'

'She found a way. So, the hairs came from a Caucasian male, aged approximately forty-five to fifty at the time. They match your DNA, and a sample Anna provided when Ellen went missing, sufficiently to identify the hairs as belonging to your father, Kyle Moorland.'

Liz gripped the steering wheel, pushing down anger but unable to stop her eyes filling with tears. She pulled over and wiped them away.

'Still there?'

'All that time, Terry. All that damned, wasted time when we could have been searching for Kyle. Yet nobody told me hairs had been found. Nobody cared enough to see the anomaly with their appearance compared to hairs from a young child. We would have found Ellen. At least found Kyle.' She closed her hands into fists, ready to pound the wheel.

'I know, Lizzie.'

A message popped up from Pete.

Call me. Urgent.

'Pete's after me, Terry. I'll send you through the address Darryl gave me. It has to be where Kyle's gone with Eliza.'

'Don't go alone.'

'Got to call Pete.'

Liz hung up and quickly texted Terry the location. Her phone began ringing again with Terry as the caller and she rejected it, then dialled Pete as she got back on the road.

A siren was in the background when he answered. 'Got some news.'

'Me too. You go first.'

'We have good intel that Kyle and Eliza left the Collaroy Street address about one hour and fifteen minutes ago. There's been a possible sighting of his vehicle heading along the M1 near Altona Meadows. Have airwing coming and have an alert out.'

'Makes sense. He rents a boat in Williamstown. If he's been spooked enough to run with Eliza then we might never see either of them again. I'm going there now.' Liz turned on her lights and siren. 'At least fifteen minutes away though.'

'Don't confront him alone, Liz.'

'Sure, *Terry*. I'll just wait for the men to arrive.'

'Haha. If Terry already told you to wait then do it. Didn't you learn anything from getting a baton in the guts?'

'Tell Liz to stand down.'

'I can hear you, Andy and I'm not only the closest body but the one who can at least delay him, if he is taking off. Kyle took Ellen from me and Anna and I'm not going to let him take Eliza from her mum.'

'And I'm telling you, Detective Sergeant Moorland, to stand down. I'm ordering you to go no further than Melbourne Road and wait for—'

Liz terminated the call.

She knew the area well. Liz and Vince had been beat cops in Williamstown for a few months and although it had grown, much remained the same.

The pier where her father's boat was— allegedly—was out of the way and small. It reminded her of one in Altona where the family of Ben Rossi's now-girlfriend kept their yacht. Less likely to have prying eyes see what someone might wish to hide.

Liz left the car two blocks away after putting on a protective vest and checking her weapon. Her phone hadn't stopped ringing or beeping with messages and she wasn't about to start responding. She'd blown everything by ignoring not one, but two superior officers and she no longer cared. Liz turned it to silent.

The police force had let her down.

Uncovering the truth about the hairs in Ellen's file was the final nail in the coffin.

The coffin of my career.

Once the pier was in view, Liz approached cautiously, using what cover there was in the way of trees and other people. It was almost closing time for the shops and businesses in the bayside suburb. Then would come the joggers and dog walkers and families out for a stroll or swim. This had to be resolved before there was a higher risk of the public getting caught in the middle of anything.

Only eight boats were tied up, a mix of type—mostly decent-sized yachts, and then at the far end was just one. Smaller, perhaps a twenty-footer and old in style. There were two people on the pier beside it.

A man and a little girl.

Liz positioned herself inside the doorway of a toilet block where she could keep them in sight but hopefully not be seen. She texted Pete.

I have them in sight. Both on the pier. Boat is at the far end. I will watch unless he makes a move to leave. Come in without sirens.

She took a series of photographs of the boat, the pier, and of the people and sent those to Pete. Then she used her phone to zoom in on the child.

Eliza sat on the timber boards of the pier holding onto a stuffed unicorn with one hand and a bottle of water with the other. She wore a dress and a little sunhat and was looking around. Not afraid, but perhaps a bit worried or unsettled, and who wouldn't be, being moved from place to place and not knowing if she was ever going home? What lies had she been fed?

Almost afraid to see his face, Liz forced herself to move the focus to the man. Kyle. Her father. Her throat constricted.

He was stowing bags onto the boat. Two at a time, a mix of shopping bags and luggage, stepping on and then off the pier. His eyes roamed constantly and for one heart-stopping moment he stared directly in Liz's direction. But then he looked away. It was too far and she was in the shadows.

She knew his face. Not just from the new profile image Meg had distributed. But from her childhood. He might have aged but the lines of his jaw and his nose were the same.

This was unreal and she almost faltered. He was her father. A man she barely remembered and would have loved to have known, flaws and horrible beliefs and all. Her flesh and blood.

Who killed a man and took his identity as part of some grand plan to steal his grandchild.

The bitter taste of bile filled her mouth and she retreated into the toilet block to spit it out. He wasn't going to control her.

She was only a few seconds but when she stepped out, Eliza wasn't on the pier. Her little hat was visible walking around the boat.

Liz zig-zagged toward the water. A tree here. A group of walkers there.

And then she was at the land end of the pier and had to make a decision.

She felt for her gun. It was a last resort.

But Eliza is coming with me today.

THIRTY-FOUR

'Is she really so stupid as to disobey orders?' Andy couldn't stop ranting about Liz cutting off the call. 'Her decision making has turned to crap today.'

Pete gritted his teeth. All he cared about was getting to Williamstown before Liz had to make herself known to Kyle. They'd left the freeway and were winding their way through arterial roads which were too busy for his liking. Too many minutes of driving ahead. Anything could happen in that time.

'Nothing to say? Usually can't stop you,' Andy said.

'Do you want to get there alive?'

'Did you just threaten me?'

'Not even close,' Pete said. 'I'm trying to concentrate on avoiding us being hit by a truck.'

As if to prove the point, Pete overtook a container truck and dived in front of it to miss an oncoming one, resulting in horns blasting them. Andy was holding the grab handle and stayed blissfully quiet until they'd moved onto a narrower road and Pete was forced to slow.

Terry rang and Andy reached over to accept the call on speaker.

'How far, Pete?'

'Under ten minutes. Are you in a car?'

'Liz needs back up.'

'Terry, its Andy. This could be a volatile situation. Isn't waiting for Special Ops appropriate?'

'They're thirty minutes away.'

'Then we take a look and evaluate.'

Pete opened his mouth to speak but Terry was already responding.

'What I need from you, Detective Senior Sergeant, is to know you can do what's asked of you, irrespective of whatever code it is you hold yourself to. There is no black and white answer to a situation such as this but I can guarantee that Liz is the right person to be there at this moment. Our job, your job, is to support her instead of stepping back waiting for the so-called right team to arrive.'

Andy's face had reddened at the stern words.

Pete didn't feel the least bit sorry for him.

'I'm about to park near Liz's car and will meet up with her.'

'Watch your back, Terry,' Pete said.

'That's your job now.'

After Terry disconnected the call, Pete turned off the sirens. He took a back street which was quiet, then another. The bay came into view and he stopped at the end of the road.

'There's the pier.' He pointed across rooftops. 'I'll get us closer.'

Andy looked but remained quiet.

'Still want to join Homicide?' Pete asked. He wasn't being smart but saw Andy shoot a glare at him from the corner of his eye. 'There's no glamour, mate. We don't get to pick our cases when there's an emergency. We don't get to stand back and wait for the right people to get there first… whoever the right people are. Not all rainbows, Andy.'

'Yeah, I get that.'

'But what we *do* get far outweighs the glorified myth of being the elite squad.'

'Which is?'

Pete was as close as he dared and slid into a parking spot along the waterfront.

'We get to save lives. Not nearly often enough, but when it happens then it is worth more than any glory. And today we're going to save lives.'

Andy met his eyes and nodded.

'We will.'

THIRTY-FIVE

Kyle had disappeared from view and Eliza was at the stern, giggling and waving at seagulls which hovered above the boat.

Liz took the opportunity to get onto the pier and made it as far as the second boat before Kyle's voice carried across the short distance. She ducked low so that the bulk of the yacht would hide her.

'Do you like the birds, Liselle?'

The little girl answered in a bossy voice. 'Not Liselle, Pop. Eliza Sharney Singleton.'

'I think Liselle is perfect. It means God's promise and you, little one, have a whole life of promise ahead of you.'

Oh my god, he is insane.

'I'm hungry.'

'Me too. That's why we stopped to buy all those groceries because we can make a nice dinner for ourselves very soon. Would you like to help me decide what to make?'

'I'd like pizza.'

Kyle chuckled.

Liz knew that sound. He used to laugh softly at her attempts to boss him around or any one of a hundred things kids did. He'd been patient. Helped her learn. Been a great dad.

To me. Not to Anna.

Her fingers undid the clip on her holster.

Beneath her were small gaps between the timber boards. The sea ebbed and flowed. The pier moved ever so slightly under the pressure of the water. All of the boats rocked and bumped against the sides. Salt air stung her eyes.

'Pizza it is then. Would you like to see your cabin?'

'I don't know what that is.'

'A bedroom. But on a boat. Actually, enjoy the seagulls and I'll come back up once I've made your bed.'

'Okie dokie, Pop.'

Another chuckle.

He might not have embraced Eliza as his own at first but something had changed. Now he knew his real daughter was forever out of his reach, had he decided Eliza would do?

Liz waited a minute before cautiously taking a look at the boat.

Eliza was close to the pier, leaning over to gaze at something in the water.

She needed back up. Someone to put a gun in Kyle's face if he tried to stop her taking Eliza. Nobody was close. No sign of Pete yet. Liz moved from boat to boat, checking and rechecking for the reappearance of her father. There was a gap of perhaps five metres to his boat with no cover.

Grabbing Eliza and running wouldn't work. The child didn't know her. She'd scream.

Liz walked at a normal pace, wincing at every creak of the timber.

Eliza glanced up.

'Shh… I'm Pop's friend.' Liz whispered. 'Can you be very quiet for a surprise?'

The child's eyes rounded and she nodded.

Another few steps. She could almost reach her.

'Do you like hide and seek?'

Another nod.

Let this work.

Liz extended her arms as she closed the gap. 'I know the best hiding spot and Pop will have so much fun finding us.'

There was doubt in the child's eyes.

'My name is Liz. And you are Eliza. I know your mummy.'

'Mummy?' She squealed the word.

There was a thump from below deck.

Liz slid her arms around Eliza and lifted her from the boat, almost dropping her as pain rippled through her stomach muscles. 'Grab my neck,' she gasped.

'My unicorn.'

It was on the deck.

'We'll come back for it. Hold on, sweetheart.'

'Liselle? Are you alright?' Footsteps were stomping up the steps from below deck.

Liz's heart pounded as she carried Eliza away from the boat. She could barely run. All she could do was grip the child and pray she wasn't about to be shot in the back.

'Stop! Elizabeth, no. No!'

Liz was only a dozen steps from the boat and not close enough to the next one to use it as cover of any kind.

'I'm pointing a gun at you, Elizabeth. Stop now.'

His voice sent a shiver down her spine. It held pure evil in its depths and she remembered. It was the tone he'd use just before he'd hurt her mother. And now he was threatening her, his golden child, all because he refused to let go of a stolen girl.

'Pop's angry.'

If he shot her, the bullet might hit Eliza.

Liz abruptly halted and turned to face him.

Kyle was on the boat, training a rifle on her. His eyes held such fury that Liz feared he would lose whatever control he had if she made one wrong move.

'Hi, Dad.'

'Bring Liselle back to me.'

The little girl clung to Liz, head buried into her shoulder and legs wrapped around her.

'I can't. She isn't yours to have, Dad. But I'll come with you. I'll go wherever you want me to go.'

His aim didn't waiver but the anger drained from his face.

'There are so many questions I have. We lost all those years,' she said.

There was someone behind her. Footsteps, carefully placed. *Please let it be Pete.*

'What questions?'

'Some are better not asked in front of a child. But one is burning me up. The day you took Ellen... how did you know I would be there at the park with her... how did you get her away without being seen?'

'Feeling guilty about not watching over her?'

'Yes. I still do, every single day, Dad.'

'Good. You already know the answers, Elizabeth. You're nothing if not intelligent and resourceful. If Garry Ford's properties were raided then you know I took over his life after his tragedy. It helped that he was reclusive. Ran his businesses remotely. I spent a lot of time putting people in places where I could use them when it suited me. Even in the police force.'

She drew in a sharp breath.

His lips curled up in a cruel smile. 'Didn't expect that, did you? Now you'll be looking over your shoulder forever.'

'Liz, I'm going to step out.'

It was Terry.

The chill returned. Terry had been around when Ellen was taken. Not as her superior officer nor in Homicide but hadn't he worked in evidence for a while? The list of names on the boxes containing the files hadn't included Terry. Liz couldn't be sure because she'd never properly read it. Kyle had someone working in the force for him back then. She'd be looking over her shoulder... Terry was behind her.

Liz put her mouth close to Eliza's ear. 'I need you to keep holding me tight. There might be some noise but I'm taking you home to Mummy.'

Terry would never be that person.

'Kyle Moorland? I'm Detective Senior Sergeant Terry Hall and I'm going to move next to Liz and Eliza. That's all.'

Kyle's body tensed and he tightened his grip on the rifle but kept it pointed at Liz.

Terry stopped to Liz's left and a foot ahead. His gun was trained on Kyle.

There was a pause, a moment when the air stilled. Eliza's heart raced against Liz's chest.

'Take her home, Lizzie. You did good.'

Then Terry stepped between Liz, right in the line of fire.

Liz turned and ran.

There were shots. The rifle. The handgun.

A heavy thud.

They were beyond the bigger yachts. Kyle would need to follow them to shoot.

'Liz! Keep coming.'

Pete was drawing his gun as he followed Andy, both pounding their feet onto the timber boards.

Then Liz was off the pier and somehow behind the trunk of a tree and Eliza was screaming.

With the arrival of more police, Liz managed to get Eliza into the safe arms of Senior Constable Annette Benski.

'There's paramedics coming, Liz. You need to sit.'

'I'll be back. Eliza? Annette is going to take care of you.'

'Mummy. I want Mummy.' The screams had turned to sobs.

'We're going to phone your mummy in a few minutes, love. Come on, let's go over near my patrol car and you can take a look inside while we wait. Okay?' Annette winked at Liz but didn't look any less worried.

Terry.

Only minutes had passed since she'd fled the pier.

There'd been noise, more gunshots, and a motor.

Now, as Liz stepped onto the pier, it made sense. The boat was under power and already a few hundred metres away.

And where she'd left Terry…

'No!'

Pete was slumped on the boards beside Terry, who lay in a pool of blood.

Tears poured down Pete's cheeks. 'I was too late, Liz.'

She sank next to Terry and took his hand in hers. There was no response. No returning squeeze. Just a bullet hole in his forehead and another in his stomach. How could this be? Terry was her friend. Her boss. He'd come to help her save Eliza and he'd done that.

It was curious. Her body was on fire with pain but she felt no emotions.

'Why did Kyle escape?'

Andy appeared from wherever he'd been. He squatted near Liz. 'You okay?'

'What happened to my father?'

'He had the ropes off while Pete and I tried to help Terry. We were only a few seconds because… anyway, Kyle had gone below and as we approached the motor fired up. Couldn't get there fast enough.'

'Boat has some bullets in it.' Pete sighed heavily and got to his feet. 'We'd already alerted Water Police and there's a copter coming. He won't get far.' He held both hands out to Liz.

She released her hold on Terry and let Pete help her up.

'Ambulance just arrived. Go and get checked, Liz.' Andy said, also straightening.

'Eliza first.'

Liz made her way to the end of the pier. The boat was moving at a steady pace.

'You saved Eliza.' Pete came to stand beside Liz.

'At what cost?'

The sound of a helicopter drew their attention. It flew fast and low in the direction of the boat. At the same time, a police water vehicle was closing in on Kyle.

'Catch the bastard,' Pete muttered.

With a flash of red and a thundering boom, the boat exploded.

Pete threw his arms around Liz to protect her. But the debris raining down was hundreds of metres away and he released her.

'What the hell?'

Andy joined them.

The helicopter and police boat had veered sharply away.

'Tell them to find him, Andy. Don't let him escape.'

Liz shaded her eyes. The sun was low and glaring. There was no way she could see from this distance but somewhere in the water, her father was holding up his middle finger at them.

THIRTY-SIX

Terry wasn't coming back. Liz stood in his office, expecting to see his face, hear his voice. Both gone forever along with the rest of the man who'd put his life at risk for hers today, and lost. Not just her life, but Eliza's. And that little girl was spending one night in hospital and no doubt had her mother in a chair at her side.

You did what you promised. You brought Eliza home.

Liz returned to her desk. She shouldn't even be here but the alternative was a visit to the hospital and right now, she couldn't stand being around people.

'Liz?'

She'd thought herself alone.

'Um, Meg, I'm sorry, I'm not up to talking.'

But she should have saved her breath.

Meg came around the desk and hugged her, gently, but still enough to hurt. Everything hurt despite more painkillers. Exhaustion didn't help but how could she sleep, knowing her father might still be out there?

After stepping back, Meg smiled. 'I have something to show you.'

'There's not any point. I know about the hairs and thank you for whatever strings you pulled.'

'Oh, I have strings everywhere and rushing DNA samples past certain friendly places is the tip of the iceberg. Would it encourage you to come with me if I tell you that Anna is waiting for you?'

'Why is Anna here? I've already spoken to her about our father.'

'You won't know if you don't hurry up.'

Tempted to tell Meg she wasn't in the mood for guessing games, Liz pushed herself to her feet anyway. There were things she still had to say to her sister.

Meg was chatty all the way. 'I heard you have a new front door. And your keys will still work seeing as the lock wasn't damaged. Darryl is going away for a long time because now he can't stop talking and is spewing information about the gambling ring and who knows what else.'

They approached the conference room, which made no sense. It was after nine at night and apart from the officers still working through the fallout from today, the place was quiet.

'Wait a sec,' Meg said, stopping them both outside the door. 'I'm gutted about Terry so can only imagine how you feel. But you need to know that he only ever had your best interests at heart. And he knew there was a good outcome for you and Anna.'

'I don't understand.'

Meg opened the door.

Anna was pacing the room and when she saw Liz, ran over and threw her arms around her. 'I thought I'd lost you.'

'Ouch. Stop squeezing... please.'

'Sorry.' Anna dropped her arms. 'Do you know why I'm here?'

'I do.'

Pete wandered in. He'd showered and changed but the shadows on his face told Liz how heavy his heart was.

'Let's sit. There's news.'

'I wasn't letting go of my gut feeling about your father,' Pete said. 'Things weren't adding up about how he'd allegedly died, not when I factored in some of the information from Brian Bisley's interview. I took it upon myself to do some off-duty digging around.'

Pete had begun the conversation by saying that Terry had made a mistake keeping certain intel from Liz, but he'd been under pressure.

'From Andy?'

'He was one but it was from higher up as well.'

Today had been a nightmare which might never end. Barely any sleep, being on that news broadcast in a bad light, her father's attack at Brimbank Park… and then Terry and the explosion of the boat. All along Liz had been certain she was being excluded from something important.

It doesn't matter now. Just hurry up and let me leave.

'I'm happy to go through everything that led me there, but not tonight.' Pete exchanged a glance with Meg. 'I found a young woman.'

The hairs on Liz's arms rose.

'She grew up in Geelong as Lena Ford and—'

'Ford? The name Kyle took?' Anna's eyes were huge.

'Yes. She knew Garry Ford as her grandfather.'

Meg slipped out of the door.

'I knew from the minute I met her… I had to get proof, Liz. Anna. I couldn't just blurt out that I thought I'd found Ellen,' Pete said.

Anna had both hands over her mouth and her whole body was trembling.

'Meg had a DNA sample rushed. Never knew it was even possible to get one done so fast.'

'Pete. Is it her?'

A smile lit his face. 'Ellen's alive and well.'

With a small cry, Anna burst into tears. 'My... my little girl is safe?'

'Couple of things and I need you to hear me, Anna. And Liz. She was told her mother and father had died in a plane accident. Most of her early memories are sketchy. This has been a shock to her. Candace Carroll has spent time with her today and says Ellen will need a lot of time to come to terms with her past.'

'She doesn't believe who she is?' Anna kept wiping tears away and more kept falling. 'Can we go and meet her? Will she let us?'

Pete's eyes moved to the doorway and so did Liz's.

The young woman standing just inside the door, with Meg at her side, was like looking at herself in her early twenties. Same eyes. Facial structure. Same height and build.

Anna's chair fell over in her haste to stand but then she seemed frozen in place.

Ellen's eyes flicked from Anna to Liz and back to Anna.

You look so frightened.

'Ellen?' Anna managed a step.

The young woman glanced at Meg. 'I can't.'

She turned to go.

Liz stood. 'Not goodbye.'

Pete and Meg and Anna looked at Liz.

'Ellen? It's not goodbye.'

The answer was soft. 'Only 'til next time.'

And louder. 'Only 'til next time, Auntie Liz.' Ellen spun around. 'It's not goodbye.'

Terry's funeral was over. The ache in Liz's heart was dulling but she'd never forget the man who'd fearlessly lost his life to save a child. And to save her.

As officers, friends, and family gathered in groups outside the church, Liz wandered away. She didn't go too far, finding a bench beneath a tree. Being too close to some of the police was hard. People like Andy. Liz was a long way from dealing with the fact that he'd probably end up in Homicide now that he'd been part of the team which brought a child home and resulted in the death of her kidnapper.

Alleged death.

'Prefer to be alone, Lizzie?'

'Only from most of the others. Not from you, Vince.'

Her old partner settled on the bench and for a while they sat in silence. People were slowly dispersing. In a few days she'd visit his grave and talk to him properly.

'Come and stay with us for a while,' Vince said. 'Melanie would love to have you. I would as well. And there's plenty of places to walk and spend time alone. I go up to the orchard I planted with Melanie's mum when she was small. Restful there.'

'Would you settle for dinner one evening? I'm helping Anna clean up her house so that Ellen and Parker can come and stay when they want.'

'Can't get my head around you being a great-aunt now,' he chuckled. 'Dinner, breakfast, anything, anytime.'

Andy was heading toward his car and he hesitated when he noticed Liz. She gazed back and he nodded, then continued. Since Terry's death, they'd spoken only when necessary and Liz felt he was likely to paint her in a poor light in his reporting. Pete even more so.

'How's shithead?'

Now you can read my mind.

'He's the shining light in all of this, Vince.'

Vince nodded. 'He found Ellen.'

'I still can't believe it some days. Long way to go before she's entirely trusting of us because she had a lifetime of lies from Kyle, but now there's a chance that we thought gone for good.'

'He has his moments, I guess,' Vince said.

'He's leaving the force.'

'Not surprised. And you?'

Liz turned to look at Vince. 'For the first time in my life, I don't want to be a cop. I'd never disobeyed an order before and the result was rescuing a kid, and seeing my boss killed. He wouldn't have been there if I hadn't ignored him.'

'Be kind to yourself. That's what Terry would say.'

It was. But it wouldn't change a thing.

Liz and Pete were at the end of the pier at sunset. They'd just laid flowers on the water and watched the tide carry them out into the bay. Twenty single stems of purple iris, a flower Terry's family had said he loved.

'Don't like losing, Lizzie,' Pete said.

'You mean Kyle?'

'We both know he's alive somewhere. He'd have planned ahead for an emergency exit just like he did with the river escape and the cruise ship.'

'Agree.'

They began to walk back. It was a month after that fateful day and Liz had taken leave to recover from the injury and spend time with Anna, Ellen, and little Parker.

'I'm due back next week, Pete.'

'But you don't want to go.'

'No. Except I don't know how else to serve the public let alone be there if my father reappears.'

'What if there was another way?' Pete asked.

A tall man stood on the grass where the pier ended. His face was familiar but it took Liz a minute to recognise him.

'Ben? Is that you?'

Ben Rossi grinned and then leaned down to kiss Liz's cheek.

'Hello, Liz. Pete.'

'Aren't you living down the coast somewhere, arresting overstayers at the beach in between surfing?'

Liz had known Ben a long time and he'd headed up Missing Persons before Andy.

'I am. At least, the first bit. I'm here to offer you a job.'

'Okay. I can't surf very well though.'

The smile disappeared. 'But you can police very well. You detective even better. And I'm putting together a new squad.'

'Hadn't heard anything new was happening.'

Pete looked just as serious. 'You would never have heard of at least one covert unit I was in, Liz. This one? Nobody will know unless they have a particular need or are at the receiving end of an arrest.'

'I thought you were going to go private.'

'It is. Kind of.'

Both men were waiting and Liz didn't have an answer. If there was a way to work in law enforcement but with more resources and less bureaucracy then perhaps she didn't have to rethink her future. The future without a badge.

'Besides, you can keep working with me,' Pete said, his voice hopeful.

Ben slapped his own forehead and rolled his eyes. 'Pete, shut up, that's not an incentive.'

It is though.

She could trust Pete.

Liz stared back at the bay. Somewhere out there was a man who still wanted to do harm, either to Liz or Anna, or even Ellen. One way or another, Liz had had every intention of finding him. And with a whole team on her side, what else could she achieve? The last rays of sun fading were a sign. She'd worked her entire life in the light as she'd followed every rule. Now it was time to take a walk in the dark.

NEXT IN THE SERIES...

Liz's new covert team faces its first case... the disappearance of a woman with a mysterious past. Lyndall once saved one of their own and now they are her only chance at survival.

ACKNOWLEDGMENTS

To my wonderful readers who keep me going - thank you. A special thanks to my superstar ARC team as well as Rosie A., and Carolyn W., who stepped in to help me straighten out a few point on short notice.

I had a lot of help with insights into procedures around a missing person - particularly a missing child - from a retired Sergeant of Victoria Police. To John L. - sincere thanks for taking the time to chat.

I'd like to acknowledge Brimbank Park (and Alex, one of the rangers who helped me with logistic advice), Keilor Cemetery, and all places mentioned.

ABOUT THE AUTHOR

Phillipa lives just outside a beautiful town in country Victoria, Australia. She also lives in the many worlds of her imagination and stockpiles stories beside her laptop.

She writes from the heart about love, dreams, secrets, discovery, the sea, the world as she knows it… or wishes it could be. She loves happy endings, heart-pounding suspense, and characters who stay with you long after the final page.

With a passion for music, the ocean, animals, nature, reading, and writing, she is often found in the vegetable garden pondering a new story.

Phillipa's website is www.phillipaclark.com

ALSO BY PHILLIPA NEFRI CLARK

Detective Liz Moorland
Lest We Forgive
Lest Bridges Burn
Lest Tides Turn
Connected to this series through several characters is
Last Known Contact

Rivers End Romantic Women's Fiction
The Stationmaster's Cottage
Jasmine Sea
The Secrets of Palmerston House
The Christmas Key
Taming the Wind

Temple River Romantic Women's Fiction
The Cottage at Whisper Lake
The Bookstore at Rivers End

Charlotte Dean Mysteries
Christmas Crime in Kingfisher Falls
Book Club Murder in Kingfisher Falls
Cold Case Murder in Kingfisher Falls
Plan to Murder in Kingfisher Falls
Festive Felony in Kingfisher Falls

Daphne Jones Mysteries
Daph on the Beach

Time of Daph
Till Daph Do Us Part
The Shadow of Daph
Tales of Life and Daph

Bindarra Creek Rural Fiction
A Perfect Danger
Tangled by Tinsel

Maple Gardens Matchmakers
The Heart Match
The Christmas Match
The Menu Match
The Cookie Match

Doctor Grok's Peculiar Shop Short Story Collection

Simple Words for Troubled Times
(Short non-fiction happiness and comfort book)

———

Prefer Audiobooks?
The Stationmaster's Cottage
Jasmine Sea
The Secrets of Palmerston House
Simple Words for Troubled Times
Till Daph Do Us Part
Lest We Forgive
The Cottage at Whisper Lake

Made in the USA
Coppell, TX
21 December 2024